TRAIL BOSS

TRAIL BOSS

PETER DAWSON

THORNDIKE
CHIVERS

This Large Print edition is published by Thorndike Press, Waterville, Maine USA and by BBC Audiobooks Ltd, Bath, England.
Thorndike Press is an imprint of Thomson Gale, a part of The Thomson Corporation.
Thomson is a trademark and used herein under license.

LIBRARY OF CONGRESS CATALOGING-IN-PUBLICATION DATA

Dawson, Peter, 1907–
    Trail boss / by Peter Dawson.
      p. cm. — (Thorndike Press large print western)
    ISBN-13: 978-0-7862-9346-9 (alk. paper)
    ISBN-10: 0-7862-9346-2 (alk. paper)
    1. Large type books. I. Title.
PS3507.A848T73 2007
813'.54—dc22
                                                  2006039154

BRITISH LIBRARY CATALOGUING-IN-PUBLICATION DATA AVAILABLE

Published in 2007 in the U.S. by arrangement with
Golden West Literary Agency
Published in 2007 in the U.K. by arrangement with
Golden West Literary Agency

U.K. Hardcover: 978 1 405 64050 3 (Chivers Large Print)
U.K. Softcover: 978 1 405 64051 0 (Camden Large Print)

Printed in the United States of America on permanent paper
10 9 8 7 6 5 4 3 2 1

PEOPLE IN THIS BOOK

Dave Santell. A tall young man from Texas with a lot on his mind and a price on his head.

"Major" Jacob Wilce. An Indian agent with money-making ideas.

Gail McCune. A city girl with coppery hair whose first impressions are inclined to be wrong.

Ray Breen. A gentleman who likes cattle — a thousand head at a time.

Tucker. Wilce's precise clerk.

Erbeck. A bad man who discovers an honest bone in his body.

Doc Faris. A physician who knows people inside and out.

Martha. Erbeck's girl.

Ed Torrence. A power in the unsavoury town of Scalplock.

Howard Mordue. He sat down to a game of poker and never got up.

Blaine Shotwell. A man who spends a lot

of his time with men named Spence, Birkheimer, and Holmes.

Jim Land. Dave Santell's foreman who bossed Fred Harkness and Red Rhea.

Tom Warren. A good man in a bad town.

Sheriff Moore. A man of law who understands justice.

I

They saw him quartering in to the fire, the faintly grayed dawn sky outlining his high shape and the clean-limbed horse. One of them called, "The boss, T-bone."

The cook eased down off the chuck-wagon's tailgate and moved with unaccustomed alacrity about his dutch ovens and smoking pans, heaping a tin plate with enough edibles to fill two ordinary men. Meanwhile, the rest watched this Dave Santell turn his pony over to the wrangler and go to the buckboard to take a long drink from the barrel there and pour a dipper of water over his head.

When he came to the fire, his stride choppy and short from saddle cramp, his spurs jangling musically, one of them asked, "How about turnin' in for a couple hours, Dave?"

"Wouldn't wake up for a week," was Dave Santell's sparse answer. He squatted on one of their grounded saddles and took the plate and the steaming cup of coffee the cook offered.

They saw that his face was leaner looking than usual, its angles shadowed by a heavy beard stubble. The crows-foot lines webbing from the outer corners of his eye sockets were deep with tiredness. His wide shoulders sagged with fatigue; yet not enough to take away their squareness.

"Much farther, Dave?"

"Don't know yet. I'm goin' on ahead directly."

The five men from then on silently watched him wolf his meal, feeling a little guilty about being caught here tarrying over their breakfast smokes. They shouldn't have, for they were the day crew not due to take over the herd, that had passed the cook's camp sometime during the night, for another hour. They had worked until midnight and had slept only these four hours, on the same schedule as the night before.

Nevertheless, they knew that Dave Santell hadn't hit the blankets in the past two nights and a day and, to a man, they felt they owed him more than they had given him in this gamble of his to save a hundred miles of distance and an extra week on the trail. Time was running out on them and there was nothing they, or Dave Santell, could do about it. Except, of course, to hope that his hunch wasn't playing him false.

As he finished and laid his plate aside to reach for his tobacco, the cook spoke. "You can take that black horse of mine if you want him, Boss."

They took some notice of that. T-bone would ordinarily have taken a meat-cleaver to any man who laid a hand on the black stallion.

But Dave Santell seemed too tired to be aware of this magnanimous offer, for he only said, "Red's already got my hull on the buckskin." He stood up then, lit his smoke and stretched. He drawled, "Keep pushin' 'em," and walked back over to the horse line, there to swing up onto a big white-stockinged buckskin.

He was out of sight over the near stage-studded rise before anyone said anything. Then:

"Hope he knows what he's doin'."

"Why the hell wouldn't he?" Querulously. "Ever know him to go wrong?"

"But this desert's awful damn' wide. One more day and these critters'll boil every pound of fat off."

"You rannies clear out before I put you to work cleanin' up," T-bone said sourly; and,

9

faced by this threat, they drifted out from the fire toward the *remuda* and another day of work.

When he rode away from the grey blob of the chuck-wagon, Dave Santell swung left across the sandy hummocks and in three miles came up with the dust of the drag. In the strengthening light he made out two riders in that heavy-lying fog. But he cut away from them without speaking and rode up along the snaking shadowy line of plodding steers vociferously bawling their thirst.

This was the biggest single herd that had been driven beyond the Kansas line in the past two years and, unless an obscure memory was serving Dave incorrectly, these three thousand steers were due for a thinning. So it was more than a bone deep weariness that lined his face. He was worried, more worried than he would have admitted.

It was the worry that made him hold the buckskin to a fast trot all the way up past the swing, past the leadsteers and the single point rider and on from there into the distance. He rode straight for the tallest snow-shrouded peak of that low and broken blue line of mountains quartering the hazed northern horizon, constantly nagged by the doubt of having misjudged the desert's

10

width.

But an hour later, on a high rise of ground, he brought the buckskin to a stand and all the tension went out of him.

Off there toward the mountains that now seemed higher in the day's full light, he could make out the detail of broken land, of buck brush and cedar dotted flats, of barrens below timbered foothills.

But what caught his eye, much closer, was a wedge of bright emerald edging this waste of rolling brown sage land.

Unless he was mistaken, and he knew he wasn't, that spot of lush greenery marked the seep of American Creek, the southern boundary of the reservation. By noon, the herd would be slacking its long thirst there.

When he was sure of this, sure he wasn't wrong, he reined about and rode back to the herd's point and spoke a brief word to the rider there.

"Seven miles more, Jim, maybe eight and you'll be to water. See you in Grade in three days."

"By damn! You've done it!" Jim said, and his face broke into a wide grin.

Dave carried the rider's relieved grin with him as a token of what they had accomplished when he once more cut on ahead of the herd, the buckskin at a high lope. He

11

had won his gamble. Now all that remained was to collect on it.

Forty minutes later he was letting the buckskin drink under the big cottonwood at the edge of the seep. He shed his clothes and, buck naked, waded out through the cattail thicket and sloshed around in the clear knee-deep water.

There was a quality of feline grace about this man. His flat-muscled body seemed, and was, wire strong. That leanness so prominent in his face was in his rangy build, in narrow hips and powerful wide shoulders. He was a big man without appearing so because of his tallness, much heavier than he looked. It took a sixteen and a half hand horse like the buckskin to carry his weight well.

This Dave Santell was four months out of Texas. Wind and sun had darkened his hands and wrists, neck and face, until the contrast between them and the whiteness of the rest of him was startling. The sun had bleached the blond hair above his temples to the color of oat straw. Squinting against strong sunlight and rain and wind had put those webbing lines at the outer corners of his eyes. When he smiled, which was often, these lines added a warmth to the expression of the eyes, a dark brown. A great many men liked Dave Santell; and a few feared him, with reason. The weighty responsibility that was his had added a maturity beyond his twenty-eight years. Without it he was as carefree and wild and reckless as the next man. But lately he hadn't had the chance to let down. He was hoping he'd get the chance soon.

That hope was the reason for his not wasting too much time at the seep. Ten minutes after he had ridden in there he was on his way out, headed northwest into the higher country, the ragged banner of dust trailing the buckskin the token of an urgent errand.

The untidy room was sweltering hot. Dust lay over everything, greying the worn carpet, the chair arms, the desk. There were flies too, their constant buzzing a lazy undertone to the heat-deadened late afternoon sounds echoing in off the square facing the agency.

The girl at the window fanned her flushed face tiredly with a lace-edged handkerchief and tried not to listen to the flies or breathe too deeply of the dust laden and dead hot air.

Jacob Wilce, Sioux agent for the Ironstone reservation, took out his watch and noted the time to be six forty-two.

The girl saw him returning the watch to

13

the pocket of his black alpaca vest and said, rather sharply, "That's the third time in the last five minutes, Major. I trust you understand that I'm quite aware of the time."

The agent nodded his shiny bald head. "Wasn't thinking, ma'am," he said mildly, and sucked almost inaudibly on his bad tooth.

That nervous habit, so often repeated in the hour she had been here, now grated once more against Gail McCune's frayed nerves. She didn't like this Jacob Wilce, for he was a thin dour man wholly devoid of any emotion; or so he seemed. She was slightly in awe of him, chiefly because of his title, Major. She supposed, wrongly, that he was a retired Army man; later she was to learn that every Indian agent in the west was referred to always as "The Major."

She felt his glance striking her and pulled her blue velveteen skirt down so that it hid her ankles. She felt it necessary to say something, for the stillness was oppressive.

"I don't know why my father would sign such a contract," she flared, with an unintended edge to her voice. "It's ridiculous to have to pay such a penalty simply because these cows of mine don't arrive by a certain time."

The agent smiled thinly at her referring to

14

the McCune steers as cows. "Your father signed that same contract four years straight running, ma'am. Don't think I make anything by applying the penalty. The money'll go back to the government."

"Whoever gets it, it isn't fair. A dollar a head! Three thousand dollars!"

"But we've got to have some guarantee that your drovers will get us our beef on time," Wilce said in that same mild unemotional way that so irritated her. To add to her vexation now, he sucked at his tooth again before continuing placidly, "These Indians are already starving. They've been camped here around town for days. I'm threatened by an uprising if I don't issue them beef. That's why the contract sets a deadline."

Helplessly, angry beyond words, Gail McCune turned to the window again, sitting stiffly in the horse-hair rocker. And now Jacob Wilce's bold glance studied her at leisure. He wasn't too old to admire this girl's well-turned ankle, her slender waist below the gentle curve of her tight bodice and her coppery hair.

Never was a better looker than a red head he was thinking, which made him mistaken on two counts. Gail McCune's high-piled hair looked red in the strong sunlight but

15

was really a deep rich chestnut; and her face showed more character than prettiness, for it had the flaw of a wide mouth, clearly not of that rosebud variety associated with "pretty" women, and her nose was uptilted slightly from a truly straight line. She was more striking looking than pretty.

What she was seeing beyond the window was more of the filth and confusion and drabness that had so depressed her the past five days in Grade. Before that had come the two-day stage ride across here from the railroad way station; and with each dusty jarring mile the awesomeness of the reservation's isolation had made a deeper impression on her. She was a city girl, accustomed to security and niceties and cleanliness. Here she found none of that.

Now, across by the squat log trading post, she was watching a group of loafing Sioux bucks who looked as alike as old pennies in their wide high-crowned black hats, their dark pants and tails-out shirts. Two reservation police sat on the edge of the plank walk, one with his dark blue uniform buttoned crookedly, the other seeming misshapen and dwarfed by a big Navy Colt's strapped in a holster high at his waist. They sat with their boots in the littered gutter, seeming not to pay any attention to the dirt and the filth. Nearby a mangy cur dog licked at a puddle where the post swamper had just emptied his bucket of slop. The bony runted horses tied at the rails nearby switched their tails constantly at the torment of the flies and stood down headed and drowsing miserably in the fierce blaze of the lowering sun.

At the upper end of the square another knot of Indians stood admiring a sleek clean-limbed chestnut horse. To this side of them was a saucerlike depression some sixty feet across, the topsoil at its center cracked and curled to mark where standing water had been sucked dry by the sun. Years ago this had been a buffalo wallow; the town had had its beginning when a hide buyer's crew had settled here.

The thing that impressed Gail McCune most unfavorably at what she had seen these past days was the countless fat squaws and their dirty children who roamed the plaza at all hours of the day on seemingly pointless errands. They were out there now, sitting on the walks, getting in the way of the slow traffic of saddle horses and wagons and buckboards. She didn't understand how children could ever grow up in such unhealthy conditions and blamed their mothers, the squaws, for it. She turned from the

17

window once more, facing the agent behind his battered deal desk, and asked abruptly, "What time is it?"

He took out his watch. "Nine to seven," he said.

"I wish my father was here!" Gail said in a tired voice.

Wilce gave a slow shake of the head, his expression grave. "We'll all miss John McCune," he said. "A fine man."

All at once Gail found this unbearable. She got up quickly out of the chair. "Please let me know if there's any word for me," she said, and started toward the door.

Wilce was there before her, holding the sagging mended screen open.

"I'm sorry about this, ma'am," he said as they stepped out onto the complaining boards of the porch. "As I say, it's nothing to me if —"

His words broke off and, looking up at him, Gail saw his glance directed down the square. Looking that way, she at first saw nothing that could have taken his attention. Then the man on the white-stockinged buckskin rode around the group of bucks loafing in front of the Blue Belle, the saloon, and he headed toward the agency tie rail and she knew that it was this man Wilce had seen.

Beside her, the agent said, "Here's Santell."

"Santell?" Gail asked.

"Your foreman."

"Oh!"

That low-breathed word was eloquent of a vast relief within Gail that lasted until Wilce said flatly, "But he couldn't have made it. I'd have had news if the herd was close."

The fury that instantly gathered in Gail dwarfed the emotion that had held her this last hour. She stood silently watching this Santell approach, targeting him with a fierce and raging contempt. The closer he came, the more there was about him that she didn't like.

First, she saw that he badly needed a shave; his face looked dirty, grimy. Next, she noticed the long expanse of grey cotton underwear exposed by the rolled sleeves of his white blue-pinstriped shirt. Her involuntary thought was that, if a man was foolish enough to wear long underwear in this pressing heat, the least he could do was to keep his shirtsleeves down to hide it. Finally, as he swung aground and ducked under the tie-rail to saunter up the walk toward them, she saw that his eyes were bloodshot and the lids a trifle swollen. She immediately labelled him a drinker.

Dave came to a halt beyond the bottom step, touched his hat to her and drawled, "We made it, Major. I'm five minutes early."

"Where's the herd?" Wilce asked severely, dispensing with the formality of any greeting.

"Somewhere this side of the south line along American Creek."

"Then you didn't make it. That's thirty miles from here."

"Read the contract, Major," Dave drawled levelly. "It says we have to be on the reservation, not here at Grade, by not later than seven o'clock on the evening of the twentieth. Today's the twentieth and it's not seven yet. So there's no penalty."

Gail turned to the agent, not taking a full breath as she studied the stern cast of his long thin face.

"That's a technicality you can't fall back on," he said. "Every other year we've considered the town here as your delivery point."

"We've never been late before. Last week we were stampeded and it took us four days to make our gather. All I'm askin' is that you go by the contract and not apply the penalty. The herd'll be here as fast as my men can bring it."

"You'll drive the tallow off those steers,"

Wilce objected. "They'll be under weight."

Dave Santell shook his head, said soberly, "They won't. They'll grade better than any animals we've brought you so far."

The agent was now plainly at a loss at finding any further objection. He said dryly, "We'll have to talk this over." Then, nodding down to Gail, he added, "Santell, this is your new owner, Miss McCune."

Dave smiled pleasantly and now removed his Stetson. "Howdy, ma'am," he said. "We tried not to keep you waiting."

So confused had Gail become by the shifting possibilities of their interchange of words that now she said the first thing she thought of, said it cuttingly and without reason: "Why should you lose four days because of a stampede?"

The faintly amused look that passed between the two men only angered her further. Wilce said mildly, "A stampede is something you'll have to learn more about, ma'am." He nodded down to Dave. "Better come in and get something to wash the dust out of your craw, Santell. Sorry we don't have some lighter refreshment for you, ma'am."

Gail was still smarting under that unreasoning anger as they went into the shabby office. Dave held the screen wide for her and she purposely didn't look at him in passing, nor as he drew the rocker from the wedge of strong sunlight at the window, offering it to her before going across to the desk to join the agent there. Wilce had taken a bottle and two none-too-clean glasses from a drawer of the desk. Now he filled the glasses with straight whiskey, pushed one across to Dave and said, "Well, here's to a long count. That's evidently all I can hope for."

They drank on that and for the next several moments talked of things quite at odds with Gail's understanding, of the long hard drive, of cattle prices and of the dry summer and how it had affected the condition of the cattle.

"They'll do, though," Dave Santell said at length. "We took our time and they're up to weight. By the way, I turned those three hundred head over to Breen three days ago."

Gail understood that something was wrong as an expression of bafflement and surprise crossed Wilce's face.

"You gave Breen some steers?" the agent asked. "Why?"

Dave frowned, peering hard at the agent; his dark eyes were no longer pleasant and warm but surface lighted with a strange quick hardness.

"He had an order signed by you. Said you wanted him to take three hundred head to the north end of the reservation to issue to that big camp on the Squaw."

"But I fired Breen sixty days ago." Wilce's expression was one of blended amazement and contriteness. He said hollowly, "My God, Santell! You've been stolen blind!"

"Here's the order in your handwriting." Dave took a crumpled piece of paper from his pocket, smoothed it out and tossed it onto the desk. His eyes didn't once leave the agent.

Wilce shook his head slowly, helplessly. He looked down at the paper, read it. "Breen would naturally be able to make a good imitation of my writing. But it isn't mine, Santell. I let Breen go because I suspected he was rustling from the reservation herd. I even had him in jail while I hunted evidence against him to turn him over to the army at Fort Bewell. But there wasn't any. I had to turn him loose."

"What are you saying?" the girl asked sharply. "Do you mean you've lost some of my cattle?"

Dave was still looking at the agent in that hard probing way. His ignoring of Gail now only increased the intensity of her antagonism.

23

But Wilce was affected differently. He seemed to squirm under Dave's glance, although he didn't move visibly. "This is an out and out forgery," the agent said, looking down at the paper. "I'd like to do something to help. But what can I? Would it help to get the police out after Breen?"

Dave shook his head. "No. He had only sixty or seventy miles to drive to wild country. He's across the reservation line by now."

"But you can certainly get those cows back!" Gail put in.

Dave turned now and regarded her gravely. "That depends on a lot of things, ma'am. I'll certainly try."

Gail felt her face grow hot with anger. This man had not only mismanaged things so as to be inexcusably late, but he had lost a tenth of the herd her father had started up from Texas four months ago, just before his death. John McCune had borrowed heavily on that herd. He had left his affairs in such a muddle that Gail didn't even now know but what she would be heavily in debt when they were settled.

But she did know that the contract price on the herd had been twenty dollars a head and that the loss of those three hundred steers represented six thousand dollars. And here before her stood the man who was responsible for that loss. She had her father's hot blood, along with his stubbornness. She was proud and the experience of the past week in these strange surroundings had unsettled her more than she knew. So now she blurted out unthinkingly,

"You fool! You careless muddling fool!"

Dave took her scathing reproach with no visible reaction beyond a tightening of his broad lips.

"Now Miss McCune," Wilce said soothingly, "don't let's lose our heads. I'll get my police out on this. Let's wait until we're sure those steers are gone before we start blaming anyone."

"But he's already admitted that they're as good as gone," Gail blazed.

"Let's just wait," the agent replied with that endless patience that had so disturbed her before Santell's arrival.

Dave went to the door. He stopped there to say, "I'll get a room and sleep a few hours. If I start at midnight I can be into that country Breen was headed for by sunup." He pushed open the screen and left, his move so abrupt and final that Gail could think of nothing to say to stop him, though she tried.

As the sound of his boot tread was fading

beyond their hearing Gail asked helplessly, "What am I to do?"

"Wait, just wait," Wilce said. "You mustn't be so hard on Santell, ma'am. He's a good man. You act as though he'd helped Breen steal those cattle."

This suggestion was too pointed to be overlooked. "That's possible, isn't it?" Gail asked, defensively, for she was at her wits' end.

These past six years she had led a sheltered motherless life and she felt lost and utterly helpless in this strange rough country of uncouth men and filth and bodily discomforts. She was forgetting that her father had trusted Santell completely. All she could think of now in the face of the agent's suggestion was that her foreman had somehow done a dishonest thing, that he was to blame for keeping her here, for causing her worry, and now for the loss of part of her herd.

She asked quickly, before Wilce could speak: "Santell has been up here before, hasn't he?"

"He grew up in the country east of here. That's one of the reasons your father hired him, because he knows it so well. He can even talk in Sioux."

"Then he knows this man who stole those

cows?"

This time the agent wasn't amused by her use of the wrong word. "Of course he knows Breen. At least he's seen him working for me these last three summers. And of course he saw him last winter when your father sent him up here to draw up that new contract with me."

"Then why couldn't he and Breen have done this together?"

Wilce's eyes opened wide with seeming shock. At first it looked as though he was about to protest. But then his glance narrowed and a change came over him; his eyes took on a calculating look. "That's a hard thing to say of a man," he said softly. But he didn't sound too convincing.

"It could be true, couldn't it?" Gail insisted. "He could have planned this and expected to get away with it now that dad's no longer here to watch him. Working for a woman who knows nothing of the business, he might think it would be easy for him to steal, mightn't he?"

Wilce shrugged and ran a hand over his shiny bald head in a gesture of exasperation. "It's you that's deciding this, ma'am, not me."

"You're right, I am deciding it! I want Santell arrested, Major!" Gail said on sudden impulse. "I want him held here until I can find another man who can be trusted to manage things for me. If he's stolen from me, I'll have him tried and sent to prison."

"But Santell is honest." The agent's assertion sounded weak, inconclusive. "Besides, you'd need more proof against him than you've got. The army handles things like this. They'd want definite proof against him."

"What kind of proof?"

Wilce thought a minute. "Say you'd find a lot of money in his possession. More than his pay would amount to. Mind now, I don't say you will. But if he was in with Breen he got paid for it."

"Then look for money. You mentioned that you have police working for you. Search his belongings, do everything you can to get me the truth of this. Do you know where he'll be staying?"

"He said he was going to get some sleep. The only rooms in town are where you're staying, over the saloon," Wilce told her.

Gail nodded. "Then go get him."

She started for the door and he hurried to open it for her. As she went out, he said, "You're sure you won't change your mind?"

"No, I won't! Good evening, Major."

The agent watched her as she went down

the walk toward the Blue Belle; and the look of worry and concern on his face wasn't long in passing.

When she was out of sight, he turned and called, "Tucker."

The door to the back office at the rear of the room opened shortly on a small middle-aged man whose sandy hair topped a green eyeshade. This was Tucker, Wilce's accountant, helper, man Friday. Unimaginative and with a prodigious memory for detail, as neat in person as Wilce was careless, Tucker in reality ran the agency without either himself or the agent knowing it.

Wilce told him off-handedly, "Get Erbeck in here."

Tucker disappeared and shortly the agent heard him call out across the back barn lot. It wasn't long before the door opened again, this time on a medium tall and stocky man outfitted in waist-overalls, a dark blue shirt and high-heeled boots. Erbeck wore a gun hung from a heavy belt around his waist.

Wilce said, "I've got a job for you, Erbeck."

He went to a small iron safe behind his desk and knelt before it to work the combination, this Frank Erbeck meanwhile eyeing him quizzically. The safe open, the agent took out a strong box and from it drew a sheaf of banknotes. He tossed them to the desk as he put the strong-box back, saying. "There's eight hundred. Count it."

Frank Erbeck picked up the money, asking, "What do I do with it?"

Wilce told him.

II

Dave tossed his blanket roll onto the foot of the bed in the room over the Blue Belle and sat down heavily, sagging the mattress ropes nearly to the floor. For some moments he stared blankly at the cracked and peeling paper on the room's far wall, wholly lost in a sober consideration of this new turn of affairs the past half hour had brought.

He had half killed his crew these last ten days, driving them to make good the time lost in that mysterious stampede, driving them even harder to make that risky desert crossing so that John McCune's daughter wouldn't have to pay a penalty for the herd's unavoidable tardiness. He had saved the outfit three thousand dollars. But this news of Breen meant that he had just as surely lost six thousand that he hadn't even known he could lose.

His mind became so muddled that he finally rose, went to the washstand and dipped a towel into the water pitcher and wiped the dust of the afternoon's ride from his parched face. The water was fresh from the saloon well, cold, and the wet towel felt good against his fevered skin.

He shouldn't have stepped to the window to look out across the square. For at once, adding to his already weighty depression, he was feeling the strange uneasiness that always hit him when he looked upon this sorry town. It had been this way last year, the year before, the year before that.

Wonder what there is about it? he asked himself, and had only a partial answer.

He called this his country and he had never seen any he liked as well, that he missed so much when he was away from it. Yet each of these last three summers, the ending here at Grade of the long drive up from Texas had filled him with an indefinable restlessness, a wish that he hadn't come. It had been the same last winter when he was here. In the northward distance beyond the far corner of the plaza towered the snow-shrouded Ironstones. To the south and out of sight stretched the flats and beyond them the desert he had crossed yesterday and last night, hazed and limitless. As a kid he had hunted the rolling timbered prairie to the east; and the badlands footing the shoulder of low mountains in the west he knew well. All this country he liked, felt a real affection for. Yet being here in Grade, even though surrounded by these pleasing memory-awakening vistas, depressed him now to the point where this year he had almost dreaded coming.

Down in the square below the light was fading fast. The Indians, the fat squaws and the shabbily clad bucks, were straggling out of the two ends of the street to their camps. Off beyond town against the fading sun-glow, clouds of blue woodsmoke marked their supper fires. He knew some of these Indians and their language was familiar to him. Yet to see them in a town, riding in wagons and buckboards and buggies, sorrily aping the white man, cast a shadow over his pleasant memories of what they had once been. This change in them was recent, too, for he could remember the old days when they would shun a town and scorn the white man's ways.

Still, this change in the Sioux wasn't the core of his dislike for Grade. It lay in a combination of many things, he decided; of the weathered frame agency and the squat log trading post, both symbols of the white man's tawdry exploitation; of the run-down mission and school where the Sioux children went about their laborsome learning; of furtive men, some of whom never went without their guns and seemed willing to loaf endlessly upon the street — a few were outlaws depending on the awesome isolation of the reservation for sanctuary — all seeming to be the dregs of civilization washed to this far corner of a vanishing frontier because no one cared whether they came or went. There was sordidness here, with little that was pleasant to relieve it.

With an effort, he finally shrugged aside these bleak ponderings and left his room, going downstairs and turning out of the small entrance hallway into the saloon.

The Blue Belle was like everything else in Grade, shabby, run down, gloomy. The lamps were too few to give adequate lighting, the bar rail sagged to the floor on a broken hanger a third of its length along the sticky pine counter, and the mirror behind the bar was dusty and fly-specked. The air bore the stale stench of tobacco and whiskey, and the sawdust on the floor was swept out and changed so infrequently that it seemed always the color of the dirt in the square outside. But even for all this, a man might come here and, through drink and talk, for a time forget the hellhole he was in.

Fred Hamp, the apron, saw Dave and came up behind the bar with a bottle of bourbon and a glass. "On the house, Dave," he said. "You still look like you could stand one." A few minutes ago he had taken Dave's money for the upstairs room.

"Thanks, Fred, I can." Dave poured, nodded to Hamp and drained the shotglass at a swallow.

"Been expectin' you for a week," Hamp said. He was a short barrel of a man with thinning hair, a waxed moustache and pink sleeve garters pinching his heavy upper arms. Now he pointedly ignored a customer who thumped a glass on the counter below, wanting to be served, as he asked, "Run into any trouble on the way up?"

"Some." Dave half smiled at remembering the McCune girl's reaction to the news of the stampede. "Just a little," he added.

Hamp stepped away to serve his customer, then came back. "You ain't a damn' day too early, Dave," he said. "These red devils've been on the prod. We'll be lucky if they don't go after a few scalps before the Major issues your beef."

"Hungry, are they?"

"Hungry, hell! They're starved."

"What's the matter, the government short change 'em on their beef last winter?"

Hamp looked pointedly up and down the bar, then said in a lower voice, "Not Uncle Sam, Dave. But someone sure thinned down the reservation herd when someone else wasn't lookin'."

"Breen?" Dave asked. "I hear the Major let him go."

Hamp smiled scornfully. "Sure, Breen was in on it. But he ain't got enough between the ears to have thought it up himself. This was a big steal. The Major claims he lost close to eight hundred head."

"Well, you can't say he didn't try to stop it if he let Breen go," Dave said. "They were pretty thick, those two."

"That's a fact. A year or so ago I'd've said Wilce didn't give a Confederate dollar for what went on here. But lately he looks like a good man for the job. He kicked Breen out, then a month back he took money out of his own pocket and sent up to Fort Bewell and bought a hundred steers from the Army. Issued 'em right off. No tellin' what would've happened if he hadn't done that."

Here was news. Dave's dealings with Jacob Wilce had given him little liking for the agent as a man. But he did respect him, respected him for a certain animal cunning and shrewdness. Wilce, he knew, was hard to beat in a trade. Because of his opinion of the agent as a close-fisted man, he was doubly surprised on learning of this generous gesture of Wilce having bought cattle to feed the Sioux.

"We live and we learn, Fred," he said.

"Don't we?" Hamp mopped off the bar. "Me, I'll hand it to the Major. He done us all a favor."

He moved away to take care of his customers and Dave turned his back to the counter, glancing idly down the long narrow room. The whiskey was beginning to ease the cramped tiredness from his rangy frame now and he wondered if he shouldn't eat and then ride. He had at least forty miles to cover tonight so as to be at dawn in the country where he figured Breen would have driven the stolen herd into the northward hills. To be on the safe side, he should probably do his travelling first and then sleep out any time that was left until daylight. He would have to wait until it was light before looking for sign of the herd.

But there was no hurry. Just now he was enjoying this relaxation and the anticipation of a meal. The smell of cooked food drove out some of the stale beer and whiskey taint to the air and, looking down the well filled bar, he saw Hamp's Chinese cook at the rear lunch counter. He decided he'd eat here and not go up to Mrs. Cooney's boarding house.

Two of Hamp's poker layouts were running, their green shaded lamps laying their smoke-jagged cones down over them. The back table was dark. A man sat there, though, in the chair in the corner. Although the light wasn't good back there, Dave thought he recognized who it was. And at once he turned and laid a silver dollar on the bar and picked up the bottle and his glass.

Passing Hamp on his way down the bar, he said, "Send over something to eat, Fred," and went on back to that rear table.

He pulled out the bar-side chair and drawled, " 'Evenin', Doc," before the table's lone occupant seemed aware of him.

Doc Faris looked up. His drooping longhorn moustache straightened with a smile. He held out a slender delicate hand. "Dave!" he said warmly. "It's good to see you, boy."

They shook hands. Then Dave pulled down the lamp and lit it, saying, "You're a gloomy soul, Doc, hid back here in the dark."

Faris laughed softly. "Not gloomy, Dave. Just communing with my past. Afraid to shed any light on it, I suppose."

"Eaten yet?" Dave asked as he pushed up the lamp. When Faris shook his head, Dave turned and called to the Chinaman, "Make it two, Louie." He saw the empty glass by Doc's elbow and filled it, along with his own, before he sat down.

The doctor lifted his glass. "Glad you're back," he said, and they drank on that.

For a few moments they sat without speaking, two friends getting used to the look of each other again. Doc was a slight man crowding old age. His eyes, dark blue, seemed more alive and younger than the rest of him. His brown derby and neat black coat, shiny along the bottoms of the sleeves and frayed at the cuffs, bespoke a more civilized way of life than his twelve reservation years had brought him. He managed to look just that, civilized. Here was the only man on the reservation Dave ever looked forward to seeing.

"You're thinned down," Doc said shortly. "A hard trip?"

"Like all the rest. It's no quilting party."

Doc sipped at his drink as though it were some fine liqueur and he was relishing its bouquet. Presently he asked, "Met the new owner yet?"

"Just."

"Pretty, isn't she?"

"I didn't notice. She was too busy firing me."

"She fired you?" Doc appeared only mildly surprised. He laughed. "With that start, you two ought to get along well," he said. "So she has the McCune temper?"

Dave nodded. "To go with her red hair."

"Not red, Dave. It's prettier than any red hair I ever saw. So she has a temper?"

"More than she needs."

"Like John," Doc said gravely. "How was it with him, Dave? Bad?"

"No. Passed away in his sleep without a sick day, so the letter said."

"Good. He deserved it."

Louie came across with heaping plates of beef stew and steaming cups of coffee. He had a broad smile and a word for Dave and after he left they fell to their eating without preliminaries. Because Doc could see that Dave was hungry, he didn't try to talk.

Only when Dave's plate was clean and his own nearly empty did the medico say, "So she let the best man who ever worked for her father go, did she?" leaving it entirely up to Dave to make or not make his explanations.

Dave took out tobacco and built a smoke and laid the sack in front of Doc before answering anything to that. Then: "Doc, what's behind Wilce runnin' Breen off?"

Again the medico seemed only mildly surprised where another man would have been more so, for it was obvious to him that Breen somehow figured in Dave's trouble. Perhaps Doc's many years of coming suddenly upon the unexpected had taught him this perfect self control and a certain deep insight.

For now he said, "So Breen was mixed up in it."

Dave nodded, inhaling deeply of the tobacco smoke and blowing it ceilingward. "He met me with a small crew a day out from the reservation line with a forged order from Wilce telling me to turn over three hundred head to him. I cut them out and watched him drive them away. Now Wilce tells me he never wrote that order."

"And the girl?"

Dave shrugged meagerly. "She can't understand why it took us four days to round up our 'cows' after a bad stampede."

"Dave, she's a city girl. Six years in Philadelphia could make anyone forget a Texas upbringing."

"I'm not arguin' the point, Doc. You wanted to know."

Faris took a briar pipe from his pocket and filled it with Dave's tobacco. The pipe's bit was of wood, chewed nearly through. Its original amber stem was something Dave remembered from the long ago; the pipe had always been as much a part of Doc Faris as the derby. Dave watched the medico pack the briar and light it.

Then Doc was looking at him through a slow billowing cloud of smoke, asking with sure insight, "You're going up into the Scalplock country after Breen?"

Dave nodded.

"He has friends up there, Dave."

"So I take it."

Doc pulled at the pipe again, deliberately and with a deep relish. "You might have a look in the high country off east from the town. It's wild up there. Remember Pete Holmes?"

Dave had to think a moment before the name meant anything. Holmes, he now remembered, he had heard of as a halfbreed who had worked for the agency off and on for the past several years. Last winter, while Dave was here, a Sioux buck had been found mysteriously murdered after a drunken brawl resulting from several Indians securing whiskey in an unknown way. Pete Holmes had been suspected of furnishing them the whiskey, which was later found to have been stolen from the agency warehouse. When the police tried to find Holmes, he had disappeared.

"What happened to him?" Dave asked.

"He's been seen across there," Doc told him. "Lately, he's been travelling with Breen."

Dave frowned, thinking of something. "Does he have a scar over one ear? Hog fat and a crooked nose?"

"That's Holmes. Didn't know you'd ever seen him."

"He was with Breen the other day."

Doc's brows arched. He said, casually, "Then you might look up Birkheimer. And Spence and Torrence. Know 'em?"

"No. Should I?"

"They run cattle in those hills closest to the reservation. Take Torrence. His old man died and left him his outfit. Wheel is the brand. It's only an average place. Yet he seems to make a good thing of it."

"What does he look like, this Torrence?"

"Set up like you. Not so heavy or so tall. Curly dark hair. A woman would look at him twice."

The medico was staring beyond Dave. He frowned now and, after a brief pause, said quietly, "Heads up, Dave."

Abruptly, Dave realized that the room was going quiet. Turning in his chair, he saw Jacob Wilce approaching the table. Behind Wilce were two bucks in the army blue uniform of the reservation police; one was tall and flat-faced and staring hard at Dave as he came up, the other shorter, fatter and trying ineffectually to match his companion's severity. The tall buck's right hand rested on the butt of a long-barreled .45 Colt's in a belt holster. Customers were looking this way and play at the faro and poker layouts had stopped.

Wilce was plainly nervous as he moved in to the side of the table to Dave's left, saying, "We'd rather you didn't start any trouble, Santell. But we're ready for it if you do. Come along quietly."

Dave stared up at the agent in open incredulity. "Come along where?" he asked.

"Upstairs to your room first," Wilce said. "Miss McCune is waiting there. Then you're going to jail."

"You're arresting him?" Doc asked querulously. "Why? You can't lock a man up without reason, Major."

"Gentlemen," the agent said mildly, "I don't like this any better than you do. But Miss McCune asked to have your room searched, Santell. The police have found something that looks bad for you unless you can explain it. Now let's make this as painless as possible."

"What did they find?" Dave asked, coming to his feet. He saw now that his horn handled .38, which he'd left in the room, was thrust through the belt of the tallest police.

"You'll see directly," Wilce said. "Come along."

Dave looked down at the medico and Doc asked resignedly, "Anything you'd like me to do for you, Dave?"

"A last will and testament?" Dave drawled, smiling thinly. "Well, when the crew pulls in you might tell Jim Land he's in charge."

Doc nodded. "Anything else?"

"No. They can't hold me on a trumped-up charge like this, whatever it is."

He turned from the table then and, with Wilce beside him, walked the long length of the bar between the two thin ranks of curious and puzzled customers.

Someone Dave didn't recognize broke the weighty silence by calling loudly, "You're out o' step, Short Horse!" evidently referring to one of the police who walked behind Dave and the agent. A few suppressed laughs greeted the remark; but for the most part the watchers were sober and respectful. For Jacob Wilce was the law on the reservation and most men had learned not

44

to irritate him.

They turned through the door to the entrance hallway and started up the stairs, the two police following closely.

Dave said, "You've made a mistake, Major."

"I certainly hope so," was Wilce's seemingly sincere reply.

They were nearly to the stair head when Dave, in the lead, asked, "What did you find?"

"You'll know presently."

Dave stopped at the landing and moved aside to let the agent come in beside him.

"I've got a right to know before I go in there," he said flatly, noticing with some satisfaction that the two police, blocked by his standing there, had halted two steps below. Then he repeated, "What did you find?"

"Enough to convict you if it means what we think it —"

Suddenly Dave lifted a boot and, thrusting out, caught the tallest of the bucks, directly below, square in the chest. The police made a frantic grab toward holster, then forgot that as he collided with the smaller Sioux behind. They went down together in a writhing tangle of arms and legs. They landed five steps below with a jar that shook the stairs and made the flimsy banister sway. The big one cried out hoarsely in pain as the other rolled onto him. Then both went on down the steps bumping, grunting, trying to break their fall but not succeeding.

Dave, as they went down, wheeled in on Wilce. He caught the agent's right hand as it slid out of sight toward his left armpit, underneath his coat. Bringing the man's arm down with a quick snap, he whirled Wilce around and doubled the arm up at the agent's back.

Wilce groaned as Dave increased the pressure on the arm. Then, lazily, Dave reached over the agent's shoulder and lifted the snub-nosed gun from the clip holster there. It was over before the two police piled up at the foot of the steps.

Dave let go his hold and prodded Wilce in the back with the gun, drawling, "You first, Major," pushing him down the hall.

The agent was thoroughly frightened now as the boot tread of the two police pounded up from below, mounting the stairs quickly. He led the way along the corridor and opened the door to Dave's room. Dave stepped in after him, swinging the door shut. Gail McCune came up off the chair across by the bed, her eyes opening wide with startlement and fear.

Then the hard pressure of a solid object nudged Dave's spine and a drawling voice said evenly, "Drop it!"

Dave let his breath out in a slow tired way. He opened his right hand and dropped the agent's gun. It thudded to the carpetless floor, making a loud sound against the momentary stillness. He looked back over his shoulder at Frank Erbeck, who had been standing behind the door.

A downlipped smile crossed Jacob Wilce's face. He was rubbing his wrenched shoulder as he said, "Thanks, Erbeck. You can go now." He stooped and retrieved his gun, then backed off to the foot of the bed, the weapon levelled at Dave.

"Sure you won't need me?" Erbeck asked, opening the door. Outside, the two police were brought up short at sight of the agency crewman holstering his gun.

"No, I'll do quite nicely now," Wilce said. "Tell those two to wait out there."

The door closed behind Dave and from the hallway came the muffled sound of Frank Erbeck's voice giving Wilce's order to the two bucks. Then Erbeck's boot tread faded down the hallway and Wilce was saying smoothly,

"Of course you don't know where this

came from."

He pointed to a thick bundle of banknotes lying on the bed.

Dave saw the money for the first time and shook his head. "No."

"It was found in your blankets."

"I didn't put it there," Dave said.

"You can't lie out of it!" Gail McCune cut in sharply. Her face was flushed and her hair shone like dark copper in the lamplight. Oddly enough, Dave's thought right then was that he'd never before seen such a striking looking woman. "I watched the police untie your blanket," the girl went on. "The money was there, stuffed in that tobacco tin."

"Not by me," Dave drawled.

Gail's furious glance left him and swung over to the agent. "What's the good of our standing here arguing this?" she asked hotly.

"I wanted to see what he'd say," was Wilce's answer. "Later on, we'll use it as testimony."

"It proves nothing."

Wilce shrugged meagerly. "Perhaps not right now. But it will if he changes his story."

"There won't be any change in it," Dave said. "I've never seen that money before."

Again, Gail McCune's wrathful look came at him. "You helped that man steal my cattle," she said. "This is what he paid you to do it. I'm having you arrested for stealing from me."

Dave looked at Wilce. "Let's get out of here," he said quietly.

"You're sure you want to go through with this?" Wilce asked the girl. "You'll have to go to Fort Bewell to bring charges. You'll have to stay there for the trial. It's ninety miles away and you'd have to come back through here and go on to the railroad again, the way you came. That's a lot of travelling."

"I'd do it if it was a hundred and ninety miles both ways," Gail said scornfully.

On the way down the stairs, Dave said to Wilce, "A pretty tight frameup, Major. What're you getting out of it?"

"I'm not getting a thing," was the agent's answer. He sighed heavily. "I wish I knew who was."

III

Frank Erbeck had a drink at the bar, repeatedly professing ignorance of what had gone on upstairs to the several curious customers who questioned him. Shortly, he left the bar and went out the doors onto the veranda.

He built a smoke as he paused there, letting his restless and wary glance inspect the dusk-dimmed square. A thorough training in trouble had given him that habit of carefully studying his surroundings, even in as familiar a place as this town had become after his three months of living in it.

His smoke lighted, he sauntered down off the steps and out across the square toward the mouth of the street's upper end. He turned once and looked back at the Blue Belle, at the now darkened window of Dave Santell's room. An expression of plain disgust was on his face as he hurried on, for he was late for his supper.

He was turning in the walk across the yard of Mrs. Cooney's broad log boarding house before he saw Martha Mills standing on the porch waiting for him. He wanted to turn and leave, so bleak was his mood. Yet something drew him on and his interest in this girl was as alive and quick as always as he climbed the porch steps and touched his hat to her.

"You're late, Frank," she said.

"Had some work to do," he answered, the sound of her voice instantly making him forget the somber run his thoughts had taken on the way up here. "Do we get anything to eat?"

"If we hurry."

They went in the door. Mrs. Cooney's front room was crowded by a big table with twelve chairs ranged on its four sides. Only three of the chairs were filled now. Ott, the trader, leaned low over his near empty plate, not bothering to look up and see who had come in. The blacksmith, Phil Rust, was wiping his plate clean with a piece of bread. " 'Evenin', folks," he said. "Nothin' left."

Mrs. Cooney's ample figure appeared in the kitchen doorway. She was wiping her red plump hands on her apron. "Don't listen to him," she said. "I've kept it hot and I'll bring it right in."

The third man at the table, who wore a suit and shiny buttoned shoes and looked like a drummer, got up from his chair as Martha and Frank took the two places at the table's far end. He reached to the toothpick jar, took his hat from the back of his chair and went out.

Rust finished his coffee and leaned back in his chair. "What's this about Dave Santell bein' arrested, Frank?" he asked.

"You've got me, Phil," was Frank's noncommittal answer.

"Santell?" Martha asked. "Isn't he the McCune foreman?"

"Sure is. And worth any two men that ever hit this hole." Rust rose, stretched his thick frame and yawned. "Well, guess I'll get down and see what I can hear. When they start jailin' gents like Santell, it's time for me to pick up and leave this country. Means it ain't safe for honest men no longer."

As the blacksmith left, Mrs. Cooney came in with a stoneware baking dish of crusty chicken pie and two plates. She smiled down at Martha. Leaning over to put the plates before them, she said in a low voice, "All nice and hot. Now don't hurry, you two. I have an hour's dishes to keep me busy." There was a friendly meaning in her smile which made Frank uncomfortable and embarrassed.

Maybe the old lady's right. Maybe it's Martha that's keepin' me here, was Frank's thought as he gave Martha a quick glance. Her rather plain face was flushed at Mrs. Cooney's words. When she felt Frank's glance upon her the flush deepened. She quickly spooned some food onto her plate and pushed the baking dish across to Frank.

The pie was good and Frank ate with relish. The trader Ott's presence at the other end of the table was a damper for their talk, for neither of them liked him nor his business of bleeding the Sioux of their money.

But when he finally left and they had the room to themselves, they still sat silent. It was as though something so delicate lay between them that they dared not speak for fear of bringing it to the surface. It had been like this lately with them even though they had been much together.

Martha Mills had spent five empty years here in Grade, teaching at the mission school. In this, her twenty-fourth year, her illusions were failing away before a suspicion that she was wasting the best part of her life, throwing it away. No longer did she go about her work with that intensity and devotion of her religious training. She was now waging her private battle against grim reality, against the new and sobering realization that she had set herself a monumental, maybe an impossible, task. Teaching the Sioux was laborious work, full of disappointment and, just recently, heartache. Tonight, sitting here beside the one man she had ever cared for, she was filled with a feeling that all she was doing was futile, impotent.

"Have you got those kids so they don't take their shoes off once they're out of your sight, Martha?" Frank asked abruptly.

His remark touched her problem so deeply that she answered without thinking, "That's not very kind of you, Frank."

He was taken aback. "Sorry," he said, and

went on eating.

She saw that she would have to make it up to him and said haltingly, "I — I didn't mean that. You're right. They don't wear their shoes when they aren't in school." And she went on bitterly, "They forget what I teach them, forget it by the next day. I'm afraid I'm not a good teacher, Frank."

Amazement made his face go slack as he put down his fork and looked at her. This matter had, until now, been a lighthearted and bantering feud between them. Never before had they discussed it in any seriousness.

"Girl, don't talk like that," Frank drawled. "You're doing the best you can."

"But they don't want to learn," Martha flared. There was a moistness in her blue eyes and she looked away to hide that, the rounded line of her jaw firming as she held back this rise of emotion.

"Now you're talking straighter," he said in sudden seriousness, all pretense gone. "It's what I've tried to tell you. They don't want being taught, won't have it. Martha, ten years ago their fathers were hunting buffalo. Before that they were scalping people like us. You can't expect them to shed the old ways overnight."

Martha laughed nervously. "Watch out,

54

Frank. You're sticking up for them."

He shook his head soberly. "No, not where you're concerned. It takes something different than you've got to give them. I've said it before and I say it again. If you were a spinster and hard enough to take a whip to them, you'd get further." He tempered his words with a warm smile. "Give it up, Martha. Get back among your own kind and start livin' again."

"I've told you there's no place for me to go. This is my work, my duty."

"Go anywhere, go back to Denver or Kansas City or even Chicago. You could teach there. As to duty, there's plenty of whites who could take what you have to give."

Mrs. Cooney called, "Ready for more coffee?" and Frank answered, "No hurry."

But in another moment she came in carrying the big granite pot and filled their cups. Then, because she liked this man and this girl who most times came late to meals, she sat down and talked with them a while. In her barren life as a widow there had once been romance. But it was long gone and she liked to think that maybe she was helping to bring these two together.

Afterwards, Frank walked up the street toward the mission with Martha. The air was cool and crisp, seeming to have cleansed itself of the dust that hung by day over the town. Off beyond the head of the street was the rosy glow of a late fire in the Sioux camp and overhead the stars shone like a sprinkling of diamond dust against a rich coal black blanket.

Yes, Frank was thinking, *she's the reason I'm staying on. And will stay 'till it's too late.* But no regret came with this thought. It was as though this had always been meant to be and that there was nothing he could do about it.

"Frank," Martha said, to break in on his thoughts. "You blame me for wasting my life here. But how about you? Aren't you wasting yours?"

He laughed, softly, brittlely. "Let's leave me out of this."

"Why should we? Won't you take your own medicine, doctor?" she asked him in mock flippancy. "Why is it, Frank?"

"Why is what?" He was playing for time, trying to put down the impulse that made him want to trust this girl, to tell her the thing that was so constantly nagging at him.

"You work for Jacob Wilce. Why? You're young, you must have ambition. They say you're a good man with cattle. Haven't you ever thought you should be working for yourself rather than at a job like this that has nothing but wages to it?"

Had Martha put it any way but this, it is doubtful if that impulse for confession in Frank would have overcome his habitual reserve. But now anger was blended with it, a hot and sudden anger against what he had done tonight there at the Blue Belle. And Frank spoke out, without hesitation, flatly.

"Once I did work for myself."

"What happened?"

A bleakness was in his voice as he said, "A herd from below the quarantine line, from south Texas, was driven through my land. My cattle caught the fever and died a month later."

"Oh, Frank!" Martha laid a hand on his arm and pressed it firmly. "You never told me."

"I burned the carcasses, then got on a horse and went after the man that owned the outlaw herd." He was started now and he went headlong, his words edged with strange bitterness and hate. "It took six months to find him. I asked him for damages. He wouldn't hand over a dollar."

"Couldn't you have started over again, Frank? You had the land."

"I could've. But I didn't. This Texas man sicked his crew onto me. I took a beating.

He stood there laughing down at me when I was too weak to stand."

Now her grip on his arm hurt. Still he went on, wanting her to understand, not to forgive. "It was a week before I walked again. When I was strong enough to ride, I got a gun and killed him."

He heard her catch her breath and felt her hand on his arm go limp. He wanted to leave her knowing that now he had destroyed the one decent and clean thing of his life. Yet something took him on, his stride even and unbroken, and she stayed beside him.

All at once the pressure of her hand was there again. And she was saying, low-voiced, "Does Wilce know?"

"Yes. There's a dodger out on me. He spotted it. Do you think I'd work for him a minute if he didn't have something on me?"

She stopped and turned so that she could look up at him. He could see that her face was pale. "Frank, you have to get out of here! Tonight! Now!"

He shook his head. "No. I'm safer here than anywhere else. Wilce won't give me away as long as I —"

"As you what, Frank?"

"So long as I toe the line. His crooked line."

"But you can't let yourself be like him, Frank," Martha said softly, her voice awed by the full realization of what his words meant.

From down the walk sounded the steps of someone approaching. Frank turned and saw a man's shape come out of the obscurity. And then a voice was hailing him, "That you, Erbeck?"

It was Hult, one of the agency riders. Frank answered him.

"Boss wants to see you," Hult said. "Right away."

"Go ahead," Frank said. "I'll be right down."

They listened to Hult's step fading into the stillness.

"Do you have to go?" Martha asked.

"I'd better."

Martha was silent a moment. Then: "Frank, promise me something."

"Name it."

Again, she didn't speak for a long moment. Finally she said, "Promise that you'll let me know before you leave here, that you'll not go without telling me. I — I'll want to say goodbye."

He laughed softly. "We won't be saying goodbye for a long time." Then, more soberly, "I've never had much use for a man who spills his guts to a woman."

"You had to tell someone, Frank. And something might come up that would mean you'd have to leave in a hurry. If it does, will you let me know, will you promise to see me before you leave?"

"If you say so."

She said, "Now I won't worry so much," and left him, going on up the hardpacked dirt walk.

He stood watching, then listening, until the night had taken her from sight and sound.

IV

Long before the time Dave Santell had breakfasted at the chuck-wagon on the desert that morning, a rider had come in on Wheel with the news that the McCune herd would cross the reservation line sometime that day. Ed Torrence took the information stoically and, some minutes later, saddled and left the ranch, the stars still bright overhead.

Torrence could have reached Grade by a shorter way than he took, for the reservation town lay some fifty miles south from Wheel. Instead, he rode west and down-country. When he reached the hill town of

Scalplock, he paid a visit to a house there, where he roused a man and talked briefly with him. He started the climb for the pass at dawn.

He knew this trailless north slope of the Ironstones like the back of his hand and by nine was high in the aspens, Scalplock hidden in a downward fold of the pine-blanketed hills. Crossing the pass, which marked the reservation's northern line, he continued southward and down. Shortly, he spotted a rider climbing toward him across a boulder field far to his left.

Because it had often paid him to know of the comings and goings of men in this country, he swung off there and, from the concealment of a spur of fox-tail pine, had his furtive closer look at the horseman. He could have saved his trouble, for the unknown was Gillis, the new mail rider, on his way across to Scalplock with the mail from last night's stage picked up at Grade. Torrence knew Gillis but didn't hail him; he didn't care to have it known that he was on the reservation.

By noon, he was low in the southward foothills and travelling the rolling pine and grass country that was the watershed of the Squaw. He cut a mile wide circle around the Sioux encampment at Mineral Springs.

He had little use for the Indians, and they for him.

Riding the long granite rim twelve miles north of Grade just before sundown, he found that he had miscalculated his time. So he stopped below the rim, built a fire and cooked a leisurely meal of stewed jerky and canned tomatoes. At dark he went to the saddle again and headed on.

An hour after dark he rode past the dying supper fires of the Sioux camp close above the agency town. He swung out before he reached the head of the street and rode well beyond the back lots until he came even with the feeble lights of the agency. He tied the gelding in a thicket of scrub oak and went in on the big shed-flanked compound afoot.

He had a long wait, standing in the deep shadow of a lean-to at the rear of the lot. Finally the bunkhouse door opened and a man started across the yard toward the house.

Torrence called, "Send Wilce out, will you?"

The man froze at the sound of his voice, wheeled toward him and his right hand fell to his thigh and the gun there.

Torrence repeated, "Tell Wilce to come out."

"Who the hell're you?" The agency rider spoke belligerently, half out of fear.

"Just tell Wilce I want to see him." Torrence didn't move, knowing he was well hidden.

The man stood stock still another moment. Then, abruptly he swung around and hurried to the back door of the agency, passing quickly in and out of sight.

Wilce appeared sooner than Torrence had expected. The agent stood in the door a brief instant, then closed it behind him and came out across the lot. He stopped near the barn, calling softly, "Torrence?"

"Here," the Scalplock man answered; and enjoyed the start of surprise Wilce gave at hearing his voice come from behind him.

"Why so spooky?" Wilce asked as he came in on the lean-to. He hadn't located Torrence yet and his tone was edged with nervousness. "Why not come inside?"

Torrence gave a soft unamused laugh that let the agent know where he was. "I'd rather be your silent partner, Major," Torrence drawled. Then: "Did it work?"

"Just like you said," the agent told him. "The girl had him arrested. He's in jail." In the feeble starlight, Torrence thought he saw Wilce's face take on a worried frown. "There's only one hitch. Santell's well thought of. What do I tell his friends?"

"Nothing. You won't have to. By morning he'll be off the reservation and headed home."

"You mean? —"

"You're to have at least two men take him as far as the reservation line tonight," Torrence cut in impatiently. "Let him know what'll happen if he ever comes back. You can let on like you're not sure he's guilty. Tell him you're lettin' him go because you're too busy to be bothered with him. Let on like you don't think much of the girl."

"But you can't turn him loose," the agent protested. "He isn't the kind that forgets easy."

"Maybe he isn't. But he won't come back if you make him understand he's to be a wanted man. Tell him you'll fix it so it'll look like he broke jail. Tell him there'll be a U.S. marshal after him inside a week." Torrence spoke deliberately, as though he had memorized this explanation. He had actually done this, long ago.

"Now about this other," he went on, and Wilce could see that his aquiline handsome face tightened in expression. "I hear the herd came across the desert and beat the time it lost in that stampede."

"Who told you?" Wilce asked quickly, and wished he hadn't.

"Never mind. How did it happen?"

"Santell's idea," Wilce said dryly. "The girl won't have to pay the fine now."

"Forget that." Torrence gave a careless lift of one hand. It wasn't his right hand, which hung close to his hip. "It wouldn't have amounted to much anyway," he added.

"Three thousand is a lot of money, Torrence," the agent reminded him.

"Not when you stack it against what's coming. When will the herd pull in?"

Torrence seemed abruptly impatient; and this reminder of the man's unstable temper laid a cold hand of fear on Wilce. He had reason to fear this dark-haired man from Scalplock. Lately, he had pondered the possibility of getting rid of Torrence, of hiring his killing, although he wouldn't have known how to set about this. Thinking of that now was what made Wilce afraid; for when he was with Torrence the man's driving cold will seemed unbreakable.

"Tomorrow maybe," he said in answer to the other's query, "the day after at the outside."

"And when's your beef issue?"

"Right away. The same day if I can manage it."

"Good. You'll make your regular issue and then push the main herd on up to the camp on the Muddy, like we planned?"

"That's what I agreed to."

"Then by Friday everything'll be set?"

"Unless something goes wrong." Wilce wanted to make that one reservation. Accustomed as he was to giving orders, he couldn't take them with any good grace.

"It won't," Torrence drawled.

He stood straighter now and stepped deeper into the shadow, away from Wilce, as the rear agency door opened and the man who had crossed the lot a few minutes ago recrossed it to the bunkhouse. Wilce heard Torrence's breath leave his lungs in a slow exhalation. Then Torrence was saying quickly, "All right, I'll have Breen down there the night the herd hits the Muddy."

The agent had nothing to say and Torrence, with his quick insight, asked, "What's the matter, Jake? Gettin' cold feet?"

"Hell, no!" Wilce said angrily. "But what if something does go wrong?"

"Nothing happened last winter, did it?" Torrence asked coolly. "We swung a bigger loop then than we're swingin' now."

"I can't help but consider everything," Wilce protested. "Last winter hardly anyone was around. Now we've got strangers in town. If anyone gets to askin' questions, it's liable to break us."

"Or make us," Torrence drawled. "Why is this any different than your deal with Ott?" he asked, tauntingly. "You give him the trading concession and he agrees to hand you a quarter of the profits. He kicks up his prices and takes it out of the hides of those damn' Indians. Why is this any different than your sellin' these red devils that rot-gut whiskey on issue days? No, Jake, your record's no blacker now than it was before we agreed to this thing."

Torrence laughed softly again, and now that laugh was mocking, as though he dared Wilce to back down. "Besides," he continued, "you were the one that thought up that neat little idea of firing Breen and having him stampede the McCune herd so you could collect a fine when it was late. Not only that, Jake, but you dreamed up that steal Breen made before the herd ever hit the reservation. You've got good ideas, my friend. But not good enough. You missed a few bets. I'm only callin' 'em to your attention."

Anger hit the agent so suddenly, so violently, that he forgot for a moment. "You're a cold blooded devil, Torrence!"

"I look out for myself, Jake," was Torrence's sober answer.

"You'd never have been in on this if Breen hadn't told you what I was doing."

"Careful, Jake!" Torrence said softly. He wasn't a big man, not so tall as Wilce, in fact. But the way he said this jerked the agent up short, making him at once regret his outburst.

"Jake, if you're going to be crooked," Torrence drawled, "go at it whole hog. Never hire a man like Breen unless you can pay him enough to buy him outright. Breen needed money. So he sold me information. But what're you growlin' about? The way it's turned out, you'll make four times what you would've on your own."

"With four times the risk," Wilce said, again unthinkingly.

In the shadow, Torrence's face twisted in a look of contempt. "Better go in and get out your bottle and have yourself a shot of nerve, Jake."

Sultry anger was again alive in Wilce. But this time his fear of the Scalplock rancher outweighed that anger and he made no retort.

Shortly, Torrence said, "We've been over everything, haven't we?"

"You said something about the McCune horses."

"Four dollars a head is my offer. Five if they're delivered. Better make the deal through the girl's new ramrod, whoever he turns out to be. Anything more?"

Wilce said, "No."

"Go careful, Jake," Torrence drawled gently, meaningly.

The agent didn't know exactly when Torrence left him, it was so dark here under the lean-to's overhang. One moment Torrence was there, the next Wilce knew he was gone.

After fully a minute had passed, the agent called softly, "Ed!" just to make sure.

There was no answer.

"Damned Indian!" the Major breathed, and turned and went back across the lot.

He didn't feel exactly comfortable until he had closed the door behind him and was in Tucker's small lighted back office, mopping his bald head and sucking noisily on his bad tooth.

The lamps in the trading post went out sharply at nine, as always. A minute later Ott padlocked the three bars across the post door, then made his solitary way around the plaza to the Blue Belle, not speaking to any of the several men he passed, nor being spoken to.

He went into the bar just long enough to

drink the same vile concoction he had taken at this hour each night for as long as Fred Hamp could remember. It was four ounces of straight gin followed by a bottle of beer from the trader's private stock that was brought in by stage twice monthly. Ott drank alone, his stooped figure and wizened scowling face forbidding enough to forestall even the conversational forays of occasional friendly strangers under the influence. Fred Hamp always said, "Good night, Mr. Ott," when the trader left the bar for the door leading to the second floor stairway. He rarely got an answer.

Ott's lonesome trek from the post to the saloon was invariably the signal for idlers around the plaza to yawn and drift away toward their beds. Tonight the square was empty a quarter hour after the trader disappeared and the stillness shrouding the town became a shade heavier for the absence of an occasional voice. Presently, even the fitful bursts of loud talk from the saloon seemed muffled by that curtain of silence. The eerie chant of a prowling coyote, and the answering howls of cur dogs from the Sioux camp on the lower flats was like the last restless turning of the town before it dropped off to sleep.

Shortly after ten, several shadows moved

across the littered agency warehouse lot toward the small log jail. One of those shapes approached the jail's single barred window and whispered a hushed yet harsh,

"Santell!"

That first summons brought Dave only half awake.

But when it was repeated, he swung his long legs off the cell cot and came erect before the window that framed a cobalt rectangle of star sprinkled sky.

"Doc?" he queried.

"No. Wilce," came the answer.

Dave wheeled violently away from the window, his back hugging the wall alongside it. He stood tense and not breathing for several moments, not knowing what to expect; it had flashed through his mind that the blasting charge of a shotgun raking the cell might be a fit accompaniment to the obscure pattern of his arrest.

But nothing happened, except that shortly the agent's voice sounded again, impatiently: "Santell! I want to talk with you."

"Get started," Dave drawled softly, and at once ducked down and moved soundlessly to the wall at the other side of the window, behind the end of the cot.

"I'm letting you go," Wilce said, and paused.

Dave made no sound.

Plainly irritated, the agent went on, "Damn it, are you listening? I'm turning you loose. Two of my men will take you as far as the east line. It'll look like you broke out."

Again he paused; and again Dave remained silent, even his breathing shallow and wary.

"You'll have a seven hour start on the police," Wilce said. "Make the most of it. They may follow you over into the Territory. You'll have to keep travelling."

Dave was plainly baffled, his wariness growing tighter with each passing second. In the few minutes he had lain on the cot before dropping off to sleep two hours ago, his fatigue-muddled thinking had revolved around only one hazy notion — that Jacob Wilce had somehow been responsible for his framing, that this affair tonight was in some obscure way related to Breen's theft of that small herd; for, try as he would, he couldn't dissociate Wilce and Breen.

Yet here was a direct contradiction to that theory. Or was it to be proof of it? He was remembering *ley del fuego,* the law of flight, a form of murder indulged in mostly by conscienceless officers of the law interested chiefly in collecting rewards and no questions asked. In its simplest form, the trick consisted of breaking an unwanted prisoner from a jail under the pretense of helping him escape, then coldbloodedly shooting him down in proof to the public of the law's alertness.

"Speak up, man!" the agent said now, to end Dave's speculation. "We don't have all night for this." Then, while Dave was seeking an answer he snapped, "All right, Erbeck! Open up."

A moment later the big lock bar rattled at the front of the jail and the heavy door swung back. A blocky shape moved in across the faint grayness of the night patterned there. Dave's stomach muscles knotted against the expected slam of a bullet and he hugged the wall tighter, a clawing and real fear keeping him rigid. The lock on the cell door clanged, there came the protesting squeal of unoiled hinges and then the same drawling voice that had earlier surprised him in his hotel room said,

"Let's go."

Dave had no choice but to walk out of the cell and through the door. He would have bolted then except that Wilce and another man stood waiting outside. There came the restless muffled stomp of a horse. Turning that way, Dave saw three saddled horses close by. One was his buckskin, marked by the faint grayness of the white stocking on the off foreleg.

Wilce said, "I hope you make it, Santell. Get back to Texas and lose yourself."

Behind Dave the heavy jail door thudded against its frame and his back crawled with the threat he felt there. Yet he managed a toneless drawled answer: "Why the favor, Wilce?"

"Why? Because no woman can tell me how to run things. The easiest way for me is to let you go and forget the thing, if that girl will let me. Stay out of sight for a while and this'll blow over. Now you'd better be on your way."

Dave sauntered across to his horse, weighing his chance of a quick jump to the saddle and a fast getaway, for he was still unsure of the agent's good intentions. Then he remembered the miles the buckskin had travelled that day and knew the chance was a thin one. When the man beside Wilce backed over to one of the other ponies and swung up into leather before he did, the chance was gone.

He noticed that his blanket roll was thonged to the saddle cantle as he climbed stiffly up, thrust boot in stirrup and said, "Give the lady my regards, Major."

He saw the agent's pale long face tilt up to him. "This is no joke, my friend," Wilce said gravely. "You're just plain lucky to get the benefit of the doubt."

"Don't I know it."

Wilce turned and spoke sharply to the other man, the one who had been in Dave's room: "All right, Erbeck. Take him all the way." Then, as Frank Erbeck was mounting, the agent said to Dave: "I couldn't get your gun. The police have it."

Looking down at him, Dave drawled, "I'm revisin' my opinion of you, Major."

"Don't thank me," Wilce retorted. "This is just the easiest way. I'll even wish you luck."

"So long," Dave said, and followed Frank Erbeck away across the warehouse lot. Behind him came the other agency rider.

They struck obliquely away from the line of the street and its houses. Within a quarter of a mile they came to a low rise. As they topped it, Dave looked back and down on the town.

A dim scattered sprinkling of lights marked Grade. That earlier regret of Dave's at coming here was now replaced by an even keener regret to be leaving this way. Suspicion and doubt would be coupled with his name now and he saw that this outwardly helpful act of Jacob Wilce's might well become the final proof of his guilt in the eyes of Gail McCune and the law. But there was nothing he could do about it.

So, resignedly, he rode on. And now that he could take his time to think back over the past quarter hour, that barb of fear he had felt in the cell just before his release was pricking him again, much as he tried to ignore it.

A few minutes after Dave and his guards had ridden away from the jail, Doc Faris stepped quietly behind a mound of empty crates in the jail yard, warned by a sound close ahead that he wasn't alone.

Gradually, he made out a figure standing beside the small barred window of the jail. For five minutes he watched that figure's meager movements and several times the sound that had first warned him came again, the dull ring of metal on metal. Excitement came alive in him as he realized that Dave must have another friend who was here doing the same job he had come to do. He wondered if he should walk over there and help, then decided against it.

Abruptly, the figure moved back along the wall from the window, rounded the far corner of the building and went from his sight. Listening, Doc heard the furtive step of that man, whoever he might be, fading out across the rear of the lot toward the hulking shadow of the agency warehouse.

When he was sure that this unknown person wasn't returning, the medico walked over to the jail and up to the window.

"Dave!" he called softly.

There was no answer.

Doc scanned the surrounding blackness carefully, then lit a match.

The first thing the medico saw was the pried loose bars of the window, their lengths bent and torn from the holes in the thick lintel log. *Good job,* Doc mused, and softly laughed.

But just then a thought sobered him and he went closer and reached through the bars with his still burning match. Before the flame died, he glimpsed the deserted cell, the mussed blankets on the cot, the closed and padlocked door at the cell's far end.

His face went hot and prickling as a stunning realization came to him. Dave was gone. But he hadn't climbed out of the window! And, with the cell door locked, the window was the only way he could have made his escape!

Afraid now, Doc went around to the front of the low building. The big lock bar was in place, the heavy padlock closed.

Dave hadn't come out of the window. Doc's own eyes could prove that. Then it followed that Dave had left by way of the door. But what friend of Dave's had access to the jail keys so that he could release him in this way and then pry loose the bars to make it look like he'd gone by way of the window?

Doc thought hard and in the end was more bewildered than before. No one except an agency man would have access to the jail keys. And Dave had no friends at the agency.

Suddenly Doc knew, or thought he knew. Jacob Wilce himself had let Dave go. But why?

He could find no answer to that and his first impulse was to go directly to the agency, rouse Wilce and question him. But that would only handicap Dave by putting the police on his trail hours before they would otherwise be after him — if it hadn't been Wilce.

Baffled, worried, miserable, the medico finally went out to the street and turned up it toward his house, the mystery of Dave's escape deepening with each new turn of thought.

And now came the nagging suspicion that he had seen the last of Dave Santell. At least the last of a live Dave Santell.

V

They rode steadily, not slow, not too fast, and time and again Dave lost his fight against drowsiness and dozed in the saddle. Each time he would waken abruptly, crowded by that helpless expectation of a gun's sudden explosion, of a bullet slamming into him. But the miles dropped behind with monotonous regularity and no spoken word or tell-tale move on the part of the two agency men broke the rhythmic hoof-pound of their horses.

They halted at the ford on American Creek to water their animals, all three building smokes as they sat with slack rein. By the light of their matches, Dave had the chance to study the Wilce men.

One had a plain and stupid and unshaven face broadened by a flattened nose. The other he had seen before and now he examined him more closely. Frank Erbeck looked intelligent and pleasant even for the soberness written on his face. He gave Dave but one swift look and thereafter avoided his eyes, even when they started talking.

"Much farther?" Dave asked as he let out the first satisfying lungful of smoke.

Frank Erbeck shrugged. "Call it twenty miles."

"More like fifteen, ain't it?" the other asked.

"Fifteen then," was Frank's sparse reply.

Dave's buckskin tossed his head, seemed to listen to some remote night sound a moment, then dropped his head and went back to his drinking.

There was an insistent impulse in Dave to get this over with, to have his doubts answered finally and definitely. For he could see no reason behind the agent's act of freeing him except that he was wanted out of the way. And that meant dead. Yet pride was strong in him, so strong that the only thing that mattered now was matching the casualness of these two agency men.

"Anyone ever fish this stream?" he asked. "Looks like a good pool there above."

"How about it, Hult?" Frank asked idly. "You know more about it than I do."

"Indians sometimes," Hult said. "But fishin's better up in the hills."

There seemed no more to say and presently they rode on. The very unimportance of their talk back there should have reassured Dave; instead, it had the opposite effect on him and, his wariness heightened, he managed to stay awake.

They came to timbered stretches where the stage road wound among thick stands of jackpine with a dense undergrowth of seedlings and scrub oak. Here, if at all, was the place for Dave to make his try at a getaway. But, as though they read his thoughts, the two closed in on him until they were riding close together. They held that abbreviated distance until they were out of the timber two miles farther on.

From then on Dave rode listlessly, accepting the fact that a break was impossible. He had a bad scare once. The road was climbing stiffly along the face of a steep rock-strewn hill where an enormous boulder blocked the main ruts and shallower ones cut off around it. Breasting a high rock outcrop, Hult's horse, behind Dave, suddenly shied violently.

Dave's instant thought at that abrupt and nervous hoof pound was, *This is it!* He rammed blunt spurs into the buckskin's flanks, bent low in the saddle and stiffened against his gelding's lunge ahead.

Then, as the buckskin swerved, Frank Erbeck's roan gathered into a quick run and drew out of the way. Frank turned in the saddle and looked behind. Dave pulled the buckskin in, the absence of any sound behind reassuring. He stopped the gelding and up ahead Frank pulled the roan to a halt.

Hult's vicious and obscene swearing rolled across the stillness, coming up on them. Then Hult said, "Damn' fool jughead! Shied at that white rock layin' back there!" He stopped his rebellious animal with a cruel jerk on the reins.

Frank said quietly, to Dave, "Lucky you stopped."

"Lucky?"

"Yeah. Thought you were makin' a run for it."

They went on with Frank's casually ominous words adding weight to Dave's foreboding. But instead of that dulled apathy toward what he was sure now was to happen, Dave was feeling a slow rise of anger and impatience. Why didn't they get it over with? They were at least thirty miles from Grade and not close to any Indian encampment so that the shots would be heard. What were they waiting for?

And now Frank, still in the lead, began whistling softly and lifted his roan to a faster trot. He held this pace steadily for twenty minutes, so that Dave's buckskin began breathing hard.

Abruptly the roan slowed and came to a stop, Dave drawing rein alongside. Hult closed in behind. Dave faced the buckskin away from the trail, gathering himself for sudden explosive action.

Frank drawled, "Far as we go, Santell."

The mildness of Frank's tone, the fact that he sat with hands folded idly on the horn of the saddle, seemed but a casual prelude to the final and all consuming act Dave had been expecting over the last five hours.

He played for time by asking, "How about a gun?"

"No can do," Frank told him.

Dave shrugged, momentarily eyeing the upended stock of Frank's carbine, almost within his reach. But then he ruled out a try for the weapon, knowing that he had Hult to consider. All he would do was await the right moment, then rush for it. He felt the palms of his hands getting moist.

"We wrapped Jerky in your blanket," Frank said shortly. "Ought to keep you fed until you can hit a town and buy grub."

Dave said "Thanks," and sat there waiting.

He felt Frank's glance full on him. Then Frank said "Well, get goin'. Good luck." He didn't move his hands, just sat there relaxed and waiting.

Dave groped for a way to gain more time, for something to say that would keep them from guessing his suspicion of them until the last possible instant.

He drawled, "Tell the Major he's a better man than I thought."

"He'll be touched," was Frank's dry reply. Yet he blunted the sarcasm of his words with a soft pleasant chuckle.

Suddenly all the tension drained out of Dave, leaving him tired and relieved and wondering why he had inflicted himself with the needless torment over these long hours. Instinct told him that no man who contemplated murder could laugh this carelessly, that Wilce's only purpose in sending these men with him had been to make sure he left the reservation.

He turned the buckskin out the trail, lifting a hand and saying, "Be seein' you."

From behind him sounded Frank's easy, "Next year maybe," and Hult's mild, *"Adios."*

He rode a hundred yards and knew that he was out of their sight.

He drew rein and instantly caught the steady hoof beat of their going. He waited there until that sound had died into the utter stillness of this before-dawn hour. Then he began laughing. He couldn't stop.

The laughing sobered him, did him good. He swung down out of the saddle and walked a few steps to sit on a high bank flanking the trail. He built a smoke and by

84

the time he had finished it his thinking was coming straighter, the last remnant of his night-long tension gone.

And now he began wondering for the first time what he was to do. Strangely enough, it didn't once occur to him that he could do as Wilce suggested, ride to Texas and lose himself and wait until the law's certain hunt for him petered out and he was finally forgotten.

Just as surely, he dismissed the prospect of ever working with the McCune outfit again. John McCune's fiery tempered daughter had finished him there with her suspicion and distrust of him. There was a brief regret in him over the possible mismanagement of the herd's arrival at Grade, of the snarl of detail that he had kept straight in past years — such as the sale of the horses, the chuck-wagon and the two buckboards, the paying off the crew and the seeing to it that they didn't gamble or drink away the money that would get them back home after the long drive. But that would be taken care of. Jim Land was a good man for the job and someone would have the sense to see that he was put in charge.

But what was he, Dave Santell, the newborn outlaw, going to do?

At first he didn't have even a remote idea.

But then the thing that had been in his subconscious mind all along gained prominence. Finally he knew that he could do only one thing, no other. He must head across those northward hills whose high and jagged outlines were now strengthening with a first faint hint of dawn. He would go across there and find Breen and, somehow, get to the core of the intrigue that had managed the theft of the herd and his own present circumstance.

Not for one moment was Breen anything but a minor pawn in his mind's eye picture of this obscure game. Breen didn't have the brain to think up the nicely timed circumstances of the past few days. The herd's theft had been remarkably simple in conception. But the pattern of his arrest, the fact of the money being found in his room above the saloon, was far from simple. A keener brain than Ray Breen's was behind this obscure maneuvering.

So he would go across into the Scalplock country. He would find Breen and deal with him. After that, he would have to follow whatever leads he uncovered.

But right now a minor item became very important. He couldn't cross those mountains and run the risk of meeting Breen unarmed. He had to have a gun. How to get one?

He doubted that he could buy one at any of the Indian encampments; besides, the risk of being seen on the reservation was too great, for the police would be on the hunt for him this morning. There was just as great a risk in riding straight to Scalplock and trying to buy a gun there; he might meet Breen before he got his hands on one. Sixty or seventy miles on East was that way station on the railroad and he supposed he could buy a gun there. But he would waste two days in riding that distance and getting back here, and by that time whatever sign Breen had left up in those northward hills would have cooled.

There was one final way. Both of Wilce's riders had guns.

He thought back over the long night ride and remembered that steep climb in the trail where Hult's horse had shied. And at once he tossed away his smoke, watching the bright red ash burst into a shower of sparks in hitting the ground. He mounted the buckskin and started back up the trail into the reservation.

He rode a mile, fast, then swung off the trail on a wide circle.

As Frank Erbeck started up the rock-strewn shoulder of the hill, the heavy night shadows were thinning, for the sky in the East was light now with the dawn. Hult, thinking of his lost sleep, had ridden on ahead. But Frank was in no hurry. He had much to think about; and that thinking revolved around Martha Mills, Jacob Wilce and Dave Santell.

He found himself trying to fit Martha into a plan he had made long ago for his escape from the reservation. Sooner or later he would have to make his break with Wilce. He had planned how he would leave Grade by night and strike straight west. Three days of hard riding would put him in a wild mountainous country of few settlements. He could live off the country and be on the west slope of the Rockies, in Oregon, by the time winter set in. He had a hazy notion of working his way down to California, 'Frisco probably. Eventually he would buy his passage around the Horn and land at one of the eastern ports. There, he felt, he could forever lose his identity as Frank Erbeck. His problem now was to think out a way of taking Martha Mills with him. Well, he had plenty of time to do this.

Or did he have the right to ask Martha? Would it be safe to take her? A woman couldn't travel as fast as a man. Wilce would certainly make some attempt to bring him back. And if he was ever caught, the agent would collect his reward.

His muddled thinking had gone this far when he sensed a shape hurtling toward him from the crest of a high rock outcrop close to his left. He started to roll from the saddle. His horse lunged forward. Then a driving weight crushed the breath from his lungs and he was falling groundward. His boot was torn from the stirrup. His right shoulder drove hard against the ground and his chest felt as though it was crushed as a man's weight piled onto him.

For an instant Dave's frame rolled clear of Frank. Frank tried to get his knees under him and lunge away. Then a hard blow on his cheek drove him face flat into the dust again.

Dave was breathing hard. He stood over the agency rider, waiting for him to recover from that stunning blow. He held Frank's .45 Colt's in his left hand, having jerked it from the man's holster as they were falling. Ten feet ahead and beyond the near wheel-rut lay Frank's carbine. The roan horse had run on a few steps and now stood waiting as he had been trained, with trailing reins.

When Frank moved, Dave reached down and took him by the arm, wanting to help him to his feet. But with a sudden vicious grab, Frank clutched Dave's arm and pulled him over onto him. There was a moment of furious violence. Frank's elbow drove into Dave's lips, crushing them. Dave's mouth was filled with the salty taste of blood. He rolled free, got to his knees and swung both fists at Frank's face, close before him. Those blows connected and the agency man fell into him, groggily, clutching wildly for a hold. Dave lunged erect and pulled a leg free of Frank's feeble grasp.

"Quit it," Dave drawled, wiping the blood from his mouth with the back of his hand. "Give up, fella. All I want is this iron."

Again, Frank tried to reach out and get a hold on Dave's legs. But he was still groggy. Dave merely stepped out of his way.

They stared at each other over a long moment, Frank's eyes dull with anger in the strengthening light, Dave looking down with a patient wonder. He had hurt this man, hurt him badly. Yet he hadn't taken all the fight out of him.

"One o' the Major's tin stars has my gun," Dave said. "You can get it from him and we'll be even. But I'll need some extra shells."

Frank reached down instinctively and clutched his heavy shell-filled belt. "Go to hell," he said thickly.

Dave came in on him, sidestepped nimbly and, when he had Frank off balance, pushed him flat again. He yanked at the heavy shell belt buckle while Frank struggled under him. He opened it, then pushed erect and, with a tug, jerked the belt from around the agency man's waist.

He stood buckling it around his thighs, looking down at Frank to drawl, "I'll take the rifle, too. When my outfit hits town, go see Jim Land and tell him to give you thirty dollars out of my pay. Tell him why you want it and he'll hand it across."

Frank said nothing. He managed to get to his feet and stood with boots spread wide to steady himself. His face was pale with fury and bleeding from a gash along one cheekbone where Dave had hit him. He was dragging in huge lungfuls of air, trying to get his wind back. And he wasn't licked yet; for Dave could see him calculating the distance between them, gathering himself for a lunge.

Dave stepped back from him and went over to pick up the Winchester. Then he went across the road and around the high boulder from which he had leaped. Frank started after him, his gait stumbling, uncertain. Frank lost his balance when he stepped into the first wheel-rut. He fell flat. He got up again and came on.

By now Dave was twenty yards up the face of the hill. Looking back at Frank, still coming on, he had his keen regret at having given this stubborn gutty fighter such an unfair beating. Then he went on around the high shoulder of the hill to where he had tied the buckskin.

In the saddle, he rode back so that he could look down toward the road again. Frank Erbeck was standing there, one arm across his aching chest, staring up in the direction in which Dave had disappeared.

Dave lifted his hand in a brief salute, got no answer, and dropped down the far side of the hill.

It was a little better than sixty miles across to Scalplock. He would be there by nightfall.

Frank Erbeck was back in Grade by eleven that morning. He turned his horse into the big agency corral, forked down some hay for the animal, then went to the crew shack to wash up. Hult was the only man there; he lay snoring in his bunk.

Frank's face ached with a throbbing deep pain and the gash on his cheekbone smarted and started bleeding again. It was hard for him to breathe and he wondered, hardly caring, if he had any broken ribs.

Over the past four hours, the beating he had taken at Dave's hands had become a shameful smarting thing, a blot he must somehow erase. So deep was his feeling of humiliation, and so final the stubborn resolve that he would again meet Dave and this time whip him, that he had made up his mind to leave Grade at once. Instead of riding west, he would go south. Texas wasn't big enough to hide this Dave Santell from him. And he had completely forgotten that only last night he had been feeling sorry for Santell!

As he washed at the bench alongside the bunkhouse door, he began wondering at Dave having taken both his guns, at the fact of Dave having risked so much in waylaying him. Why had Santell been so intent on having a weapon? The man had been lucky. Any number of things could have happened back there, any one of which would have involved great risk for the Texas man.

Then, as knotty as the puzzle had become, it abruptly straightened out. He knew that Dave wasn't the kind who would easily forget his arrest. Nor would he forget what had caused it, Breen's theft of the herd. So long as he was innocent, this Santell had everything to gain — and not much to lose — by trying to find out who had framed him. And the only clue he could possibly have so far was an obvious one. That clue was Ray Breen.

It naturally followed, then, than Santell wasn't headed for Texas, that he wasn't going to run from Wilce's threat of putting the law on his trail. No, Santell had wanted those guns because he was going on the hunt for Breen. Then wherever Breen was, there also would be Santell. Eventually, of course.

Short of noon, Frank left Grade and hit the hill trail that led across the mountains to Scalplock. In his saddle bags he carried grub enough to last him three days. He had borrowed the sleeping Hult's six-gun. Hult could make his guess on who had taken the weapon. So could Wilce make his guess on where his crewman had gone. So could Martha wonder why he didn't show up at Mrs. Cooney's for his meals. He didn't like doing this to Martha, for she would worry, maybe think he had left for good. But he couldn't help that.

All that mattered was that he had the chance of finding Dave Santell. And this time it would be a different story.

VI

The day's dying burst of sunlight was creaming the upper snow fields of the Ironstones as Dave dropped down out of the trees and saw Scalplock lying below in the gathering dusk of a timbered hill fold. He had often heard about this town, heard of it as a place to avoid; and now he reined in and had his long look at it, strongly resisting an insistent urge to turn back and wait until he had the full light of day to go on down there.

Vague rumors of what went on here in the Scalplock country had even years ago travelled as far as Dave's home range, three hundred miles to the east. Because he was ten years gone from this land of his upbringing, those rumors had become hazy of detail. But he could remember enough to keen his wariness — tales of lawlessness, of renegades and outlaws periodically run off the reservation and coming here, of small ranchers who in earlier days had preyed on the Fort Bewell herds for their shady beginnings.

There was one story clearer than the rest. The Army had finally tired of issuing warnings to the rustlers living in this tangle of hills. A cavalry detachment had been sent across here from Bewell to recover stolen cattle. They had found the town empty, deserted. It had been the same with the ranches; even the cattle had been driven off into the hills. The irate lieutenant in charge of the detachment had ordered the torch put to the town and the ranches closest to it.

The scar of that old fire was still visible on the near bank of a creek in the ravine below the new town. The present buildings flanking a short street were all of log or slab and clung precariously to the face of the high hill that formed the ravine's eastern shoulder. Pine timber backed them closely on the upper side. It wasn't much of a settlement. There weren't over twenty buildings in all; and in a few, lights were already glowing against the thickening darkness.

Dave shrugged aside his hesitation and rode on, thinking that before he did anything else he would have to find feed and shelter for the buckskin. The animal had covered close to a hundred miles these last thirty hours and needed rest badly.

He stopped in a clump of jackpine halfway down the slope and hid Frank Erbeck's Winchester in a hollow rotting windfall. He also left the heavy shell belt and holster there and shoved the Colt's inside his shirt, wedged by the belt of his waist-overalls. Then he went on, fording the creek presently and then topping a lift of the trail to bring the town into sight again, close now.

Riding down the street, he spotted the feed barn almost at the town's center, across from a squat log building with a weathered sign on its wooden walk-awning proclaiming *Merchandise, B. Shotwell, Prop.* He left the buckskin with a close-mouthed and suspicious hostler, paying the man half a dollar extra and telling him, "Give him grain, lots of it."

In the store across the way, the owner treated him with the same too obvious indifference and surliness. Dave bought a two pound chunk of bacon, some coffee which he had ground, salt, flour, three big cans of tomatoes and a skillet. He asked for a flour sack to carry his grub in and, as he paid, inquired the way across to Fort Bewell.

His query seemed to thaw the storeman; for he received an almost polite answer: "Bewell? Head north, down the valley. Just keep goin' and you'll get there."

"Reckon I can make it in a couple of hours?" Dave's seeming ignorance of the country was bland and disarming.

"Not without killin' a couple of horses, you couldn't! It's over forty miles."

Dave whistled, then gave an easy laugh. "Hell, I thought I'd make it easy tonight."

"Better lay over here," the store owner said, apparently convinced now that here was a stranger, an out of country man, with no other reason for being in Scalplock than that he was just passing through.

"Place to stay, is there?" Dave asked, adding, "I got ground sores from sleepin' out so much. A bed'd sure feel good."

"Tom Warren might put you up over the saddle shop. But it ain't fancy."

"Don't have to be." Dave took his change and pocketed it, and began dropping his purchases into the flour sack. Abruptly, he looked up. "You wouldn't know of a stud game goin' on anywhere tonight, would you?" he asked.

He could see the storekeeper debating something and added, "Low stake, o' course."

"How low?"

Dave grinned. "Depends on how my luck runs to begin with," he said. "Nickel limit, maybe."

The store owner chuckled dryly. "There's always the saloon. You might run into a game your size there. If you're out for blood, ask the barber and he may let you in on the game in his back room. Half a buck limit."

Dave said, "Too stiff for me," slung his sack over his shoulder and carried it across to the feed barn. Then he went to the saddle shop toward the lower end of the street and found that he could sleep on a straw-mattressed bed in the upstairs room for fifty cents. He paid his half dollar in advance. He liked the saddlemaker's face. Warren had a kindly look and at first didn't want the money. But Dave made him take it.

The street, almost empty as he had come in it, was now beginning to come to life with the dark. There were an even dozen saddle animals standing at the rails along it as he went over to a grimy-windowed lunch room and ordered steak and pie and coffee.

As he ate, he was wondering what luck he'd have in finding Breen. The chances were much against him that the ex-agency rider was even in town. But this afternoon he had remembered Breen's weakness for poker, known to him through his other trips to Grade. He had settled on this as his one lead. If Breen was in or around Scalplock, a poker game would eventually attract him. Not tonight, maybe, but certainly soon.

Now, having established himself as a harmless stranger on his way to Fort Bewell, Dave could take his time about moving on. If he had any luck at poker tonight — he had only a few cents over four dollars in his pockets — and if he found a friendly game, he could lay over another day or two longer without arousing any suspicion. In whatever time he found it safe to stay here, he would have to locate Ray Breen.

An hour after finishing his meal he was in a draw game at the small saloon, the *Elite,* and three dollars the winner in a game with a nickel limit. By nine he had won six dollars and a quarter. He cashed in then, with the promise that he would be here tomorrow night and the excuse that he wanted to get some sleep. Of the thirty-odd men who had gone to and from the bar since he had come into the *Elite,* he had seen no one he knew. This evidently wasn't to be Breen's night.

Starting down the street toward the saddle shop, he saw that the barber shop's light was still on. He sauntered on across there and looked in. The two scarred black mahogany chairs with their red plush foot rests were empty and there was no sign of a barber waiting for customers. But in the back wall of the small room the frosted glass upper panel of a door glowed with light from the other side.

He went into the shop and was halfway to

that back door when it opened narrowly on a plump short man in shirtsleeves. The man came out, closing the door quickly behind him, saying, "I've closed for the night, stranger."

Dave remembered the name on the awning of the *Merchandise.* "Shotwell told me there was a game on here tonight," he said. "What's the chance of sittin' in?"

The barber eyed him with a suspicious scowl. Shortly, he asked, "Blaine Shotwell sent you?"

Dave nodded.

Another hesitation. Then: "It'll cost you ten to buy in."

Dave brought out his money, counted it. He had ten dollars and thirty-four cents. He let the barber see the ten, then put the money back in his pocket and turned back to the street door, drawling, "Guess not. Wasn't aimin' to horn in on a private game."

Behind him, the barber said quickly, genially now, "It ain't so private but what we can use your ten."

Dave was grinning as he faced around again. "Feelin' lucky tonight, eh?"

"I'm fifteen the winner." The barber stepped back and opened the rear door, his next words a bantering, "Come along, sucker."

Dave followed him into the room. The air was close and fogged heavily with smoke. Four men sat around a small square table. There were two empty chairs, six stacks of chips. Counting one as the barber's, there was a player missing. The man on the far side facing the door was Ray Breen. He looked up from his cards a second too late.

The gun slid out through the opening in Dave's shirt and lazily lined at Breen. Dave reached out with his free hand and pushed the door shut and leaned back against it. The man to Breen's left was the last to see the gun. He, too, had been looking at his hand and now as his glance lifted his mouth sagged open. He said hoarsely, "God A'mighty!" and dropped his cards and tilted back out of line with the gun.

Dave drawled, "Better reach and get on your feet. Slow!"

No one said anything. The barber's sallow face had gone paler and he was the first to lift his hands. He moved farther from Dave down the side wall. Two others scraped their chairs back and rose. Then another.

Finally it was only Breen who sat, his hands flat on the table, his massive shoulders hunched forward, as though he would lunge when he moved. He had a broad and square face that was now impassively set.

Pale gray eyes reflected a cold steady wariness.

Dave's thumb drew back the hammer of the Colt's. "You weren't hard hearin' the last time I saw you, Ray," he drawled. "Get up!"

Breen said, "What is this?" without moving.

"Just a friendly —"

Dave had said that much when the sixth player, who had left the game to go across to the saloon for a bottle of whiskey, opened the door at his back hard and pushed him off balance. As Dave stumbled, he tried to keep the gun in line.

He could have killed Breen had he wanted to. For Breen was an easy target as he lunged up out of his chair, heaving the table up and over. Instead of shooting, Dave wheeled away from the door, letting the gun off cock.

An instant later the table crashed to the floor on its side, spilling chips, empty glasses, cards. And in the sweep of one arm Ray Breen knocked the overhead lamp from its holder. It burst apart with a metallic jangling sound as it hit the floor. The room went dark except for the light coming through the door from the shop.

"Down, Ed!" Breen's deep voice bellowed.

The man who had unwittingly opened the door against Dave's back ducked out through the opening into the shop. Dave dimly saw Breen's right arm sweep up from his thigh and at the same moment threw himself to the side, colliding with the nearest man and dragging him down with him as he fell. Breen's gun exploded, a man fell heavily and loosely into the swung back door.

Suddenly all was confusion, a blend of fear-edged shouts and the sound of violent movement as men crowded into each other or fell flat to avoid the threat of more shooting.

Dave slugged the man under him with his free hand as he rolled onto his back before the overturned table. He was facing the door and lying full in the light shining through it. He lined his gun and shot twice through the empty doorway. The chimney of the lamp in the shop disintegrated, the flame guttering out. Quickly, Dave went belly down in another half roll, slashing out in the total darkness with the gun.

His blow hit a man sharply in the shins and his victim bellowed hoarsely and kicked out at him. Dave sensed the blow coming and raised his gun arm to ward it off. The boot caught him on the forearm, numbing the muscles of his hand so that the Colt's spun from his grasp. He caught the man's boot, twisted it hard and then got to his knees and drove his head into the man's middle as he went down.

Someone piled into him from behind and he sprawled face flat on the floor. The glass panel of the door broke and clattered to the boards: the next instant and the man on top of him breathed, "That you, Spence?"

Dave struck upward with an elbow and connected, feeling the hard bone structure of a man's face against his elbow. Then, bringing his hands under him, he pushed up and the man's weight slid off him as a fist drove into the small of the back.

He got his feet under him and, arms outstretched, dove at the table. It slid backward three feet, then jammed with its legs against the rear wall. Dave pulled himself up and fell belly down across it and lit hard on one shoulder behind it.

He came erect hearing the hard breathing of a man close by, the scrape of boots beyond the table, the grunt of a man further out as he took a blow. He struck out savagely in the direction from which the breathing came. His fist hit a shoulder heavily padded with muscle; he knew it was Breen. He was slashing out with his other hand, his aim higher, when a rock-hard big fist caught him in the throat, and knocked him backward.

He was retching, gagging for breath, as Breen's weight piled into him. He managed to turn a little as he fell back across a table leg. It broke under him and he went to the floor. Its jagged broken end must have ripped Breen in the side as the big man's weight came over on him; for Breen cried out hoarsely and rolled away, shouting, "Here he is!"

Dave thrust out a boot and pushed the table aside. It collided with a man who went down mouthing an obscene oath. Dave was crawling away when Breen caught a hold on one of his legs. On knees, Dave turned and struck downward with all the weight of his upper body behind a fist. But there was nothing there and the force of the blow carried him off balance and his fist struck the floor in a knuckle-aching drive. Quickly, he kicked away Breen's hand hold and crawled away, then got to his feet. He had barely climbed over the table when someone hit him hard in the stomach.

He struck out wildly as the blow doubled him over. His right smashed into a man's face. He felt his knuckles mash a pair of lips against teeth that cut him bone deep. He drove his head into the man's midriff and went down again as he stumbled over another's outstretched legs.

Dimly, he made out the shadow of the door's outline and a man's high broad shape in it. This was Breen. He stood up, jarred but still erect as a man stumbled into him. He pushed this one away and went to the door and, throwing weight behind his fists, hit Breen twice in the head. In the feeble light coming through the street window, he saw Breen go down, limply. He stumbled out the door to where Breen lay and reached down to pull him to his feet.

A man rushing out the door shouldered him aside from Breen. He fell against the wall, against the ceiling-high rack in which were neatly cubbyholed the shaving mugs of the shop's customers. Trying to catch himself and to keep from falling, he pulled this rack over on him and fell anyway, the mugs spilling to the floor in a shattering brittle wave of sound.

He booted the rack off his legs, picked up an unbroken mug and threw it at the vague shape he saw rising up off the floor, knowing this was Breen. The mug missed and crashed into the big mirror behind the nearer chair. The mirror broke and fell to the floor with a jangling musical sound. A man stumbled out the rear room door and into Breen. Dave dimly saw Breen knock this man down and then drop on him, knees first.

Someone out on the street was shouting lustily as Dave got to his feet. The man under Breen screamed, "Don't, Ray! It's me, Spence!" and Breen stood up.

Dave stepped in at him and swung on him once more. His knuckles hurt as his fist tilted Breen's head around. He swung his other arm but missed and would have fallen if he hadn't lurched forward into Breen. He twisted free of Breen's powerful hold and swung again. But before his blow landed one of Breen's fists hit him in the temple. Weakness went through him for a few seconds and in that time he took four more punishing blows, one in the face, three in the chest.

Groggily, he closed on the big man, trying to get inside the brutal swing of those ham-like fists. His first blow must have done Breen much damage, for the man forgot his strength and kept trying to shove Dave away. They were near the front of the shop now and Dave could see men running across from the *Elite.*

Finally, the numbness cleared from Dave's brain. He was slugging once more, weaving aside from Breen's powerful swings. He hit the massive man so that each blow counted now, hit him in the face, feeling his fists slide over blood-slippery flesh.

The window was only four feet behind Breen when a man's driving weight took Dave in the back and threw him hard against Breen. He caught hold of the bigger man to keep from falling. Breen, off balance, staggered backward, crashing through the window. The sill of the window caught Breen at the back of the knees and he fell out, Dave on top of him.

Dave drove two half-effectual blows in at Breen's chest and wrenched free of the man's encircling arms. As Dave was coming to a stand, someone knocked him down with a stiff driving blow to the jaw. He fell across Breen, kneed him in the face to break his quick hold, and rolled clear.

A pair of legs was coming in at him and, from hands and knees, he dove into those legs. The breath was driven from his lungs as this second man fell onto him. Another was close now and kicked Dave in the side. He twisted onto his back and slugged a face close above his, hit it twice, hard, viciously.

For a long moment they struggled there on the walk, Breen, Dave, the third man. All at once Dave was in the clear and stood quickly erect, Breen and the other man struggling at his feet. Too late, he sensed the rush of another of Breen's friends out of the shop door. A shoulder knocked him off balance. At the last moment he reached out and grabbed the man and they fell out and across Breen and rolled off the walk into the gutter.

Twice Dave felt the numbing jar of a fist driving into his jaw. He struck out feebly, connected, and watched the man's head rock back hard against the edge of the walk planking. The man's frame all at once went limp. Dave pushed the weight of his victim's legs off his thighs and stood up again. He was unsteady, weak, and stood with head hunched, dragging in huge lungfuls of air, waiting for the next man to come at him.

Breen was up now. So was the other on the walk. Two more stood here off the walk's edge, one to either side of Dave, waiting for Breen's word before they rushed their victim. Beyond them stood a loose group of eight or ten men who had come across from the saloon.

Breen advanced a step until he stood almost within Dave's reach. His broad heavy face was battered and swollen, his look ugly.

"Where'll I hit him?" he asked, with a soft unamused laugh.

Dave stepped in at him, swung hard. Breen easily backed out of the way. Dave fell headlong across the walk. Breen booted him in the side so hard that it rolled him halfway over. Dave laboriously pushed up onto elbows, then hands and knees. Breen put a boot against his side and pushed and Dave sprawled face down. One of the watchers guffawed loudly, then went silent when no one joined him.

Dave was once more trying to rise when a voice from the middle of the street said, "That's enough, Ray."

Breen swung around. The rest looked off there. "Who the hell says so?" Breen asked.

A rider drifted in out of the deep obscurity. It was Frank Erbeck. He reined the horse in just beyond the tie rail. He sat the saddle loosely, one hand holding a .45 Colt's that rested lazily against his thigh.

"He's licked, Ray," he said. "Lay off."

"You want some of what we gave him, Erbeck?" Breen asked.

Frank lifted the gun now and laid it across the broad swell of the saddle, lining it carelessly in Breen's direction.

"Let him get up," he said tonelessly.

By now Dave had rolled over and was sitting. He got his legs under him and was nearly erect when he stumbled and went to his knees. He made another try and this time succeeded in standing. He squared away at Breen and tiredly brought his hands up.

"Santell!" Frank called sharply. "Don't! Get out here."

It was a moment before Dave seemed to understand. In that interval Frank Erbeck knew that this was to be a close thing, that these men would all turn on him if he gave them the chance. And Santell was no help. He was too stunned, too tired to know what he was doing. He stood there now, staring stupidly, making no move.

Frank said, "A couple of you bring him out here." And he motioned toward the two nearest men with the gun.

They looked at Breen. Frank said, "Get a move on!" Only then did they grudgingly move over to the walk and take Dave by the arms.

Dave twisted loose from them, nearly falling. He stumbled down off the walk and into the tie rail, holding onto the sagging pole to steady himself as he stooped under it. He was walking straighter as he came out to the horse. Frank reached down and caught him by the shoulder, offering the stirrup. Dave put a boot in the stirrup and heaved himself up and belly down behind

112

the saddle. He managed to get a leg over and sit straight.

Breen called, "You'll never make it, Erbeck!"

Frank lifted his gun, lined it over Breen's head and fired as he raked the horse's flanks with spurs. The bullet must have come close to Breen, for he and two others near him dodged back into the barber shop door. The horse, lunging away suddenly, scattered the group of saloon watchers.

Frank threw another shot back there, aiming well over the heads of the remaining men on the walk. A gun winked redly against the shadows under the *Elite's* wide awning across the way. Frank felt the horse break stride momentarily, then run smoothly again.

Within brief seconds, he was in the clear, Scalplock's last cabin dropping past in the darkness.

Ed Torrence had witnessed the finish of the fight from across the street. He was the one who had made that tardy try at Frank Erbeck's horse, to the last moment expecting that Breen would call the agency man's bluff or that one of the watchers, several of them Breen's friends, would stop him. He'd had no wish to become involved in what was happening across at the barber shop;

113

for his own reasons, he thought it best to keep out of the town's affairs. But that shot had involved him directly. So now, as he rocked open the loading gate of his Colt's and punched out the empty and reloaded, he started across there.

Two riders, more headstrong than wise, pounded past him and on out the street on the avowed errand of overtaking Erbeck. Torrence smiled meagerly at the futility of their night ride and pushed into the wrecked shop with the tag ends of the crowd.

Someone had brought a lantern. Its wavering light now glowed from the back room, but faintly lighting the shambles of the debris-strewn main room. Glass crunched under men's boots as they packed the back stairway and one or two had to kick aside the refuse to find a place to stand.

Torrence heard someone in that back room say in an awed voice, "Why stand there starin' at him! Someone cover him up!" A sudden urgency took Torrence to the rear room doorway and through it, roughly shouldering aside the men in his way.

The dead man lay sprawled loosely on the littered floor, a small blue hole through his left cheek and a pool of blood under his mousy hair. His blue eyes were open and staring and a gruesome smile twisted his broad face. This had been Howard Mordue, operator of Blaine Shotwell's sawmill below town.

Torrence took one brief look at the body before his glance swept the room, seeing who was there.

He said sharply, "Don't touch a thing! Huck, you and Spence and Shotwell stay. Breen, hand over your gun." He stepped over and lifted the long-barreled .45 from Breen's holster before the big man knew what was happening. Then he waved the weapon doorward. "The rest of you beat it. Anyone feel like a long ride tonight? We'll have to call in the sheriff."

Sid Apple, the barber said, "The sheriff? Why call him in?"

Torrence swung around on him. "Because this is murder."

"There's been murders here before and we ain't needed the law."

"This is different," Torrence stated. "Mordue was shot down in cold blood by that man that got away. Don't you think we owe it to Mordue's wife to do something about it?"

"Let's get out ourselves and run down this ranny."

"All right. How many of you can be ready to ride in five minutes?" Torrence addressed the crowd.

Some gave quick assent, others hesitated. But in the end, Torrence had his way and better than a dozen men left to get horses and rifles. One of Torrence's own Wheel riders was sent down to the livery barn for Torrence's fast bay to make the long ride across to Fort Bewell, where Sheriff John Moore lived.

Finally the room was cleared of everyone but Breen, Mel Spence, Huck Birkheimer, Blaine Shotwell and Torrence. As the last man of the crowd stepped out of hearing through the street door, Torrence said in a low tense voice, "Make it quick, Ray! Who did it?"

Breen let out a gusty and perplexed sigh, running a hand across his battered and bleeding face and avoiding Torrence's eye.

Before the big man could speak, Shotwell said tartly, "You know damn' well he did it, Torrence."

"Take it easy, Blaine," Torrence drawled. "There's more to this than you know anything about."

"For instance?" The Merchandise owner bridled.

"For instance, the man that got way was Santell, the McCune ramrod."

A change came to Shotwell's fat face. He

116

sobered. "Why didn't you say so?" he growled.

"The rest of you get it?" Torrence asked, his glance slowly going from one man to the next. "It was Santell that cut Mordue down."

"Like hell!" Huck Birkheimer drawled, with a pointed angry look in Breen's direction.

"Forget what you know, Huck," Torrence said. "I'm telling you what we'll say happened. You'll have to sell the others on thinkin' the same way. Now do you get it?"

"You mean we hang this on Santell?" Birkheimer asked, slower to grasp Torrence's meaning than the others.

"That's it."

"What about Sid Apple?" Spence asked. He was a thin small man with a perpetual scowl on his foreshortened face. He and Birkheimer were the owners of small ranches in the neighborhood of Wheel, Torrence's place.

"What about him?" asked Birkheimer, anxious to help now that he saw how things were shaping. "He was scared silly. He'll believe the lights stayed on if we tell him they did. Don't worry, I'll handle Sid."

Torrence looked from Birkheimer to Spence and finally to Shotwell. "We're all in on this," he drawled slowly and with a pointed emphasis that reminded them of an unspoken understanding. "We've got our story and we'll stick to it." He seemed now to be doubting Spence, for his glance clung longest to him. "Mel, you understand?"

Spence nodded. His face had been tight with alarm and indecision. Now he looked relieved, apparently glad that he wasn't being involved any deeper than having to lie to shift the blame from Breen.

"How many times did you shoot, Ray?" Torrence asked.

Breen's bruised and bloody face looked vacant a moment as his slow mind thought back. "Once," he said finally.

"What about Santell?"

Breen didn't speak and it was Spence who said, "Twice. He shot out the lamp out there."

"All right," Torrence drawled. "You fired once, Ray. You threw your shot through the door. High. Remember that, you shot high. The sheriff will ask a lot of questions. Stick to your story. All three of you can swear you remember Santell shooting twice. It was his slug that hit Mordue."

They nodded.

"Now let's get out of here," Torrence said. "Huck, you can have a talk with Sid Apple and make sure he remembers Santell's shots."

They moved toward the door, around the loosely sprawled shape on the floor there.

"Ray, you're to keep your mouth buttoned," was Torrence's last cautioning word to Breen before he led the others from that back room.

Within ten minutes the story had made the rounds. Shotwell and Spence joined the posse that was being hastily formed at the livery barn.

Torrence gained the respect and confidence of the last few doubters when he begged off joining the posse and instead offered to go down the street and break the news to Mordue's widow.

VII

Frank had pulled the horse down out of its run as they neared the creek just short of the timber spur above town. When he came within sight of the gray foaming ribbon of water, he rode a good hundred yards upstream, then slid from the saddle and reached up, offering a hand to Dave.

But Dave sat head-down, loosely, so that Frank had to shake his arm before he lifted his head and looked down, dully.

"Better get down and use some of this water," Frank drawled. Only then did Dave move; and he would have fallen if Frank hadn't steadied him. Below, from the direction of the trail, Frank heard two horses noisily ford the stream and go on.

Frank made Dave lie on the stream bank and close to its edge and, with his cupped hands, sloshed some of the numbing cold water over Dave's head. The shock of the water made Dave draw away and catch his breath. But Frank kept on and didn't stop until Dave sat up, gasping, "That's enough. Quit, will you!"

While Dave wiped the water from his cut and swollen face, Frank sat back on his heels watching. Suddenly he began to laugh, a low laugh at first, then one that became louder and finally raucous.

Dave waited until Frank was out of breath. Then: "What's so funny?"

Frank shook his head and managed to get his wind. "Me draggin' you out of there," he said.

Dave was silent a moment. "I wondered about that," he said finally. "How come you didn't pitch in and help 'em finish me off?"

"That's what I'm tryin' to say," Frank drawled. "Why didn't I?"

He was sober now, trying to call up that

vast and bitter hatred he had nursed all the way across here today. But it was gone, drained out of him because he had ridden down the street just in time to see the finish of the fight in the barber shop, to see this Dave Santell taking punishment that would have killed most men, not only taking it but coming back for more.

Grudgingly now, Frank had to admit a deep respect for the McCune foreman. And he was seeing what he hadn't been able to see before — that Santell wasn't the kind who would ever run from anything, that he'd simply needed a gun this morning and had taken the most direct means of getting one.

Yet Frank's pride was too stubborn to admit this consciously. He was uncertain but, on the surface, still resented what Dave had done to him. So now he slowly came erect, looking down at Dave's battered face, indistinct in the starlight.

"You're such a hell of a tough *hombre,*" he drawled, "supposin' you look after yourself from here on."

He sauntered over to his horse and swung up into the saddle.

Although he knew he shouldn't, he was going to leave Santell here.

He waited a moment, halfway expecting

Dave to speak. But Dave only sat as he had for the past half minute, seeming to wait while his strength came back.

Frank put his horse close in to Dave and, looking down at him, said, "You're lucky I didn't get to you first."

Dave's glance lifted but still he said nothing. It made Frank uncomfortable to be stared at that way; and he was beginning to suspect he was in the wrong.

Still, his pride refused to bend and he went on, "Don't ever lay a hand on me again, Santell. Hear that? Not ever!"

Dave drawled, "Sure. I hear."

"You take your damn' troubles and get along on your own from now on. Understand?"

Dave's head tilted down in a nod; dropped, rather, for it stayed down and he seemed too weak to lift it again.

Frank was all at once fighting a feeling of pity for this man. Before that pity could strengthen, he jerked the reins roughly, wheeling his horse away, and forded the creek and started up the trail.

He rode a mile, another half mile, all the time pulling in on the horse as his indecision mounted. Finally he stopped. He was filled with sudden shame at what he had done to Santell. He started back down the trail at a trot. Soon he was pushing his tired horse into a run.

But when he had reached the creek and crossed back over it and reined aside to the spot where he had left Dave, there was no one there.

"Santell!" he called. But the roar of the rushing water close at hand seemed to muffle his voice.

He rode out from the stream and again called, "Santell!"

He breathed shallowly while he listened for an answer. None came.

The third time he bellowed at the top of his voice, "Santell!"

Again he waited a long moment for an answer. And again none came.

Frank Erbeck wasn't a swearing man. But over the next few minutes, while he rode an ever widening circle around the spot where he had left Dave, he time on time voiced every oath he knew.

He was close to the trail, on the far side of the creek, when he caught the first feeble hoof mutter of the posse approaching. As soon as he had defined that faint sound, he spurred off to the trail and started up it, knowing that to wait here any longer was running a big chance.

Headed for the reservation, he went away

trying to believe he had been just in his treatment of Dave Santell. But that was a futile thing. He knew he had wronged a man tonight, a good man, and he was ashamed; worried, too, for Santell wasn't able to take care of himself and just now there had been proof that the Scalplock men were already on the hunt for him.

Frank was barely out of sight in the obscurity beyond the creek when Dave stood up and started climbing toward the timber. He walked favoring his right side — his ribs ached where Breen had kicked him — and when he would have liked to stop and rest he kept on with a dogged resolve not to quit until he reached the rotted windfall where he had left the Winchester. He had sensed enough of strangeness in Frank's deserting him to have the warped idea that the man could be dangerous. A deep instinct of self-preservation now warned him that he would be safe only when he had the carbine once more.

Wading the creek, he stumbled and fell full length. He went under, the current rolling him over twice before he pushed his head above water, gulping at the icy shock and struggling again to his feet. He had swallowed some water and the numbing cold seemed to have cleared his head and given him new strength, even though he was half choking. He coughed his throat clear and waded out on the far bank and found that it was easier now to stand.

He walked faster as he went on, for his soaked outfit was clammy against the night's chill. Fifty yards above the place he had crossed the creek he came to the windfall. It was while he was on his knees, groping inside the hollow log for the Winchester, that he heard Frank call.

He bellied down behind the log, the carbine lying on the ground and ready by his shoulder, while Frank's call was repeated. Once Frank rode within twenty yards of him before fading out of sight toward the trail. Then, from far below, Dave caught the sound of trotting horses. He came erect then and walked as quietly as he could back to the creek. This time he didn't fall as he waded it.

When he started downstream along the Scalplock side, the hoof mutter of the posse growling faint along the trail above, a stubborn resolve added to his slowly returning strength. The sting of the cuts and bruises on his face helped that resolve; so did the places on his long frame that ached bone deep. He even managed a smile with his swollen lips when he realized that there had been many riders going up the trail.

The feel of the Winchester's weight added the only touch of reassurance he needed as he came abreast the first sorry tarpaper and slab shack at the upper end of Scalplock's rutted street.

He took to the dirt walk and shortly was passing the darkened grimy window of the lunch counter where he had eaten his supper, the lights of the *Elite* close ahead. Across the street a man came out of a store doorway, seemed to look at him a moment, then turned up that walk, paying him no attention.

There were only three men in the saloon, none of whom Dave recognized. This fact he learned by looking in through a hole where some of the aged kalsomine on the lower half of the window had flaked away. Just as he straightened and stepped back out of the light alongside the window, one of that trio pushed out of the saloon's batwing doors. Dave stiffened, gripping the carbine a little tighter. But the man turned down the walk and went away.

Dave stood there, wondering what to do next, watching the townsman's shape fade into the obscurity at the far end of the awning. Then, abruptly, he heard a voice down there. Another answered, a deep powerful one, and two shapes came up out of the cobalt void of the lower walk toward him, their boots setting up a hollow echo as they trod the planks. If he hadn't recognized that second voice, Breen's high and massive shape would have told him what he wanted to know.

He hugged the heavy shadow of the saloon wall alongside the window, waiting, carefully sizing up the second man, Birkheimer, who was tall but not heavy. He fully expected them to turn into the saloon and was planning what he would do. But Breen and the other man came on past the swing doors.

They were only three paces away when Dave eased out from the wall and rocked the carbine into line. Breen saw him and halted abruptly. Birkheimer came on another step before he sighted Dave. He caught his breath audibly and stopped dead in his tracks.

Only then did Dave realize that his threat with the Winchester had been unnecessary. The holster at Breen's thigh was empty and Birkheimer, in shirtsleeves, didn't have a gun in sight.

Dave lowered the carbine, reaching behind to lean it against the wall, drawling softly, "Gentlemen, hush! We have some unfinished business."

Savagely, having no choice, he wheeled out and without further warning hit Birkheimer full on the jaw with a knuckle-aching blow.

The man fell forward into him loosely and out cold on his feet. Dave turned behind his body to avoid Breen's powerful rush. He let go his hold on Birkheimer and the two Scalplock men went down, Breen on top. Birkheimer didn't move and as Breen rose Dave hit him with a long looping left that dropped him again.

He knew he would have to be fast with this, for those inside the *Elite* couldn't help but hear. Once again he let Breen come erect and square away with his back to the street. Then he came in at the big man a second time. He stopped Breen's first sledge-hammer blow with his right forearm and chopped in a short vicious jab to the man's broad chest. The wind left Breen's lungs in a pained groan. Dave hit him with his right, his left, again with his right. The next blow he missed because Breen had staggered backward out of reach.

Dave came on, boots spread wide, his flat upper body swinging powerfully to the slow solid rhythm of his flailing arms. Some blows he missed; but he kept his balance.

He took the heavy smashing of the bigger man's fists unfeelingly, sheer ecstacy in him as he felt Breen giving ground.

Suddenly Breen dropped away from one of Dave's slashing swings. He fell backward, whirled in time and went only to his knees as he dropped from the edge of the walk. Dave dove in at him from the edge of the planks, swinging both fists and missing. He collided with Breen with his boots clear of any support. At Breen's back the hitch-rail sagged and bent and then splintered apart. Luckily, Dave fell short of the big man and was on his feet first.

He let Breen stand, then hit him. He took a blow on his shoulder and hit again, hit for the jaw and connected beautifully. That blow knocked Breen half senseless, staggered him. Twice more Dave swung; and twice he connected squarely with that hard jutting jaw. He saw Breen going down and looped in a hard jolting uppercut to the chin. Breen's head tilted back as his knees went loose. Dave rocked that head twice, first to the left, then to right, as the big man went down.

He didn't wait to see Breen stretched out but wheeled and ran for the walk. Someone in the saloon doorway shouted, "Get him!" but by that time he was across the walk and snatching up the carbine. He swung it hip high and threw a shot into the awning overhead as he raced down the walk for the nearest opening between two of the buildings. He was several strides down that narrow passageway before the first answering shot exploded from the saloon front, its blast echoing hollowly up the street.

They hunted for him through the next hour, all the men who had been with Torrence down at Mordue's house joining in the search. The *Elite* bartender and Huck Birkheimer, still groggy and with a swollen jaw, worked over Ray Breen. It was twenty minutes before Breen came around. Meanwhile, the search through the town went on systematically, with lanterns casting their wavy light along narrow alleyways, through the scrub oak thickets down by the creek and even up both slopes and well into the timber.

Ed Torrence, at the end of the first half hour, came back to the saloon. By that time, they had put three drinks of raw-straight bourbon into Breen and he could move his bruised jaw enough to talk.

"So he came back, did he?" Torrence asked as he sauntered up to the big man sitting loosely in a chair at the bar's end.

Breen grunted something unintelligible

and glared up at the Wheel man.

"And you could lick any two men alive!" Torrence jeered.

Birkheimer gave Torrence a wary look and said, "He ain't feelin' so good, Ed."

"So I see." Torrence glanced steadily down at the pitifully subdued Breen. "Well, Ray, there's always another day. Maybe we'll catch him after all. We'll rope him and tie him good and give you another crack at him. Think you could handle him then?"

Breen went pale at this stinging tongue-lashing. But he didn't have anything to say, wouldn't even look at Torrence. And, presently, the Wheel man tired of the one-sidedness of the argument and turned away in disgust and left the saloon.

The cold woke Dave at two in the morning. He was wholly miserable the moment he opened his eyes. For a time he didn't know where he was. It was a good thing that his soreness and stiffness prevented his moving during this long moment of half awareness; for, had he stirred too violently, he might have fallen the twelve-foot drop to the alley between the saloon roof and the icehouse.

His clothes were still soggy from his wetting in the creek and his rangy frame was trembling with the chill and he couldn't keep his teeth from chattering. Gradually, memory came alive and, as he stiffly worked himself to hands and knees, a deep chuckle welled out of his chest at thought of his meeting with Breen.

Before he left the roof, he went to the front of the building and looked up and down the dark and sleeping street. Then, sure that he was safe, he climbed down the sturdy slab trough-spout to the rainwater tub, then aground. The water in the tub felt pleasantly warm when he reached in for the carbine. He took care of the Winchester the first thing, levering the four water-damaged shells from the magazine and then loading with the three he had had time to lever out before he dropped the gun in the water some three hours ago. Then, leaning the carbine against the tub, he bathed his face and arms.

He was beginning to feel a little warmer by the time he had paced the alleyway alongside the *Elite* and was crossing the street. He took another between-store passageway on the street's far side, following the alley down to the livery corral.

The buckskin was in that corral and came at his soft whistle. There was a halter hanging on the gatepost and he tied the animal. He found the barn empty, its big back door

132

closed. But the small door in the face of the big one was unlocked. He remembered seeing the saddle pole up front and groped his way up there. By the light of a single match he found his saddle, bridle and sack of grub.

Five minutes later he stopped farther up the alley, ground-haltered the buckskin and walked around the far end of the barber shop onto the street again. The shop door was locked, so he stepped in through the dark empty hole of the window. The crunching of glass under his boots brought a soft laugh out of him, a laugh that hurt his sore chest.

He didn't strike a light until he had made his way into the back room. By the flare of the match he saw the room a shambles, the broken-legged table, cards and chips and spilled whiskey and broken glass littering the floor, the glassless door sagging inward from one bent hinge. He tried to remember where he had been lying when the gun was knocked from his hand — and then he saw the dark stain on the floor and the dirty strip of tarpaulin lying near by.

By the second match he had another look at that drying blood and the tarp. And, abruptly, he knew that a man had died in here tonight. That rectangle of canvas hadn't been here earlier. It meant only one thing; it had been used to cover a body.

He stood there soberly taking in the meaning of all this, knowing surely that he would be hunted for this killing if there had, as he guessed, been one. And suddenly he was tired, so tired he could hardly stand. He found Frank Erbeck's .38 Colt's the first place he looked, in the back corner of the room behind the broken table. He turned and left and didn't even inspect the street before climbing out of the window. Gone was that small satisfaction he had felt in having beaten Breen. For now his mind was dulled with a new shock and, his body complaining, he was miserable and baffled and worried and badly needing rest.

An hour after he rode east out of Scalplock, shunning the trails, he staked the buckskin out in a grassy draw deep in the timber of one of the higher hills. He was, he judged, some ten miles from the town.

He rolled into his blanket postponing any thought of what the day would bring, knowing only that he was to be hunted and that, as before, he wasn't running.

VIII

Gail found a disturbing likeness between this Jim Land, who was in charge of the

134

herd now, and Dave Santell. True, Land was short and heavy boned, whereas Santell had been tall; and Land's hair was straight and black while Santell's had been straw-blond. Still, the two were of a like age, they both spoke with a drawl that irritated her northern-trained hearing and both seemed exceedingly stubborn and inclined to argue.

In these past five minutes since Jim Land had met her here in the entrance hall to the Blue Belle, Gail had become increasingly angry. Nothing she could say would persuade this man that Santell had cheated her, that he wasn't to be trusted.

Just now Jim Land said, "You're wrong about Dave, ma'am. But it's no good hashin' over the thing. Doc Faris sent me here to talk business. Said I was to be in charge. Now about —"

"And who is Doc Faris?" Gail cut in, witheringly. "Am I to say who's to take Santell's place? Or is it up to someone I don't even know?"

Jim Land shrugged. "It's up to you, I reckon," he drawled. "But there's nothin' much left to do except sell the horses, pay off the crew and witness the delivery receipt and I can do that as well as the next man."

His casualness and patience caught Gail unawares. She was still angry at him for standing up for Santell and said defensively, irrelevantly, "He broke jail, didn't he? Isn't that proof that he was guilty?"

Again, Jim Land lifted his shoulders in an unknowing way. "He ain't the kind that any jail could hold, ma'am," he said respectfully. "And don't kid yourself that he run away, either. Like as not he'll hunt down Breen and swarm all over him. I'd hate to be Breen right then, big as he is."

"They found the money in Santell's room," Gail insisted.

"Sure. Because it was put there to be found." Jim pulled at the brim of his Stetson with a nervous gesture, obviously wanting to avoid further argument. "Will you want me for anything more this evenin'? If you don't, I'll go see the Major about them horses. He might know somebody who's in the market."

Gail didn't reply for a moment. And when she did speak, it was again on the subject Jim was trying to avoid. "Why is it that everyone sticks up for Santell? I've talked to a dozen people these last two days since he broke jail and they all argue with me, telling me I'm wrong."

"Maybe you are."

"But I can't be!" Gail said hotly, indignantly. "The man has stolen money from me. He's a thief. Furthermore, there's a price on his head now."

Jim appeared more surprised at this than he had at her original indictment of his old boss. "You mean you put out a reward on him?"

"No, of course not," Gail said. "It's enough that the federal law officers will be after him. Naturally, the government will offer a reward."

Jim had a hard time to keep from smiling. She saw that and flared: "What seems to amuse you so much?"

"I was just tryin' to think how a marshal would go about catchin' up with Dave. Let Dave get as far as the Texas line and you couldn't find a town where he wouldn't have half a dozen friends who'd hide him."

"I thought you said he wasn't going back to Texas."

"That's right, I did," Jim drawled mildly. "What about the chuck-wagon, ma'am? Will you take fifty dollars for it? I can get that."

"Get anything you can for it." Gail turned toward the stairway, curtly dismissing him.

"Ma'am," Jim said. She stopped and faced him once more. He looked down at his hat and fingered it in that nervous way again. Just as she was about to tell him to get on with whatever he had to say, he drawled reluctantly, "It's about tonight. You see, the boys are pretty dry and now that they're through the job they . . ."

"Yes?" she said when he hesitated.

"Well, they're likely to get a little likkered up. And you better stay to your room and not let 'em see you for a day or so."

"You don't think I'm able to take care of myself, Mr. Land?"

"It ain't that. But with a few drinks, there ain't a man in the outfit that wouldn't . . . well, y' see, they're pretty riled over the way you treated Dave. And I'd hate you to get the idee we ain't gentlemen."

Gail's face flushed. But she held her temper, saying evenly, "I see." Then, "Thank you for warning me, Mr. Land."

He muttered an embarrassed apology over having to mention what he had and quickly went out the door and across the veranda and out of sight down the steps.

Gail stood there letting her anger subside, trying to believe that she was in the right, yet not quite believing it. And now for the first time she began to wonder if she had too severely and too hastily judged Dave Santell. Then, as her doubts began to strengthen, she quickly put the matter from her mind.

She didn't want to go to her room now

138

and so went out onto the veranda and took a chair at its far end, the end opposite the saloon entrance. It was dusty out here and the horizon-reaching sun beat in under the veranda roof with a pressing heat. But this was better than staying in her room hour after hour, day after day. She had read all of the dozen or more books she had brought along to help pass the time. There was nothing to do upstairs but sit and look out the window or try and sleep. Besides, she was lonely. Although she was almost nauseated at the sights and smells around her — at the countless filthy, poorly clad Indians, the innumerable stray dogs, the dirt and the drab appearance of the town — just sitting here looking out across the plaza eased somewhat her restlessness and boredom.

The girl was climbing the steps before Gail noticed her. She was a plain looking girl with dark blond hair. She wore a severe brown dress and her bonnet, of a matching material, was without ornament. Yet on second glance there was something appealing about her face, her blue eyes and, as she looked to this far end of the veranda, Gail was curious as to who she might be.

Then she came across the veranda toward Gail, her face taking on a warm smile that washed away its plainness. She stopped beside the chair, saying,

"You're Gail McCune, aren't you? I'm Martha Mills. I teach up at the mission. I thought you might be wanting company."

Gail stood up, pressing the other girl's hand warmly, all at once glad to have someone to talk to.

"This is nice of you," she said. "I've been wondering if there wasn't someone I could — could visit with. Won't you sit down?" And she moved the nearest chair closer to her own.

They sat down, Martha saying quickly, "You'll tell me when you want me to go, won't you? But I had to meet you. You're the first woman my age I've seen in almost four years."

"You must be lonely," Gail said, impulsively, with an unaccountable feeling of tenderness for this girl. She didn't often like women but there was something about Martha Mills that appealed to her.

"Lonely?" Martha said, as though surprised that Gail should have chosen that word to describe the reason for her visit. She laughed nervously. "No. I don't have the chance to be lonely. I'm teaching all day, you see. But I do miss some things." Her glance ran quickly over Gail. "That's an awfully pretty dress."

140

For some time their talk was of the things that interest women, of recent fashions, of Martha's work and of the contrast in their lives. Neither noticed the passage of time, for they were both hungry for companionship and this pleasant conversation was what they needed.

At length, Martha said, "I must go or I'll be late for dinner." Then, impulsively, she asked, "Why can't you come and eat with me? Mrs. Cooney's food is good. And she can easily set another place at her table." The sun had set now and the light was beginning to weaken.

"Are you sure she wouldn't mind?" Gail asked. She had eaten every meal in her room since coming to Grade. Her food was brought up three times a day on a tray from the saloon. And the Chinaman's chuckwagon variety of cooking could have been improved upon.

"Of course she wouldn't," Martha said. "Would you like to get a coat?"

Gail said quickly, "No, I'll go as I am," for she couldn't interrupt this exceedingly pleasant interval by going up to her room, which would have brought a return of that lost bored mood she had been in earlier.

The plaza was more crowded than on any of the late afternoons Gail had seen it and as they passed the agency, she said, "There are so many of them tonight. Why?"

"There's a beef issue in the morning," Martha told her. "Your herd didn't arrive any too soon. They need the meat."

"What's a beef issue?" Gail asked. "Do they butcher and give the meat to the Indians?"

Martha had to smile; but her smile wasn't belittling. "Why don't you come out with me tomorrow and see what it's like? There's never school on an issue day. And it's a sight you won't believe until you see it."

When Gail hesitated, Martha added, "We could have Mrs. Cooney pack us a basket dinner. And I know where I can borrow a buggy."

"You're sure it wouldn't be putting you out?"

"Of course not."

"Then I'll come," Gail said. She had her misgivings about what the day would be like, for she was wholly ignorant of things concerning cattle; "beef" was what Martha called them, while Santell had named them "steers," and that confused her. Still, it was nice to spend time with a girl like this Martha Mills. So now she forced herself to add, "I'll love it."

Wilce didn't know why, but he wasn't entirely satisfied with Frank Erbeck's explanation. He sucked gently at his bad tooth as he thought back over Erbeck's story, meanwhile pointedly staring at a spot on the wall in back of the crewman's head. He had found this device of seemingly staring through a man, yet not quite doing so, quite convenient at times. By his victim's reaction to it, he could usually tell whether or not he was being told the truth.

But a minute of this, the Major drawing deliberately on his cigar to blue-fog the cone of light under the agency's front room lamp, brought no noticeable change in Erbeck's expression.

So at length, Wilce asked, "Why didn't you take Hult along?"

"He was dead for sleep. Besides, he's about as much help as a broken arm," Frank said bluntly.

"Why didn't you tell me you were headed across there?"

"You weren't on the place," Frank lied. "I didn't want to let anyone else in on it."

"So you followed your hunch and went to Scalplock and found Santell," Wilce went on. "You found Breen's bunch combin' him over. Why didn't you stay out of it and let Breen finish the job?"

"Santell's got friends, hasn't he? Would you want 'em to start askin' questions when he turned up dead?"

The agent took his time answering that, finally admitted, "No. But he's still alive. He can still make trouble."

"He was more dead than alive when I left him. He doesn't have a gun." . . . Again, Frank told the lie calmly, matter-of-factly . . . "He'll hide for a day or so, until he can walk. Then he'll probably steal a horse and head away from this country as fast as he can ride."

"What if he stays?"

Frank shrugged, said patiently, "Major, two nights ago you sent me out to do a job. I did it the best I knew how. If Breen messes it up, it's his fault, not mine."

Unsatisfactory as this answer was to Wilce, he had to accept it. Frank, having known he'd have to tell most of the truth because the agent would eventually hear it anyway, now felt a bit easier. He had subordinated his own part in the Scalplock affair, had made it appear that he had merely followed orders. Now, by the look on Wilce's face, he could tell that he had made his story stick.

Whatever happened from now on as concerned Santell, he was well out of it.

Wilce took the cigar from his mouth, waved the hand that held it. "You'd better wash up and get some sleep," he said. He couldn't overlook adding, "It's a good thing you came back, Erbeck."

Frank said nothing to this and left the room. He crossed the compound to the crew shack and washed and shaved by the light of a candle stub and pulled on a clean shirt. He heard a pair of riders come in the gate off the square and, as they passed the shack, caught Hult's voice. He uncinched Hult's belt and gun from his waist, laid them on the man's bunk and made his hasty exit, not wanting to be there to make his explanations when Hult came in.

The lights were winking feebly against the dusk in the square as he crossed it toward the upper length of the street. Over by the blacksmith shop a group of bucks loafed, watching the finish of the horseshoe game Phil Rust pitched his helper before closing time each night. The clang of iron on iron as a well thrown shoe hit the stake seemed only to intensify the drowsy settling of the evening's stillness. There were already a few idlers under the trading post awning, gathered there for the stage's arrival. Across by the edge of the buffalo-wallow, Ott and two Indians stood appraising a leggy chestnut colt, Ott evidently being on the point of making a trade. Off in the southwest, the diamond brilliance of the evening star shone against the darkening blue of the sunset sky. All this Frank saw and took in with a greater degree of pleasure than normal. He felt he was lucky in having come off as well as he had from that talk with Wilce.

He met Martha and Gail halfway up the street to the boarding house. There was a quickening interest in him at Martha's glad smile and he returned it as he tipped his hat.

Martha said, "Frank! I didn't know where you'd gone."

"Had some work to do for the Major," he told her.

"Frank, this is Gail McCune," Martha said.

He returned the McCune girl's nod and, impulsively and before he had quite thought it out, said to her, "Your man Santell took quite a beating for you last night, ma'am."

The shocked surprise that crossed Gail's face pleased him. He had little respect for this city-bred girl because of what she had done to Dave Santell. And now he couldn't help adding, "Breen and four others all but

146

killed him up in Scalplock."

"I . . . I don't understand," Gail said. "Where is Scalplock?"

"Fifty miles north," Frank said. "He went up there after Breen and found him."

"But, I . . . why should he fight with Breen?"

"I wouldn't know," Frank drawled. "I'm only telling you what happened." He looked at Martha. "Good meal tonight?" he asked.

"Steak and cabbage," she told him.

He touched his hat again and was about to go on when Gail asked, "Then this means Santell didn't help Breen steal those cattle?"

"Looks that way," he said, and stood waiting for her to say something more.

But it was Martha who spoke. "Everyone says Santell didn't do it."

"Then why would he break out of jail?" Gail asked.

"Probably because he wanted to get at Breen," Frank told her, adding, "See you later, Martha." He went on up the walk.

The two girls went on in silence until they came to the street opening into the square. It was then that Gail asked suddenly, "Would you do something for me, Martha?"

"Of course. What is it?"

"There's a man here in town I want to talk to. I believe his name is Harris. Doctor Harris."

"Doctor Faris," Martha corrected.

Gail nodded. "He's the one. Do you know where I could find him? Tonight."

"His house is beyond Mrs. Cooney's, near the mission."

Gail stopped. "I want to see him."

Martha sensed a deep agitation in the other girl and knew it had been brought on by the things Frank had said. She saw Gail glance back up the street and at once understood that Gail was hesitating about something. Then she understood what it was.

"Would you like me to take you to his house?" she asked.

"Would he . . . Is he busy at this time of night?"

Martha laughed. "Doctor Faris is never that busy. Besides, I know he'd want to meet you. He was a friend of your father's."

"Then let's go find him," Gail said eagerly, her tone strangely relieved.

So they started back up the street.

The nooning sun shining directly on his face had brought Dave to a slow wakefulness that day. His first awareness, after remembering where he lay, was of the lateness of the hour; and, next, of the soreness and stiffness of his whole big frame. Because he knew that any movement would cause him instant pain, he lay for a moment without stirring, postponing sure agony.

He found this pleasing, for a deep languor lay through him. The air bore a piny fragrance and a cool breeze slanting down off the peaks close above laid a restless whisper of sound through the pine tops. From somewhere below came the sibilant murmur of a stream rushing over its rocky bed. Dave had always liked best these sounds and smells of the high country and now it struck him as ironic that he rarely, almost never, rode the hills any more. His part of Texas was a flat and brushy country and he wondered now at his having been so content with it these recent years. Then he knew that his peace of mind had come from a good job done well. That was over now, of course. Idly, he tried to look into the future, to see what it would hold for him. But there was nothing to look forward to.

This unpleasant trend of thinking stirred him to an impatience to finish what he had to do here and be on his way. He was no longer satisfied to be just lying here. There was work to be done.

He heard the stomp of his pony in the draw below and turned his head and saw not one animal down there but two. The second horse, a saddled brown, grazed with reins trailing and cinch hanging loose.

Quickly, Dave pushed up onto an elbow, catching his breath at a stab of pain in his side. His glance swung up from the draw and around to his other side.

A fat untidy man with a tea-yellow and flabby face and ebony hair squatted twenty feet away with his back to the stem of a jack-pine. A rifle lay across his knees. Another, Frank Erbeck's carbine, leaned against the tree at his back. On the ground nearby was coiled Dave's borrowed shell belt, the handle of the holstered Colt's conveniently within the fat man's reach.

Dave let that first shock of utter surprise subside in him before he drawled, "Must've been sleepin' like a rock."

The man's startling pale blue eyes remained impassive. He hadn't stirred since Dave had moved. The white line of a scar ahead of his right ear glistened in the strong light, marking exactly the curved line of shadow made by a high-crowned black Stetson set too squarely on his head.

This was the 'breed Holmes, the offspring of the mating between a Sioux squaw and a Scandinavian, an Army deserter. This was the second time Dave had seen him.

When Holmes said nothing, Dave asked in Sioux, "What will you do with me?"

Holmes answered in terse English, disdaining the use of the tongue he had doubtless talked most of his forty-odd years. "You killed a man last night. I'm taking you to town."

Dave pushed up into a sitting position. For the moment he ignored the 'breed, his eye going to the sack of provisions hanging from the stub of a head-high branch above Holmes. The rifle had by now swung lazily around to line at him; but, aside from moving the weapon, the 'breed had stayed as he was.

Dave drawled, "I eat before I ride."

Holmes shook his head. "No. You're comin' now."

"I eat." Without looking at the 'breed, Dave got up stiffly and, exaggeratedly favoring his aching right leg, limped over to a deadfall some paces away. He broke away enough of the rotting branches to lay a fire.

When the blaze was going, he looked at Holmes, nodded to the sack of provisions hanging above the 'breed's head and said, "Toss that grub across."

Holmes made no move for a moment. Then, carefully, without taking his impassive pale-eyed stare from Dave, he rose and lifted down the sack and swung it toward the fire. The skillet in the sack clanged against something there, laying a harsh ring of sound against the stillness. The sack fell short. Still exaggerating the stiffness of his right leg, Dave crawled over and got it.

He took out his clasp-knife and cut bacon, lots of it, enough to fill the skillet, and put it on the fire. He opened a can of tomatoes with the knife and set the can at the edge of the burning down coals to warm, noticing that the 'breed had again lined the rifle at him when he reached into his pocket for the knife. But Holmes said nothing, although his look had taken on an unmistakable arrogance, as though he was willing to play Dave's stalling game, whatever it was.

It was awkward for Dave to work at the fire, for his leg was stiff and he found it hard to lift his left arm from his tender side. He was careful to exaggerate this awkwardness. When he should have stood, he crawled, grimacing with pain although that wasn't necessary. Sitting, he held his bad leg stretched out before him and several times rubbed the thigh as though trying to relieve the pain there.

When the bacon was done, he looked across to his saddle at the head of his blanket, some forty feet away. "There's a fork and a spoon in that pouch on my hull," he said, smiling ruefully. "I'm pretty crippled up. How about you gettin' 'em for me?"

"No. You get 'em," Holmes grunted.

"Come on, friend," Dave said. "You've got my hardware and I'm whipped. Help a gent along, can't you?"

Holmes' surly defiance lessened at the abjectness in Dave's tone. Sneering a little, the 'breed got up and walked across to Dave's saddle and blanket, his bulk moving with surprising ease. He knelt by the saddle, opened the pouch and reached inside. His rifle rested against his knee. He brought out the fork and spoon and came across in Dave's direction. Three strides from the fire, he tossed the fork and spoon to Dave, then turned away toward the tree where he had been sitting. And now, his wariness eased by Dave's obviously helpless condition, he didn't keep his glance on his prisoner.

Dave lifted the sizzling pan of bacon from the fire and threw it at the 'breed, the hot grease spraying fan-wise from the pan in a glistening stream. As the pan left his hand, Dave lunged erect.

Holmes screamed as the grease seared his neck and the back of his head. It was a cry of pure agony. The frying pan hit Holmes in the shoulder and thudded to the ground. Instinctively, the 'breed let go the Winchester, his hands streaking toward his instantly blistered skin. He wheeled to face Dave, that move one of instinct, too.

Dave hit him only once, a roundhouse full swing that caught Holmes full on his cheekbone. Dave groaned as his bruised knuckles took the punishment. The 'breed dropped to his knees, sobbing in pain. Then, lazily, Dave reached down for the rifle and rocked it up under his arm, looking down at the groaning fat man.

Holmes' face was contorted with pain and rage. Tears runneled down the channel between his broad nose and full cheeks. Seeing Dave swing the rifle up, he went rigid, grotesquely, the hot fire of hate and shame wiping out the heretofore impassive expression of his pale eyes.

Dave limped around him and over to the tree, picking up the carbine and holstered Colt's. He came back to the fire and nodded across to the tree. "Over there, Slim," he drawled, no pity in his tone. "After I've had my grub, we ride."

For a brief moment longer the hostility was alive in Holmes' eyes. But then all the fight seemed to go out of him. He was breathing shallowly in pain. He sat back on his heels, a hang-dog look replacing his defiance.

"Where will you take me?" he asked abjectly.

Dave remembered now what he had heard of Holmes. He smiled thinly. "We could head for the reservation," he said.

A look of terror widened the 'breed's beady eyes. Dave knew what backed it. That whiskey-stealing charge still lay against Holmes and, could the Sioux ever lay hands on him, it would go hard with him.

"No," Holmes breathed. "I don't go back there."

Dave appeared to think a moment, his look very grave. "Either that, or you take me to Breen," he said abruptly.

His words brought another change to the 'breed's face; a fear not quite so strong as that of a moment ago. But Holmes was caught off guard only an instant. The next, he was shaking his head, saying, "I don't know where Breen hangs out."

Dave drawled, "Maybe you'll remember later," and crawled over on hands and knees to pick up as much of the bacon as was still edible.

He ate his breakfast of bacon and tomatoes, letting the Colt's lie on the ground within easy reach. He saw the sweat standing out on Holmes' forehead and knew it was the pain of the burns that brought it.

But the burns had nothing to do with that unmistakable fear that lingered in Holmes' eyes.

IX

Doc Faris wasn't often here to meet the stage. But tonight, for a change, he wasn't busy. And for two weeks now he had been expecting the five pound package of burley he had ordered from the East. He hoped it would be in the stage's express sack, for he had been smoking reservation tobacco in his pipe lately and he was hungry for the taste of his own.

He sat at the end of the bench by the trading post door, watching the figures that moved back and forth across the orange wash of lamplight shining out of the post's grimy windows. There was quite a crowd, most of them bucks down from the Sioux camps above town who never tired of seeing the miracle of the battered Concord mud wagon pulled by six horses, all handled by one man.

It was to Doc's credit that it took but little to amuse him; or rather, to interest him.

Just now he had spoken a few words in Sioux to Thunder Hawk, one of the old chiefs, who squatted across from him at the edge of the walk. In his years here, Doc had learned a great deal about the Sioux, particularly of their life before they were put onto the reservation. He was the one white man always welcome in one of their tipis; and he had painstakingly tried to meet them as equals. Because he had the intelligence and patience not to appear ever to be prying into their affairs, they trusted him and he had consequently learned more of their past than any other white man in this country.

Doc's word to Thunder Hawk had been a simple greeting and an inquiry as to the health of the proud old chief's family. He had expected a brief guttural answer, for the aged Sioux rarely said much. He was, therefore, surprised when Thunder Hawk became voluble, almost garrulous. As their chief spoke, other bucks loafing nearby broke off their sparse talk and listened.

Outwardly, it was all for Doc's benefit; for there were only four other whites here under the trading post awning and Doc was the only one of them who understood a word of Sioux.

Thunder Hawk said his family was well

but hungry. They had been hungry for many moons. In the old days they could have hunted the buffalo when they needed food. Now the white man had killed off the buffalo and they had to wait for their food to be handed them by the Major. And it was poor food. Beef wasn't as good as Buffalo meat; and a steer's hide was good for nothing but money, while the buffalo's hide had been useful for many things, for the building of their tipis, for clothing them against the bitter winters and warming them while they slept.

But Thunder Hawk made only brief mention of this. What he spoke of at greater length, and bitterly, was of the passing of the buffalo hunt. In the old days the men were gone for many weeks hunting the buffalo. They had no worries about meat then; more often than not they killed the buffalo and used only the hide. Thunder Hawk couldn't count on all the fingers of his people how many buffalo there had been here at one time, right here on the edge of this southward reaching flat.

Most important of all was that the hunt told them who their warriors were, which of the younger men had the makings of leaders. Today — and on this point the old chief spoke with an intensity none of his listeners missed — the young bucks did no work beyond gathering a little wild hay or cutting wood in the summer and selling what they could to the agency. They had become lazy. They let their women do all their work. They were taking up the white man's ways, wearing his clothes, learning how to write and speak his tongue.

Doc only listened. When Thunker Hawk had finished, the medico said nothing. Without looking at the other bucks, he knew that they had listened even more alertly than he, that in reality Thunder Hawk had been speaking to them, not to him. This was an old story to Doc, this unceasing clash between the wills of the older and younger Indians. Worst of all, nothing could be done about it. Thunder Hawk was right. The Sioux had been better off, far better off, ten, twenty or thirty years ago than they were now. But the buffalo — the main stem of their life — were gone. And now they were a lost people, unsuited to an agrarian existence, wholly dependent on the government for food and clothing. This hurt the pride of the older Sioux. The younger ones didn't care so much, for they had either forgotten or never known the old life.

Thunder Hawk let the silence run on for many moments, squatting there with arms folded across his knees, his rugged seamed face under the high-crowned black hat set in a look of defiance. He still looked at Doc, or seemed to. Yet the medico knew that the old Indian wasn't seeing him, that he was wholly absorbed in carrying his argument to the listeners of his own race.

Finally, Thunder Hawk stood up. His glance went from right to left, disdainfully, proudly. Then he turned deliberately and walked away into the darkness out across the square.

Pete Gillis, the new Scalplock mail rider, asked of no one in particular, "What was eatin' him?" He was sitting on a bench on the far side of the window.

No one answered his question, so he resumed a conversation with the man next to him that had been interrupted by Thunder Hawk's harangue.

Doc came up off the bench and stepped to the window to look at his watch. Eight-forty, almost time to turn in. The stage was late and he wondered if he ought to wait around for it any longer. He yawned and put the watch away, disinterestedly hearing what Pete Gillis and the other man on the far bench were saying, now that he stood closer to them. He heard the name "Santell" mentioned and thought nothing of it.

Grade had been talking for two days about the jail break that still puzzled Doc.

But when Pete Gillis said, ". . . Then Santell and Breen fell through the window, Santell on top," Doc's interest came quickly alive.

"What were you saying about Santell?" he asked.

Gillis looked up sharply at the intensity of Doc's tone. He frowned. "I was only tellin' Mart here about the fight across in Scalplock last night. Why?" He didn't know the doctor at all well and was on the edge of resentment.

"I heard you say something about Santell and Breen," Doc said mildly, sensing the other's ready antagonism. "I'm a friend of Dave Santell's. What about him being in a fight?"

The mail rider's manner eased immediately. He grinned. "Never saw a better one," he said. "This Santell took on Ray Breen and half a dozen others, all by himself. Damn' near licked the whole bunch. They busted the insides out of the barber shop and ended up on the street. One man was killed. Then, after Santell had got away and they were huntin' him, he came back and managed to catch Breen alone on the street and beat his liver blue. They're huntin' him now."

"Then he got away?" Doc asked. "Was he hurt?"

Gillis laughed dryly. "Was he hurt! Ever take a good look at Ray Breen?"

Doc nicely concealed his impatience at this indirect answer and repeated the question. "How badly was he hurt?"

"No tellin'. At least he was able to get back that second time and whittle Breen down. That first time a gent from here, they said his handle's Erbeck, put a gun on Breen and got Santell on his nag and rode him away." . . . Gillis glanced at the man alongside him . . . "That's what I was askin' Mart here. How come this Erbeck would throw in with Santell when they claim he works for the agency? Ain't the Major's crew huntin' this Santell for breakin' jail?"

"They're supposed to be," Doc said. "Then you don't know what happened to Santell?"

Gillis shook his head. "No more'n I told you. He got away on his own the second time. I left there early this mornin' right after they found Santell's horse gone from the livery. Every jasper across there that can sit a hull is out huntin' him. They've sent up to Bewell for the sheriff because of the killin'. It was Santell that cut this guy down."

"You saw the fight then?"

"Only the first one, the big one. Santell was down and tryin' to get on his feet. Breen was bootin' him. Then when it looked like Breen and his crowd was gettin' ready to finish Santell off, this Erbeck shows up and stops 'em with an iron to back his say. Erbeck and Santell might've joined up after Santell come back that second time. They think it might've been Erbeck that swiped Santell's horse from the barn."

"Which way did Erbeck ride from town?" Doc asked. His face had lost color and there had been a look of cold rage in his eyes when Gillis spoke of Breen's treatment of Dave.

"Toward the pass," Gillis answered. The look on Doc's face made him add, "Wish there was more I could tell you. I kept an eye open on the way over today but didn't see no one or any sign along the trail."

Doc looked at the others, the three remaining whites and the group of Sioux. "Has anyone seen Erbeck?" he asked.

None of the whites had seen the agency rider. So he repeated his question in the Sioux language.

One buck had seen a rider he thought was Erbeck headed in the direction of town

163

along the Scalplock trail two hours before dark. This rider had been alone. None of the rest of the Indians could add to this meager information.

Doc said, "If anyone sees Erbeck, tell him I want to talk with him," and he stepped down off the walk and started across the square toward the lights of the agency.

Wilce wasn't there. But Tucker was in the back office, at work at his desk. "Erbeck?" he said, nodding his reply to Doc's question. "He should be about finished with supper. Try Mrs. Cooney's."

Doc's fast walk eased somewhat when he reached a point along the upper street from which he could see the light shining from Mrs. Cooney's front room window. This meant that someone was still eating, for the boarding house woman invariably put out the front room lamp as soon as her table was cleared. Doc hoped, almost prayed, that the late customer might be Erbeck.

It was. Frank was rolling a smoke, tilted back in his chair talking to Mrs. Cooney when the medico came in. Doc made note of the fact that Frank's face was bruised and his lips swollen. He politely asked after Mrs. Cooney's health, bemoaned the poor quality of the Blue Belle's food — his meals were eaten at such irregular hours that he

didn't often come to the boarding house —
and then said to Frank, "If you're leaving,
I'll walk a ways with you, Erbeck."

Frank gave him a quick and wary glance,
took his Stetson from the chair-back and
they stepped out onto the porch together.

"What have you done with Santell?" Doc
asked the moment the door was closed
behind them.

He could tell by the way Frank's head
jerked around that he had surprised the
man, as he had hoped he could. He added
to this surprise by saying, "You were with
Santell in Scalplock last night. I want to
know what's happened to him."

For a moment Frank didn't speak; and in
that interval Doc breathed shallowly, his
whole being rigid before the unnatural
impulse to do violence upon this man if he
didn't get a straight answer. Over the years
he had come to hate everything, every man,
even remotely associated with Jacob Wilce.
Now he didn't pause to think that he was
physically a weakling, no match for Frank.
There was only one thought in his mind,
that Frank knew what had happened to
Dave, that he was going to find out what
that something was if he had to beat this
agency man into insensibility.

He heard Frank's long slow sigh and

didn't understand it. Then Frank was saying, "I wish I knew."

Now it was Doc who was taken by surprise. "What have you done with him?" he asked, and his voice was hollow with emotion.

"I left him on the trail above Scalplock," Frank said without hesitating. "I went back. He was gone." Then Frank told what had happened in Scalplock. He didn't mention his own reasons for being in the hill town, nor why he had left Dave instead of bringing him back to Grade.

Doc heard him out without once interrupting. He saw that Frank knew nothing of Dave's second encounter with Breen. When Frank had finished, the medico said shrewdly, "Erbeck, two nights ago I watched someone prying loose the bars on the jail cell window. It was after Santell was gone. I know because I waited and looked. Now you say you left Santell up there instead of bringing him on in. Something queer is going on here. I want to know what it is."

Frank flicked his cigarette out into the darkness. Its lighted end traced a long downward arc and burst into a shower of rosy sparks as it hit the dirt walk.

Frank watched those sparks die out and only then looked around at the doctor, drawling, "I don't know a thing. But I can't call you a liar on what you've seen."

"That money the police found in Santell's room was put there to be found. And not by Santell."

In the feeble light, Frank's battered face shaped a wry grin. "It don't make much sense, does it? Especially when you figure Santell goin' up there after Breen's hide."

Doc was beginning to understand something about this agency man. Erbeck wasn't betraying any confidence. Neither was he denying that Dave had been framed. What he had just said — rather, the way he had said it — along with the fact that he could have brought Dave back to Grade and hadn't, registered a confused pattern in Doc's thinking. It seemed almost that Erbeck was trying to help him unravel the knot of this enigma. At the same time, Erbeck wasn't going beyond a certain limit that would label him as an informer.

"All right," Doc said. "Wilce turned Santell loose the first time. You let him go the second. Why?"

"I told you I went back for him and found him gone," Frank drawled noncommittally. "Maybe I'd have brought him on back if I'd found him."

"And maybe you wouldn't."

Frank frowned. "I kinda forget what I'd decided to do."

"They say his horse disappeared from the livery barn up there during the night. A man was killed in the fight and they're hunting Santell. Did you get the horse for him?"

"No." Frank shook his head. His look was worried now. "I didn't know anyone cashed in in the fight. Who says Santell did it? It's good he isn't afoot if they're huntin' him."

This was becoming a purposeless chain of subtleties that proved nothing beyond a certain feeling of sympathy in Erbeck for Dave. What Doc was after was something definite to go on, some assurance that Dave was safe and able to take care of himself. So now the medico said, "Santell must have been badly hurt. How bad?"

Frank lifted and dropped his shoulders. "He could walk. I looked around a bit tryin' to find him. I'd have spotted him anywhere within a quarter mile of where I left him. And you say his horse was gone."

"They said Breen was booting him when you stepped in. Could he have had some broken ribs?"

"Maybe. But he could hold himself up and sit straight. And his breathin' was all right."

The medico gave Frank a long level

glance, trying to read his expression in the darkness. At length, he asked gravely, "Erbeck, where do you stand in this?"

"Me?" Frank seemed surprised at the question. "I only work for the Major."

"I'm going over there, across to Scalplock. I'm going to find Santell," Doc said.

"You won't get far. They're a clanny bunch across there and crooked as hell, every man in that town." Frank hesitated a moment before he went on, "Of course, you could go over to see a patient. Ever doctored anyone across there, Doc?"

"A woman with heart trouble."

"Then you could be checkin' up on how she is, couldn't you?" Frank drawled. "She don't by any chance live over east, does she?" he added with pointed casualness.

Doc thought a long moment before he said, "So you're curious about what happens in those hills, too."

"Not curious, Doc. But a lot of things could happen up there. It's wild and no one ever rides it much."

Doc said, "Thanks, Erbeck. I'll let you know how I make out." He stepped down off the porch.

Above him, Frank said, "There's something you can do for me. Ask Santell what he did with my gun, the one he took off me night before last. You could even ask him for it if he still has it."

Doc's glance quickly lifted to the other. "Night before last?" he said. "That would be the night Santell got out of jail."

"Would it?" Frank said.

They stood looking at each other a long moment, Doc taking in the significance of this one more small but important item of information. Now he had the pieces of a complete picture if he could put them together.

He asked, "That's all?"

"Yeah," Frank drawled. "That's all."

On his way up the street to his small slab house, Doc Faris had much to puzzle over. Least understandable of all was Frank Erbeck's attitude toward the happenings of the past three days.

He was trying to pry beneath the surface of Frank's strange behavior when he turned into his yard and saw the sliver of light shining from beneath the drawn blind of his front window. He never locked his house, always leaving it open so that a patient could wait if he wasn't there. Now the prospect of having to treat a patient when he was so anxious to get started for Scalplock wasn't pleasant and he breathed a word of exasperation as he opened the door and stepped in.

Gail McCune rose at his entrance. Martha Mills was already standing, her back to him as she bent over the table on which the lamp sat, reading one of the month-old newspapers that were the medico's only tie with home. Martha turned at the sound of the door opening and said quickly, "I'll go now. I was only keeping Miss McCune company until you came, doctor. You don't know each other, do you? Doctor Faris, this is Gail McCune."

Doc removed his brown derby and laid it on the table, looking at Gail and telling her, "I knew your father well. He was a fine man, one of the few worthwhile friends I've ever had."

"It's nice of you to say that," Gail answered. She put in quickly, "Don't go, Martha," as the mission girl stepped to the door. Then she met Doc's glance again. "I came here to ask you about my foreman, doctor. I understand you know him."

"Dave Santell? Yes, I know him," was Doc's cautious reply.

"We learned tonight that he's in trouble," Gail went on hurriedly. "I . . . I was wondering if you could help me."

"With Dave?" Doc asked. "I thought you

fired him."

"I did. But I think now I may have made a mistake." . . . Doc liked the half defiant, half contrite look in Gail's hazel eyes as she made this admission . . . "I think he was innocent."

Doc's grave expression gave way before a smile. "Miss McCune," he said deliberately, "I had made up my mind to dislike you, to dislike you heartily. Because of what you did to Dave Santell. Allow me to change my opinion."

For a brief moment there was an embarrassed silence, Gail's face flushing hotly as her glance dropped. Then Martha spoke to ease the tension. "Gail wants to know what she can do to get Santell back," she said. "We thought you might help."

Doc considered a moment. It was obvious that these two hadn't heard of Dave being wanted for the Scalplock killing. He decided there was no point in adding one more worry to those already plaguing Gail McCune.

So he nodded and said, "Dave was hurt last night, perhaps badly. The only thing I know to do is for me to go across there and try to find him." He gave Gail a close regard. "You're sure you want him back?"

"Yes!" Gail's one word was eager, sincere.

"Then I'll bring him back if I can find him. And," Doc added significantly, "if he'll come."

X

From this high promontory, Dave made a long and careful inspection of the dawn-lighted country below. The dark tangle of hills fell away tier upon descending tier, still indistinct in the early morning haze. Finally, as the light strengthened, the lighter lines of several trails became distinct, all converging toward a point directly north. At that spot, far downward, the haze hung thickest, blue and obscuring even the general outline of the slopes. That, Dave was sure, was the woodsmoke of Scalplock's breakfast fires. He knew then that Holmes had deceived him.

Yesterday he had stubbornly held to his original threat, giving Holmes the choice of taking him to Breen or being returned to the reservation. In the end, the 'breed had agreed to find Breen; but only after Dave had pretended he knew for a certainty that Holmes and Breen lived at the same place. Holmes finally admitted this. And during the five remaining hours of daylight yesterday afternoon, the fat halfbreed had pretended to be riding toward home.

But now Dave saw that they were well to the south of Scalplock and far above it, up toward the pass he had ridden off the reservation. Doc Faris had said that Holmes lived east of the hill town. Which meant that in their two hours of riding after dark last night, which ended with Holmes claiming he had lost the way, the 'breed had ridden a wide circle out of that high east country footing the peaks. Holmes, had, of course, been playing a wily game, doubtless hoping they would stumble onto a segment of the posse that was undoubtedly covering all the trails.

Now Dave shrugged aside his impatience at this delay, turning and sauntering back down into the *cienega* where his camp lay. There was a spring there, greening a patch of grass on which they had staked out the horses. The rocky-edged depression had offered them sure concealment; Dave doubted that a rider passing even within a hundred yards could have spotted the glow of their fire.

Dave had eaten alone and well only twenty minutes ago, a meal that consisted of fried jerky, pan bread, tomatoes and coffee. There was a generous portion left and now he went across to where Holmes' generous bulk lay rolled and roped in his blanket. He knelt down and loosened the rope that bound the fat man. Last night he had taken this precaution, making sure that the 'breed wouldn't escape. Holmes had been warm enough, though doubtless cramped and uncomfortable.

Stepping well back out of reach now while Holmes rolled stiffly from the blanket and laboriously got to his feet, Dave nodded toward the fire.

"Help yourself," he said. "When you're through, you can clean up."

Holmes' dark scowl was evidence of his injured pride at having been so summarily and effectively trussed up during the night. He waddled to the fire and began eating. Dave could see the livid welts of the burns he had given the man yesterday and felt sorry for having had to use that panful of hot grease.

Presently, Holmes took the tin plates and cups and the frying pan and walked across to the spring. There he scrubbed the utensils well with the coarse sand at the spring's edge.

When he came back, Dave drawled casually, "Throw my hull on your nag. We'll change off for a while."

Instantly, Holmes' glance whipped across

to him, belligerent, wary. "Why?"

"Figure he'll know the way back to his corral better'n you do."

The 'breed was silent a moment. Then: "That's a borrowed horse. It isn't mine."

For just a second Dave believed this. But then he knew that Holmes would have gloated in his small triumph; instead, that sullen belligerence stayed with him.

So Dave grinned broadly, saying, "That ought to be interestin'. Anyway, we'll try it."

This high country was wild, solidly timbered, cut by few trails. Dave at the start gave the brown its head, riding with reins loose. He made Holmes stay behind and, knowing his buckskin could easily outrun the brown, warned the 'breed against trying a getaway. He sat the saddle with one boot clear of stirrup, half turned and with one of the carbines resting across the three-quarter swell.

They crossed the first trail at the end of the first hour after leaving camp. Dave paused there to study the ground. There was no sign along the trail; it hadn't been used for days, maybe weeks.

The scrubby big-headed brown, left to his own devices, displayed an increasing eagerness as the time passed and there was no authority put against his bit. At the beginning he hadn't showed any inclination but to walk unless unless Dave's blunt spurs prodded him. But after the first mile or two, and still no pressure on the reins, he lifted his stride to a steady trot, ears forward, going almost eagerly. And, Dave noticed, the animal kept to this elevation and headed directly east.

Three hours after they had left the camp, they struck rougher country, the hills no longer rounded but their sides craggy and often treeless. Unlike yesterday, there was no wind. The heat stored in the exposed rock along their way became pressing as the sun climbed higher. The sky behind them gradually lost its blue clarity and turned hazy, then definitely grey with gathering cloud. *Rain tomorrow,* was Dave's thought. *Might be a help.* It would be, too, if by then he had not found Breen and the posse came across his sign. An hour of good hard rain would wash out all traces of his movements.

When the hills became even more abrupt and steeper, the brown showed a tendency to swing downward, into the north. At first Dave used reins to keep the animal headed to the east. But when the brown seemed insistent, Dave let him go. There was a good mile of rough going, crossing the fingerlike deep washes that held a northwesterly direction. Then the timber began again and the hills rounded out and abruptly the brown walked out of the trees and into a broad well defined trail.

Dave, surprised at having come so suddenly on the trail, quickly looked both ways along it. Its climbing eastward reach, open for a quarter mile, was deserted. But when Dave looked downward it was to see a lone horseman coming toward them.

He said tonelessly, "Back!" wheeling the brown so quickly into the buckskin that Holmes was startled and flinched away. Then Holmes saw the rider approaching; and his flabby face tightened and Dave could see that he was weighing his chances.

So Dave swung the rifle around, holding it within a foot of the 'breed's waist. "Back," he drawled. And now Holmes grudgingly reined the buckskin about and climbed the bank that edged the trail and rode into the trees.

Dave followed, saying, "Just keep on going. Slow, so we don't wake the dead."

After fifty yards of going through the brush, he called to Holmes to stop. Then he swung around, nodding to the fat man to do likewise. He caught a short grip on the brown's reins and laid a hand on the animal's nose, ready to choke off his whickering if he should try to signal the horse on the road. He gaves Holmes a look that cautioned him to follow his example. Then, with Holmes a little ahead of him, he looked downward through the thick stand of short pine seedlings, watching a narrow wedge of the trail.

He heard the strengthening muffled hoof fall of the horse down there. He listened sharply, waiting for a break in the rhythm of that stride that would warn him of his sign having been spotted by the rider. But the steady rhythm held on unbroken.

The slight man on the leggy old gray gelding rode past that narrow slit along the trail that Dave could see. His brown derby and the moustache labelled him instantly. The excitement in Dave gave way before a gladness as he called, "Doc! Hold on!"

That voice ringing down out of the trees startled Doc, jerked him from his despairing mood. He looked up there, hardly daring to believe his recognition of the voice. When first Holmes, then Dave, came into sight through the trees, his pallid face took on a wide smile that held until Dave sat facing him there in the trail.

Dave looked around, then drawled, "We might get off into the shade, Doc."

"Good sense. The sun's hot today," was the medico's equally casual answer.

They rode up into the trees, Dave finally halting and swinging stiffly down. Doc stood beside him and said, "You aren't choosy about the company you keep, Dave," looking at Holmes.

Dave nodded off to the left, telling the fat man, "Sit down and take it easy. We'll let you know when we want you." Then, to Doc, "You're quite a ways from home."

"Had to come across to check up on a patient," the medico said, and made his first full inspection of the signs of violence on his friend's face. He had noted that Dave limped slightly as he came across after tying the brown; and now he saw the way Dave's left hand was held stiff at his side. "How do you feel?" he asked.

"Like I might live." Dave's flat-planed face took on a grin and Doc was at once reassured and took out his pipe and packed it.

After he had waved a match across the briar's scarred bowl, he passed his tobacco to Dave. "Gail McCune's come to her senses," he said. "Don't ask me how or why. But she wants you back."

Dave's brows lifted in surprise. "No!" he breathed.

"She sent me across here. I told her I might have a time persuadin' you."

Dave seemed lost in thought for a moment. He glanced over to Holmes, who now squatted holding the buckskin's reins. He went over there, took the reins and led the animal back and tied him alongside the brown. Then he asked Doc, "What else do you know?"

"I could use a little sleep," Doc said. "I'm too old to stay up all night."

"Come by way of Scalplock?"

The medico nodded. "To call on a patient. It was pretty dead this morning. Only a few women and some kids around. The men are all away." The brevity and casualness of his report was quite as convincing as though he had explained in detail how many men were on the hunt.

Dave took this in soberly, asking at length, "Where are you headed?"

Doc tilted his head toward the east. "Up there. I've never seen what's up in those hills. Wanted to look around. But now I've changed my mind. It's too long a ride."

"Stayin' over long?" Dave asked.

Doc frowned. "Depends on how well my patient gets along."

"Where'll you stay?"

"At Tom Warren's place in town. I haven't

told you about Tom, have I? He's new to this country, been here only three years. Has a sick wife. Runs a saddle shop. Tom's honest as a summer day is long. Which is strange, too, considerin' his neighbors. Guess he didn't know what he was gettin' into when he moved here. Now he can't pull out because his wife has spells of heart trouble." Doc pulled at the pipe leisurely. "Where do you think you're going?"

"Over east. You said I might find something interesting. And Holmes' jughead seems anxious to go that way. I thought I'd pamper him and see the color of the hay in his home stable."

Doc smiled meagerly, tilting his derby back and mopping his high broad forehead. "Makes sense," he said. "I hear you put some more kinks in Breen's face."

"Did I? Where's he now?"

"Left town about an hour before I did with one of the ranchers who lives off here, Torrence. Torrence's crew was along, too."

"You mentioned this Torrence the other night."

Doc nodded. "He's one that would bear watching. But there are others."

"Then I ought to meet up with Breen sometime today," Dave drawled.

Doc shook his head. "I wouldn't try it,

Dave. There's at least eight of them. Torrence asked them to let him go over this east country with his men." He nodded in Holmes' direction. "And you've got him to look after."

Dave smiled thinly. "I don't need him now. And I'll see he's in no shape to worry me."

"You won't come back to Grade with me, then?" Doc asked soberly.

"Not yet. Not until I've seen Breen again. And you forget I broke jail over there."

Doc's gravity held on another moment. Then it gave way as he smiled and chuckled softly. "That must've been a thing to see, that scrap the other night," he said. "Breen looked like someone had used the flat side of a meat axe on him. By the way, it was Erbeck who put me onto where to find you. I don't know what story he gave Wilce."

"I can't figure that man," Dave said. "First he drags me out of there, then leaves me stranded without a horse or a gun. A twelve year old kid could have walked up the road that night with a slingshot and taken me."

"But Erbeck came back after you," Doc said.

This evidently meant something to Dave, for he considered it a long moment before lazily lifting and lowering his wide shoulders. "Don't ask me the answers. I can't figure it." He paused briefly, his face still serious as he tried to make sense of what Doc had told him of Frank Erbeck. Then he asked, "Can we count on this Tom Warren to help if I get my hands on Breen?"

"Tom'll help all right," Doc said. "But he can't do you much good. Things up here come backwards. Instead of maybe one or two crooked men and the rest honest, here it's one or two honest men and the rest crooked. I'd sooner trust Holmes there with my wallet than a Scalplock man. Any Scalplock man."

"That's a strong statement, Doc."

"Not when you stack it alongside the known facts. How could all those cattle leave the reservation and get through this country to wherever they went without almost every man on this range wearin' blinders?"

"Then it'll be hard to put the blame on any one man, Breen included," Dave said.

Doc nodded. "It will. But any pack of wolves has a leader. How you'll find him is what whips me."

"Well, I can try," Dave drawled. He went across to the buckskin and untied his reins.

Behind him, Doc said, "Take my horse, Dave."

Dave turned to face the medico. He laughed. "That old crow bait? Why?"

"Because they're looking for sign of a horse with a bent right front shoe," Doc said soberly.

Dave's glance sharpened. He turned back to the buckskin, put his shoulder to the animal's and lifted the front leg. One of the prongs of the shoe was bent in.

As Dave let go the buckskin's leg, the medico said, "I'm not too tuckered to lay some interesting tracks for them to follow the rest of the day. Tonight, you could come down and steal a better horse than mine."

Dave said, "This means trouble for you."

"Does it?" Doc asked blandly, "if I say you stopped me and took my horse? The straying around I do can be time spent looking for the posse to tell them I saw you." . . . He glanced across to Holmes. . . . "Better put him afoot. Anywhere off here will do. Torrence and his men are the only ones working this neck of the woods today and they've already gone on past."

Dave eyed the medico with his grey eyes saying more than his, "I'd better let out your stirrups then."

XI

Jim Land, on a bay cutting horse, came out of the dust fogging the gate of the big two acre corral below Grade and rode over to the horse line.

"Make it the roan for the next stretch, Red," he told the wrangler as he swung down out of the saddle and pulled the blue polka dot bandana from his grimy face. He went to the water bucket and helped himself to a dipper of water. He rinsed his mouth and then drank the dipper empty, meanwhile glancing off through the crowd of Sioux gathered nearby to the grey-tarped McCune chuck-wagon on down the gentle slope. He wondered if he should go across there, in the end decided not to. He had done all he could for Fred Harkness.

He was having a bad day, a hell of a bad one. This morning he'd let Wilce talk him into working the crew at the corral on the beef issue while the Major's agency riders pushed the main herd on up to the holding camp on the Muddy. "It'll save you working your men on a hard day's drive," the agent had said, "and we'll be finished with the issue by noon. So take your choice."

Jim's choice to have his crew work the issue rather than the drive had turned out to be a bad one. It was already well past three and the issue nowhere near finished. The dust was bad, the blaze of the sun on this windless day worse. The McCune steers, salty after an easy drive yesterday, were almost unmanageable in the corral, big as it was. A man took his life in his hands when he rode into that enclosure for his half-hour relays of cutting out, singly and in twos and threes, the animals to be issued when an Indian's name was called. A man had to put his faith in the quickness and smartness of his horse.

Which fact, after last night's spree at the Blue Belle, had turned out badly for Fred Harkness. Fred had picked a poor pony his last time in the corral an hour ago. A mean steer had thrown a horn into the pony, Fred had been pitched out of the saddle and trampled. It looked like a broken leg but they wouldn't be sure until the doctor arrived. And Doc Faris was out of town, gone for no one knew how long. Meantime, Fred lay on some blankets in the chuck-wagon drinking straight whiskey to ease the torment of his crippled leg.

Jim now walked over to Red Rhea, the wrangler. "A hell of a mess!" he growled.

"Ain't it?" the taciturn Red said. He had just finished throwing Jim's saddle on a lean-limbed strawberry roan, the best cutting horse in the McCune *remuda.*

"Watch this," Red added, and nodded toward the gate.

Across there, a steer had just broken from the narrow opening. From a knot of mounted copper-skinned Sioux off to the far side of the gate, a young near-naked buck in breechclout and moccasins raced out on a small paint horse. As the steer shied away from the paint, the buck let out a shrill yell and swung up a carbine and fired at the steer. His bullet only grazed the animal; intentionally, for this was the proper way for a Sioux to take his issue of beef. Steer and rider pounded off into the dust swirl below the corral, headed for the flats.

"Havin' fun, ain't they?" Jim said.

He had watched this same thing happen time and again today. The Sioux bucks would take rifle or a sharpened pole lance and chase their steers well away from the corral, meantime goading their beef by bullet or lancehead, prolonging the chase as much as possible. Then, finally making the kill, they would disdainfully ride away from the dead steer, leaving to their squaws and children the work of skinning out the carcass, quartering it and loading it onto horse-pulled travois to be taken to their camps.

The four-mile-wide flat to the south was now studded with squaws at their butchering, some already leading their travois-burdened animals toward the trails which radiated from Grade like the spokes of a wheel. It wasn't like the old buffalo hunts. But it was as close to those carefree wild hunting days as the Sioux could make it with this substitute the government had given him.

Jim had been on last year's drive and had seen a beef issue then. They had worked in the mud that time and now he tried to decide which was worse, the mud or the dust. Last year Jacob Wilce's pole-stretched tarpaulin had shielded the agent from the rain. Today it was stifling hot under the tarp and the Major stood just outside it, the ever present cigar tilted up out of his mouth, the expression on his narrow face one of complete and irritated discomfort.

This was one of Wilce's chief duties, being here while the beef was issued. It was easy to see that he resented it, that he was impatient of the delays that had caused the issue to run on into the afternoon. Tucker, his accountant, sat before a table under the tarp and read off the names of the bucks and the number of beef they were to receive.

And the agent would bawl the name and number querulously, as though it was he, not the Sioux, who had been inconvenienced by this long wait for meat rations.

Jim saw the buggy coming up off the town road and, when it headed over toward the chuck-wagon he said relievedly to Red, "Here's the sawbones."

He climbed onto the roan and started across there. By the time he was halfway to the wagon, the buggy had drawn up alongside it. Gail McCune and Martha Mills got down out of the buggy. Jim was suddenly mad clear through and swore feelingly, soundly, for he had no liking for John McCune's daughter.

But he saw that he must, out of decency, go down there and try and be nice to her. He did this grudgingly and only because he didn't want Dave Santell ever to say that he hadn't treated a woman right. He had a strong faith that Dave would soon be back on the job, regardless of present complications; and he wanted to report that he had meantime done his job well.

He tied the roan to a spoke of the chuck-wagon's front wheel, sauntering on to the back of the wagon, hearing Fred Harkness talking to Gail. He nodded to Martha Mills and looked in under the tarp to find Gail kneeling alongside the injured crewman. She had pulled the blanket off Fred and was looking at his knee, where the pain seemed worst.

She spoke just then, and the calmness and strength of her voice startled Jim. What she said, without turning, was, "Martha, we'll have to get a fire going to heat some water. See if you can find the cook to help us. And ask him for some rags so we can get some heat on this knee."

Her words hauled Jim up short, jarring his mood of disgust and impatience. Was this the stubborn and helpless woman he had talked to yesterday afternoon? If so, he had missed something. Fred's leg was a sight, the knee swollen almost to the size of a ham. The inside of the wagon smelled like a dirty saloon from all the whiskey Fred had spilled in his drinking. Not such a pleasant place, or circumstance, for a city girl to find herself thrown into. Yet here was Gail McCune talking and acting like any other sensible and level-headed woman.

Jim looked at Martha. "I'll get the fire goin' and put on the water," he told her. "You could go up there to the corral and ask the redhead on the horse line to send the cook down."

Gail turned, surprised at the sound of a

man's voice. She gave Jim a quick and sure smile that tempered her, "Why didn't you send for me when this happened?"

"I didn't . . . didn't think of it," was Jim's halting, honest answer.

"You mean you didn't think I'd be interested," Gail corrected him. She looked down again at Fred Harkness. "Try not to move," she said, and climbed down out of the wagon, nodding her thanks as she took Jim's helping hand.

She wasn't the same girl Jim had lost his temper with yesterday. There was a sureness and a competence about her entirely foreign to his opinion of her. And today she didn't seem cool and aloof and so faultlessly groomed. There was a streak of black on her blue print skirt where it had brushed against the greasy wheel-hub of the chuck-wagon. Because it had been hot under the tarp, she had pulled her sleeves above her elbows, laying bare her slender forearms to the sun. Her coppery hair was slightly disordered and she didn't seem to mind the strands of it that had come loose from the crown braid; it looked more red than brown in this strong sunlight.

She told Jim, "I don't think his leg is broken. It looks like a bad knee sprain. When we've brought down the swelling we can bind it in a splint so he won't use it. But he'll be laid up for a couple of weeks. How did it happen?"

Jim told her as he got the fire going. By the time he had lighted the blaze, she had brought across two big cooking kettles and he caught her carrying the first pailful of water from the cook's barrel.

"Here, let me do that," he said severely. "It's heavy."

She willingly surrendered the pail. But from that moment on he had all he could do to anticipate her needs and be of real help. The cook and Martha came down from the corral and with four hands doing the work it went faster. Gail insisted that Harkness be lifted from the hot wagon and made comfortable on the ground in the chuck-wagon's shade, with blankets as a mattress.

It was Gail who insisted on applying the hot compress to the crewman's bad knee. Gradually, the lines of pain etched on Fred's face disappeared. He could smile now rather than giving that grimace that had passed for a smile during this past hour. He no longer gritted his teeth but lay back relaxed and exhausted. He said once, "Nothin' ever felt so good," when Gail put a fresh hot rag on his knee.

It was the cook and Martha who finally persuaded Gail to rest. But when they had relieved her of the work of applying the compresses to Harkness's knee, she at once began getting ready the splints for his leg. Jim helped, finding two long straight poles, helping her tear the strips of cloth to bind the splints.

They had been working over Harkness the better part of an hour when Jacob Wilce appeared abruptly from the direction of the corral.

"Well, that job's taken care of for another month," were the agent's first words.

Only then did Gail and Jim and Martha notice that the dust had thinned, that the corral was empty and that the many saddle horses and light rigs that had cluttered the dusty stretch of ground on the corral's near side were gone, moving up the road that led to town. Shortly after Wilce appeared, the seven remaining men of the McCune crew came down and stood at a respectful distance, silently watching what was being done for Fred Harkness.

"Taking the horses across tomorrow?" Wilce asked Jim, when his first comment was wholly ignored.

Jim said briefly, "Yeah," not looking up from his work of winding strips of cloth as padding around one of the long splints.

"Know the way?" the agent asked, seeming insistent on their giving him their attention.

Jim only nodded this time. He actually didn't know how he was to take the horses across to Torrence's place; but he would rather ask someone else than have Wilce explain to him. He had no liking for the agent nor for the job that had been wished off on his crew today.

Wilce must have sensed this antagonism in him, for now he mentioned Harkness for the first time. "Tough luck, your getting this man hurt, Land," he said. "Wish there was something I could do."

Gail, standing nearby, said, "We're very busy, Major."

"Need any medicine? Liniment?" Wilce asked, too toughened to rebuffs to take this one seriously. "I've got some up at the warehouse."

"We have liniment, thank you," Gail told him.

From then on, the agent was ignored so completely that in the end he left without a word, his narrow face screwed up in obvious bafflement and anger.

He was barely out of hearing when Gail said to Jim, "I don't like that man. I wonder why my father ever did business with him?"

"Good pay," Jim told her. "There ain't many outfits that would tackle a drive clear up into this neck o' the woods. John McCune knew that, he had the best man in Texas workin' for him and he asked his price and got it."

He immediately regretted this roundabout reference to Dave when Gail at once said, "I guess I made a mistake there. Did you know that Santell was in a fight over in Scalplock two nights ago? He went over there to get that man who stole our cattle."

"No!" Jim breathed. "Breen?"

Gail nodded, saying in a low voice, "Don't tell the others. I don't want to cause any more trouble than I have already. But tomorrow, or the next day, when you deliver those horses, I want you and the men you take with you to go on down to Scalplock. I want you to find Santell and bring him back. Doctor Faris is over there looking for him now. Find the doctor and ask his help. He seems to know what he's doing."

Jim nodded gravely, and couldn't help asking, "Why didn't you let me know before, ma'am?"

"I don't know, I guess I thought you'd hear about it," Gail said contritely, humbly. "It's . . . well, I didn't realize what was happening."

This awkward admission and what lay behind it — for she was confessing to an error, in a way apologizing for how she had acted until now — was the thing that finally and irrevocably sealed Jim Land's loyalty to her.

Afterward, around the supper fire, he had this to say to the crew, "That girl, I got her all wrong yesterday. She'll do."

From where he lay on his blankets near the fire, Fred Harkness said, "I was goin' to ask you about that, Jim. Hell, she's a damn' sight handier'n most men! Look at the way she's fixed me up. If you birds weren't so pigheaded, I'd get up and walk right now. Leg don't hurt at all."

There was much that went unspoken here, for the crew had sensed an error in Jim's judgment of John McCune's daughter, sensed, too, that Jim was as surprised at what had happened this afternoon as they were.

It wasn't until after supper that someone said, "Why are we hangin' around camp? The job's done. I've got a powerful thirst."

"Who'll stay with Fred?" someone else put in.

Harkness heard this last and said, "I'm a grown man, ain't I? I had my fun last night, the rest of you didn't. Go 'long, the whole bunch of you."

For a while, that was all that was said. But the men were restive, having looked forward to this celebration — in fact planned it last night — all the way up the trail from Texas. They had had one or two flings in the trail towns they passed near on the drive. But now the summer's job was ended. They deserved a night to howl and it looked like they weren't going to get it.

The cook had finished with the dishes and Red Rhea had gone out to night hawk the horses when Fred Harkness abruptly sat up in his blankets and threw them aside. "The hell with this!" he exploded. "I've laid away four months wages for a stud game and damned if I don't get in one! Tonight! In town!"

The others listened to this outburst in silence. All but Jim Land, who drawled, "You try that leg and it'll cave in under you. They shoot horses with a broken pin. We'd hate to have to shoot you, Fred."

"Any reason why you couldn't prop this leg o' mine across a couple of chairs at one of those tables in the Blue Belle?" Fred asked querulously, adding, "I'm rarin' to go. Never felt better."

"Why not?" someone said.

The argument went on from there, Jim alone counselling against moving Fred. But the weight of numbers finally brought his agreement. And behind it all, behind Jim's final giving in, was relief and gladness over Gail McCune having proved herself.

So at nine that night the game began in the Blue Belle. Fred Harkness rode to town in the bed of the wrangler's buckboard. They put him in two chairs at the back table of the Blue Belle; he sat in one and rested his bad leg across the other. Someone discovered a pair of crutches at the trading post. Everyone but Fred used them that night. And by midnight Fred was forty dollars the winner in a seven-hand game of quarter-limit stud.

Jim Land left the Blue Belle early, at eleven. He was in the saddle and on his way out to camp before he remembered that he didn't yet know how he was going to get the horses across to Torrence's place tomorrow. So he turned around and came back to the saloon, remembering that he had seen one of Wilce's riders at the bar on the way out.

This agency man was Frank Erbeck. He began telling Jim how to reach the Scalplock pass. But halfway through his explanation he hauled up short.

He gave a shrug, saying, "You'd never get there without help."

"Supposin' you let on like I would." Jim drawled dryly, for he had little respect for anyone who worked for Wilce.

"Supposin' I go with you," Frank said, following his impulse of a moment ago. "It'd save you time."

Jim didn't much like the prospect of having this agency rider along and would have much preferred that he and Red Rhea make the drive alone. Yet common sense told him that any time saved would be more than worth the trouble of a two day ride with a Wilce man. So he said, "We'd be obliged for any help. But I could still make it alone."

"What time you startin'?" was Frank's summary question.

"About three in the mornin'. Want to make it in a day if we can."

"I'll be at your camp at three," Frank said.

A short time later, Frank entered the agency to find Wilce at his desk, a bottle open before him, a half finished cigar in his mouth. The agent looked up and, when he saw Frank, scowled. "What do you want?" he asked sourly.

"Who told Land how to get across to Torrence's?" Frank asked curtly.

200

His question wiped out the agent's surliness. "No one I know of," Wilce said. "I tried to tell him and he said he already knew the way."

"I'll say he does." Frank smiled wryly. "Well, whoever told him is sending him up through the short cut."

"Short cut? What short cut?" Wilce asked with an unsure blandness. However, the quick anger in his eyes told Frank he had touched the agent at a sore spot. "You're the only man who isn't up at the camp on the Muddy," Wilce said. Then his curiosity overrode his caution and he asked, "Who told you about the canyon pass?"

Frank gave a slow shake of the head. "I didn't do it, Major. One of the others must've talked to him last night. And the only pass I know is the main road."

Wilce swore softly, with venom.

"Don't worry," Frank drawled. "I just offered to take him across myself. I'll see that he goes by way of the road."

Wilce eyed him a long moment without speaking, eyed him openly and questioningly. They were both thinking of the same thing, the fact that Wilce hadn't sent Frank with the rest of the crew to the camp on the Muddy today. Frank knew as well as Wilce did that something was happening at the camp that the agent would rather he didn't know about. Which meant only one thing, that Wilce wasn't trusting this crewman of his because of what had happened across in Scalplock two nights ago.

At length, the Major said in a drawling way, "Sometimes you seem to have some sense, Erbeck. All right, you'll go with Land. Only come back with him. Don't stay over there." He added, with pointed emphasis, "It might not be healthy for you."

"Don't worry, I'm not interested in your game," Frank said.

"What game?" Wilce snapped.

Frank shrugged, said carelessly, "Act your age, Major. I'm not blind."

The agent was on the defensive now and his glance refused to meet Frank's. He said gruffly, curtly, "Well, what're you standin' around here for? Get some sleep. You'll be turnin' out early."

As Frank undressed and lay down in his bunk, his square face was graven with a broad smile. He had been trying the whole day to think up an excuse to give the Major for going back to Scalplock. Now he had one.

His good humor held on even when the first big drops of rain pelted the sheet-iron roof of the crew quarters some twenty

202

minutes later. Those clouds gathering off to the west this afternoon had presaged a long hard rain and now that it was beginning there was a promise of a wet day tomorrow. But Frank gave this unpleasurable prospect only passing thought.

He was wondering what had happened to Santell and knew he would stay in the Scalplock country until he found out.

That afternoon of the beef issue, Torrence had watched Breen and three Wheel crewmen ride up across the high meadow and into the belt of pale green aspen above his place. Only when they were out of sight did he turn restlessly to his horse and tighten the loosened cinch, letting his glance meanwhile run over the layout close below.

He saw the two windows open on the near side of the low sod-roofed cabin but shrugged aside the notion of going down and closing them. Those black banks of angry clouds to the west meant certain rain, rain that would come in the direction of those windows. Yet his passing thought was, *Let 'er come. Wash the whole place out if it wants.* Such was his poor opinion of the home his father had spent half his lifetime building. Ed Torrence cared very little for Wheel.

A much more important thing than the well-being of the cabin right now was that last interchange of words he'd had with Breen a few minutes ago. And, as he mounted and rode down across the meadow to the head of the canyon, his attention was focused hard on certain possibilities.

He wasn't sure of Ray Breen any longer. Three nights ago, when he had talked to Jake Wilce, his confidence had been firm as a rock; his certainty of Breen had been one of the main roots of that confidence. But the big man's killing of Mordue had been a rash act and had come close to putting them all in real trouble. Now he couldn't help but wonder what mistake Breen would make next. Only when he convinced himself that nothing could happen on the drive across here from the agency camp on the Muddy did his worry ease off. Here, at least, was a job Breen could handle without any fumbles.

At the foot of the meadow, where the trail cut in below the rim down the canyon head, he stopped and looked back, trying to spot his men crossing one of the higher clearings. He couldn't see them. His glance involuntarily dropped to the meadow and he at once felt the same rise of sultry anger and disappointment that always hit him on glimpsing Wheel.

The clutter of weathered and unpainted sheds and corrals half circling the small cabin invariably filled him with scorn and wonder. The wonder came when he tried to imagine what had ever possessed old Ned Torrence to pick this spot for a homestead. Down lower a couple thousand feet a man had a chance against the brutal killing winters. But up here the old man had waged a long hard fight against the elements that consumed close to half his life and left him with little more than he'd had at the start. Those sixty acres of alfalfa in the meadow had meant the difference between being able to hang on and utter ruin. Those sixty acres had enabled Ned Torrence to last out winters that would have otherwise killed off all his beef. The old man had taken great pride in his foresight of damming the creek and having the water to raise his two crops of hay each summer. Yet the son had never understood this pride because, had it been up to him, he would have filed on a lower quarter section and in that absurdly simple way have won the battle against the elements.

There had been that difference between father and son. The older Torrence had been stubborn and a fighter and had taken great satisfaction in winning a battle made doubly hard because of a beginning mistake he would never admit. The son had more vision and all the ambition the father had lacked. He was just as stubborn, as evidenced by his insistence at having a better life. Had this been blended with a moderate amount of ambition, Ed Torrence might have bought another spread, lower down, and made a go of it. But he scorned the petty success of his neighbors, seeing them as nothing but pygmies when compared to the stature of out-country men whose names were well known in the cattle business.

So Ed Torrence had over the years nourished a fantastic dream of one day cutting loose the shackles that held him here and going to some other country to become one of those lords of a vast cattle empire. To do this he had to have money, lots of money. This ambition, then, was the driving force that had put him in his present circumstance. Had he been able to lay his hands on money honestly he would never have thought of being dishonest. But his opportunities in the Scalplock country were limited. He had succumbed to the temptations offered by the easy pickings on the nearby reservation and the easy blackmail of Jacob Wilce. Now he could see his dream of possessing wealth and power about to materialize. And all of his driving energy and keen animal cunning were centered on accomplishing that goal.

He was thinking far ahead, deciding on how he could increase the pressure on Wilce. And in his imagining he saw no end to it, except that in another year, possibly two, he would leave this country of limited opportunity and head for one where he wasn't cramped. It would be Montana, probably, and he would own a vast holding where Texas beef would be wintered and sold on the early spring market of high prices.

He happened to think of Holmes just then and at once was angered by that same strain of unsureness he had felt on seeing Breen leave the meadow. Holmes had been gone for two days. Why, when he had said he would be in Scalplock last night? Torrence's instinct told him that the 'breed's disappearance was somehow connected with Santell. That was what worried him with a nagging unease that now made him curse bitterly and put rough pressure on the reins so that the brown tossed his head with a hurt mouth.

Some thirty minutes later, Torrence came

to the lower mouth of the canyon where the creek spilled downward in a series of falls and rapids into the lower rolling hilly country. Taking the turning in the trail that ran obliquely out and down in a more gradual descent than the creek, his glance ran idly along that lower stretch of timber flanked trail.

He saw the lone rider on the gray horse and recognized Doc Faris, wondering idly and disinterestedly what the medico was doing out this far from town. Then, just as he looked away, he saw a second rider come down out of the trees and his eyes whipped back to the trail in a quick hard stare.

This second man was astride a brown. Shortly, another appeared, one whose bulging shape was topped by a high-crowned black Stetson. Torrence knew at once that this last man was Holmes. The halfbreed was riding a buckskin.

A buckskin! With an instinct that was sure and quick, Torrence wheeled his gelding around and into the trees above. For he knew that the third man down there must be Dave Santell.

Later, much later, Dave came up the twisting trail on Doc Faris' gray and rode in toward the creek, toward the bend where the trail cut into the canyon.

He was abreast the timber spur closing the mouth of the deep rocky notch when Torrence's voice rode harshly above the sound of the rushing water.

"Santell!"

Dave's head jerked around. He saw the man with the dark hair and the slight rangy frame who stepped from behind the stem of the nearest pine and took a spraddle-legged stance, a sixgun lined at hip level. *So this is Torrence* was Dave's immediate thought and he never questioned it. He added mentally, *A woman* would *look at him twice,* remembering what Doc had said; for Torrence's dark burned face was well moulded, strongly handsome.

Torrence's glance dropped briefly to Dave's waist, to the two rifles, one in a scabbard, under Dave's leg, the other's muzzle thrust into the scabbard and its action thonged to the swell of the saddle. He stepped out from the tree, smiling a little and drawling, "You're packin' plenty of iron."

Dave, hands held at shoulder height, said nothing.

With a motion of his gun, Torrence indicated that Dave was to dismount. That accomplished, Torrence said briefly, "Turn around." A moment later the weight of the

Colt's left the holster at Dave's thigh and he lowered his hands.

Torrence was undecided a moment. Then, because he rarely let a man know the true workings of his mind, he said, "Sorry it had to be me, Santell. I was hopin' you'd hit for a healthier climate."

Dave turned slowly and put a full look on this man who lacked half a head in matching his rangy length. He found something distinctly pleasant in Torrence's tone and manner, although the tried not to. And now he drawled, smiling wryly, "You could turn me loose if you hate it too bad."

Torrence stepped back, as though the difference in their statures grated on his pride — which it did, in fact.

"No dice," he said. "I'll have to take you in."

"Why?"

Torrence smiled crookedly. "You wouldn't know, would you?"

"I shot at the lamp there the other night, not at a man," Dave said.

Torrence shrugged. "Maybe so. But a man's been killed. You'll have to talk it over with the sheriff when he gets here."

"When'll that be?"

"Tomorrow or next day. Depends on how hard he is to find." With a deft sure gesture,

Torrence flipped his gun into holster, Dave's weapon held carelessly in his other hand. He nodded toward the trees. "You'll have to walk back here a ways with me after my jughead."

For some indefinable reason, Dave couldn't summon any resentment against this man for his turn of bad luck. Torrence had handled this nicely and his lack of any pretense or high handedness was what impressed Dave most.

Torrence even offered Dave his tobacco as they walked back through the trees after the horse.

XII

They had started out this morning under a leaden sky out of which occasional flurries of rain spit down at them, Frank Erbeck and Jim Land and Red Rhea driving the ninety-four half-wild horses of the McCune *remuda*.

The Ironstone foothills lay close to the north when the clouds closed over them and the downpour began. The rain would come in a blinding slashing curtain for long stretches, then ease off and sometimes stop altogether. But in those intervals when the rain stopped, a thick mist rose from the drenched ground and never could they see beyond a hundred yards. By midday, after two hours of seeing no familiar landmark, Frank suspected he was lost. By late afternoon, at the end of a two-hour driving downpour, he was sure of it.

Jim Land greeted the news with an offhanded, "Who cares? In a rain like this a man would lose his way in his own corral. Let's hit the timber and make camp and go on tomorrow."

So they swung first to the left through the dense haze for a while, and, deciding they were on a downgrade, turned about. At the end of forty minutes they came to timber, a thin growth of scrubby jackpine. They headed into it, looking for a small box canyon or a deep wash in which they could hold the horses overnight.

They struck a wide canyon expecting soon to reach its upper end. But by the time the light was beginning to fade, even though the canyon had narrowed it showed no sign of ending.

"The hell with it!" Frank said finally. He had just spotted a broad rock overhang in the sheer wall close by and now nodded to it. "We can sling our blankets there and keep dry and let 'er rain."

So they made their camp under the overhang, starting their supper fire with pitch-pine splinters broken from the branches of a rotting windfall. As the darkness closed down on them, Red Rhea took the first turn at riding the narrow breadth of the canyon bottom so that the horses wouldn't drift down to the lower country.

Jim Land had something on his mind that he had been wanting to mention all day. It wasn't until they had finished their meal, Frank meanwhile relieving Red for an hour's stretch while the wrangler came up to the fire to eat, that Jim saw the chance to mention it.

Jim and Frank had hung their wet boots to dry soles-up on the ground-stuck sticks well away from the fire. It had started to rain again and sleep was beginning to crowd them both when Jim said abruptly, "Miss McCune says you tipped her off on the trouble Dave got wound up in the other night. Also that you helped him out of it. How come, you bein' an agency man?"

Frank's level gaze studied Jim a moment. Then Frank drawled bluntly, truthfully, "I couldn't see that bunch of Scalplock hard-cases whittle down a man with Santell's guts."

"Why didn't you bring him back?" Jim asked. "You were supposed to be huntin' him."

"He didn't do nothin' to me," Frank said, with a meager smile. "And my hunch is he didn't do nothin' to Miss McCune. So why should I care what happens to him?"

This attitude of Frank's stumped Jim. His perplexity was evidenced by a worried frown.

He said finally, not grudgingly, "It's a good thing it was you and not one of those other rannies that works for Wilce." He hesitated a moment, apparently making up his mind to take Frank into his confidence, then went on, "Me and Red was talkin' about Dave last night. Supposin' he's still hangin' out across there? How would we go about findin' him?"

"Search me," was Frank's answer. He'd been wondering the same thing.

Jim sat for long minutes, staring at the fire, listening to the steady murmur of the rain, lost in his thoughts. Then, just as abruptly as he had first mentioned this matter, he spoke of it again.

"You know that Scalplock country. How about helpin' me and Red find Dave after we've got these nags across? Miss McCune would pay you for your time."

"And have the Major can me?" Frank drawled. "Hunh-uh!"

Jim's rugged sun-blackened face took on a guilty grin. "Well, it didn't hurt to try," he said. "Let's you and me turn in if I'm gettin' up at midnight to spell Red."

Jim rose lazily from his crouch by the fire. He stretched, yawned long and loudly.

It was at that moment that they heard the mutter of sound from far down-canyon. Jim's mouth stayed open as he listened. Frank's head tilted around sharply and his glance narrowed as he looked off into the darkness.

The sound held on, a steady low note that seemed earth-borne and slowly mounting in volume over the relentless drone of the rain.

Suddenly, out of the downward distance, the blast of gunshots rode up the canyon's narrow corridor. Its slapping echoes ripped away the curtain of the night's steady undertones.

Frank lunged erect, reaching for his boots and bridle and wheeling out into the cobalt void of the night, shouting stridently, "Red! Get across here, Red!"

Jim was close behind, running hard when Frank reached their two staked-out ponies.

And now the sound from down canyon had mounted to a low roar. Jim knew that sound and dreaded it. For he had heard it once on the trail up from Texas and his memory of it was compounded of fear and helplessness and threatening danger.

Ray Breen had been in a black mood all this day. This morning he had made things harder for the agency crewmen as they rounded up three hundred steers from the big herd loosely held near the camp on the Muddy and turned the animals over to the Wheel riders. His bad temper and bullying had been more of an obstacle to finishing the job than the storm: and when he and the Torrence men late in the morning pushed the herd away, there was a general feeling of relief at the agency camp.

It was typical of Torrence that he had discouraged any curiosity on the part of Wilce's riders as to what happened to all the cattle that had been driven from the Muddy holding ground over the past year. Each time the pattern was the same. Wilce would issue a vague order one day; the next, a strange crew would appear and drive a certain number of steers away. Once, only once, an agency rider had let his curiosity get the best of him and followed one of those vanishing herds into the higher foothills. He had been gone half a day, to return with a bullet shattered shoulder and his face scarred with the marks of a severe beating. He had never talked about what had happened to him and had quit his job shortly afterward. Naturally, after that, other Wilce riders stayed out of the higher hills.

Today Breen had ordered one Wheel man to remain behind and make sure that no agency man repeated that same foolhardiness while the herd was driven straight for the canyon pass. But the same ground fog that had lost Frank Erbeck his direction confused the Wheel riders. They took Breen's cursing stoically, knowing that the reason for it was the tongue-lashing their boss had given the big man yesterday. At last, in the middle afternoon, they stumbled onto the right trail and the delay was over. But Breen's bullying held on and when the rain commenced again the Wheel men let him strictly alone.

The man who had been left behind appeared as the gray light was beginning to fade into dusk. Breen's anger had one more excuse for boiling over because this rider came down the canyon to meet the herd instead of catching up with it from behind; and Breen naturally suspected that the Torrence man hadn't done his job.

But his explosive torrent of abuse was cut short when the man said mildly, "Hold on,

Ray! Wait'll I tell you where I been. Cuttin' over here I come across horse sign, plenty of it. So I followed it and found a big string of horses headed up the cut here. The rannies drivin' 'em had made camp about three miles above. That jasper that threw down on you and took Santell out of the fight the other night is one of 'em."

"Erbeck?" Breen breathed almost prayerfully, his temper immediately cooling. "You're sure?"

"I had a good look at him. You suppose these is the nags the boss is buyin' from the McCune outfit?"

"Couldn't be anything else," Breen said. A narrow gloating look came to his eyes as he glanced on up the canyon's narrowing corridor. Abruptly, he asked, "Where are they camped, in the narrows?"

The man nodded and the others, who had come up, looked at each other quizzically.

"Three miles," Breen said, so low voiced they barely heard him. His glance swung on them now, going from one man to another as a broad smile played across his face.

"Want to have some fun?" he asked.

When they frowned, he went on, "If we could get Torrence those jugheads without his havin' to pay for 'em he'd maybe raise our share, wouldn't he?"

"Sure," said one man, "but how'll we steal 'em unless we burn some powder. And the boss won't thank us if we hurt anyone."

"Who said anything about hurtin' anyone?" Breen asked. "We wait till dark, stampede these critters up the canyon and they take the horses with 'em. If Erbeck or the others get hurt, it'll be their own fault for not gettin' out of the way."

The man who had brought the news of the horse herd chuckled softly. "Not bad, Ray," he drawled and the others smiled as the idea caught on. They sat there in the droning downpour, looking as though they were enjoying it.

At length, Breen said, "Well, it's up to you. Do we do it?"

Of the three Wheel men, only one hesitated in at once agreeing; and he was quickly convinced by the others.

"We'll grab something to eat first," Breen said. "Once we get these critters on the move we'll have to push 'em fast all the way to the head of the pass. With luck, we'll take every damn' McCune nag across with us."

"How about Erbeck and his sidekicks?" asked that one who needed convincing.

"What would you do if you got ahead of a stampede?" Breen asked.

"Get out of the way as quick as I could,"

the man said. "Climb a tree or get behind a boulder and hope it wasn't rolled over on me."

"Then there's your answer," Breen said. "So why worry?"

XIII

The thunder of the stampede burst upon them suddenly, its first warning notes having been muffled by the sound of the rain. Frank managed to force the bit into the mouth of his jumpy steeldust pony. Jim Land, close by, was having more difficulty. Frank led his horse over there and held Jim's animal close by the halter rope while the bridle was put on, Jim meantime repeating over and over again one salty oath of exasperation.

Red Rhea rode up out of the darkness, shouting, "What the hell's busted loose here?" as Frank and Jim went to the bare backs of their horses. There was no time now to think of their saddles.

Another burst of shots spoke above the thunder of hoof pound from close below and Frank shouted, "The horses! Get 'em movin'!" He used rein ends and spurs to put his pony into a lunging run up canyon. Close on the heels of his horse pounded

Jim and Red.

There had been no time for Frank and Jim to think of their guns back there at the fire. Red alone had a weapon. As they came in on the first bunch of restlessly milling horses, Frank lifted his voice in a strident shout and Red drew his Colt's and fired it over his head, twice. The horse bunch scattered, galloping up canyon.

The three of them spread out to cover the width of the canyon and for a brief space of time their muffled cries rang between the high walls, Red's gun exploding in an occasional quick-timed burst as he came across other animals and pushed them on. All three worked with frantic urgency, with desperation, not knowing how much time they had to get the *remuda* on the move.

They were in sight of each other when the lumbering lead steers all at once charged at them through the black curtain of the rainy darkness.

Red wheeled his horse and shot the first two animals. Frank saw them go down. The ones close behind those leaders swung aside from the gun flashes. Frank shouted until his voice became a hoarse croaking, his sharp-wheeling horse gradually giving ground before the charge of more fear-crazed steers.

For a moment it looked as though they had turned the cattle back. But then the sound of more shots crashed up from below and the press of steers behind the lead animals suddenly increased and pushed them on. They broke forward in a wave of tossing horns and close-packed bodies. All Frank and Jim and Red could do was to make a run for it.

Red hesitated a moment too long, trusting too much in his gun. Frank, looking back, saw the wrangler's vague shape melt downward into the wall of shadowy running steers. Frank drew rein, half turning to go back. But then he knew that nothing could save Red. As his pony spun frantically out of the path of a head down and charging steer, Frank heard a gunshot, then a muted scream behind. That was all.

Jim had gone out of sight somewhere ahead. Frank ran his horse hard for an interval, time and again quickly reining aside to avoid horses of the *remuda*. Fear had taken these animals. Some merely trotted aimlessly, confused and terror-struck by the weighty thunder riding the night. An occasional animal, frightened by the cattle, would charge past, ears laid back, running hard. Frank could almost feel the terror strike the horses close ahead, beginning to bunch now. He saw a big pinto in a full-out run collide with another animal and go down, neighing shrilly, hooves thrashing.

All this time he was working the steeldust closer in to the sheer wall on his right, looking for a high rock outcrop behind which he could take shelter, or a wide crevice into which he could ride. Not many times in his life had Frank felt stark naked fear. But terror rode this darkness and fear struck him like a searing flame, for he knew that a rider caught between the *remuda* and the stampeding cattle stood little chance of living through until tomorrow's dawn.

Suddenly he was riding with horses flanking him on both sides and close packed ahead, blocking his path. One animal shying from another, crazed and lunging, collided with Frank's mount, crushing Frank's leg between the two horses. At that moment Frank saw a high shape loom up out of the darkness ahead. He slashed the animal alongside with rein ends and the pressure on his leg eased off momentarily. Gouging his gelding with spurs, Frank made for that shadow ahead that was darker than the night.

It was a high rock shoulder. Frank's horse was jammed against it by the press of animals and Frank's other leg was numbed by the blow. But with a mighty pressure on the reins he kept his gelding from falling and rounded the back face of the outcrop. Once behind that solid bastion, he slid quickly from the gelding's back, caught a short hold on the reins and stood with his back to the rock.

Running shapes rushed past, barely visible in the darkness, the earth trembling with the impact of hooves. And now the fear drained out of Frank as abruptly as it had hit him, leaving him chilled and wet and miserable. But he couldn't take his eyes from the solid stream of animals pounding past. He saw the pale outline of horns riding above that fast flowing tide of massed flesh.

Presently, when that rushing stream of steers had thinned somewhat, he saw the high and massive shape of a rider go past. He called out unthinkingly, his hoarse croak drowned in the roar of sound.

The next instant he knew that the rider could have been no one but Ray Breen; and he was thankful for the deafening echoes that had washed out his feeble shouting. He stood there watching the last remnant of the herd charge past the rock shoulder. He saw another rider, another; and now he drew back farther behind the outcrop, the bleak full realization in him of what Breen had done.

He waited without moving many minutes, until the sound of the herd's going had become a far off mutter. Then, wearily, he went belly down across the gelding's back, pulling a leg over. He reined out from behind the rock shoulder, calling, "Land!"

There was no answer.

For twenty minutes Frank rode the canyon's near upper corridor repeating his call, hope slowly dying in him. He had all but seen Red Rhea die and now had his doubts that Jim Land had survived those terrible moments when it had been in his power to save himself.

He came across the carcasses of many animals, both cattle and horses, animals that had lost their footing and been trampled to death in the stampede. He examined these remains, certain as he came upon each new one that it was the carcass of Jim Land's horse. But each time he was mistaken.

Finally he turned back as the rain's steady fall strengthened. He rode with chin tilted down into the upturned collar of his poncho, the rain runneling along the channels of his face and his hair matted to his head; he had lost his Stetson somewhere below in that mad rush to safety.

His thoughts were bleak and a slow hard

rage was building in him against Breen. It was a deeper and more hateful emotion than he had felt toward the man in Scalplock the other night. For he was also seeing himself in relation to what had happened tonight, blaming himself for not having made a longer search for the main pass trail, seeing himself as directly responsible for the deaths of Red Rhea and Jim Land.

In other circumstances he would have taken some satisfaction in having discovered the way by which stolen reservation cattle were taken across the Ironstones. But now that satisfaction was lacking. All that was in him was a deep sense of his own inadequacy, of his having made a failure of a gesture he had intended to be a helpful one. Here was just one more mischance, one more tally to add to the many fateful reverses of the past year. Staring down the obscure path of his future, Frank Erbeck was finally and definitely without hope. He no longer cared what happened to him. Thought of Martha, of her belief in him, only added to his dull and brooding torment.

He lost all track of time in his dismal ponderings. Shock and exhaustion had taken the keen edge from his consciousness. When a voice close in the darkness called, "Erbeck! That you?" he was only faintly relieved at hearing it, at recognizing it as Jim Land's.

But by the time he had reined over toward the sound of Jim's voice, a small thankfulness was rising in him. Shortly, he saw Jim ahead, standing by his horse. Then, as he wearily slid from the gelding's back and saw the huddled shape lying at Jim's feet, his depression once more became a heavy weight.

"Red?" he asked dully.

"Red," Jim answered. He added quietly, "We'll have to bury him here, Erbeck. He's in no shape to pack back to town."

There was a moment's silence. Abruptly Frank spoke in a grating voice, "Why don't you say it?"

"Say what?" Jim's tone was one of honest inquiry, not mocking, not understanding.

"That I'm a Wilce man, that I led you two into this trap!" The tenor of Frank's voice rose and was edged with a faint but unmistakable hysteria.

Jim stood too stunned to speak for an instant. Then he laughed harshly, mirthlessly. "Cool down, man," he said mildly. "Hell, you were as bad off as we were! The last I saw of you, I wouldn't have bet a plugged nickel against a hundred bucks you'd come out alive. You talk like you're loco!"

"That was Breen," Frank still insisted, "with more of your cattle stolen off the reservation. Go on and say that I tolled you up here so he could steal your jugheads too! You'll never see 'em again!"

Jim's glance narrowed as he studied the faint outline of Frank's face. He said in kindly tones, "You better sit down and rest, fella, while I find a place to put Red. Sure you're a Wilce man. And I'll own up to wonderin' what the catch was, you offerin' to show us the way today. But I've thought it over. You're a damn' liar when you say you tolled us up here. If you had, you'd have high tailed long before those critters busted into us."

When Frank said nothing, Jim went on, "There's only one thing I'm rememberin'. You're the gent that pulled Dave Santell out of that scrap in Scalplock the other night. You didn't do it because you had to, either. Anyone that'd do that for Dave is a good bet for my money."

"How do you know but what I helped frame Santell that first night he was in Grade?" Frank asked tonelessly. "We all know he was framed."

Jim gave a slow shake of the head. "It's no use tryin' to tell me you're a polecat," he said. "You're feelin' low because of Red,

228

maybe because you brought us this way instead of some other when we got lost."

"Well, how do you think I feel? I could've left Red back in Grade. Two men would've been enough for the job, you and me. Red would still be alive. But you can't figure it that way. Somewhere up there above there's an old man with long whiskers. When your time's up he reads your name out of his tally book and you come arunnin'. Red's name was read out tonight and he's gone. That's all there is to it." . . . He turned slowly away, beckoning toward the black shadow of the canyon wall nearby. . . . "Let's find a place to put him."

In their quarter-hour search for a place to bury the wrangler along the talus slope footing the near wall, Frank's self inflicted torment gradually eased so that he could look back over the past hour objectively. And now he saw this tragedy not as another complication to his own petty worries, but as one more piece to the pattern of trouble that had been plaguing the McCune outfit since its arrival on the reservation.

That pattern was slowly gaining clarity in Frank's mind. Adding to Jacob Wilce's frameup of Santell his certain knowledge that the agent had worked with Breen in the theft of part of the reservation herd tonight, Frank was beginning to sense a central purpose behind these separate and outwardly unrelated happenings. And once more he felt the urgency of having to find Dave Santell, of telling him these facts he was now sure of. He would have liked to talk the thing through with Jim; but he doubted that Jim even suspected the depths of the intrigue involving them all. So he held his tongue.

They found a weather-rotted ledge of rock hanging over the talus slope close below the spot where Red's body lay. "This'll have to do," Jim said, after, making sure that they could loosen the ledge's insecure foundations. So they went back down to Red, wrapped him in Frank's torn poncho and carried him up and laid him in under the ledge.

Climbing above it, they loosed a big boulder and started it rolling. It hit the ledge with a low booming roar that rose above the whisper of the rain. The ledge broke and caved in and a small rock slide fanned out and down over the talus slope, blurring the downward darkness with a faint gray fog of dust. When the last echo of rattling rock had died out between the high walls, Jim drawled gravely.

"It's lonely and wild here, and so was Red.

I remember him sayin' once that the thing he hated worst about cashin' in was all the palaver and mewlin' of a funeral. Well, he can rest easy. There'll be none of that. He was a good man and he went sudden, which is as it should be with us all."

In the pause that followed, Frank heard Jim exhale in a long tired sigh. Then, turning away, Jim said, "Let's be ridin'," and thus made his final parting with his saddle-mate.

The numbing dread that had settled through Gail a moment ago at hearing of Red Rhea's death now gave way before anger. She stood at the window of her dawn-lighted room, looking out across the plaza that had not yet wakened to the day, listening to Jim Land's story of the night. She held her robe wrapped tightly about her, the slender graceful outline of her tall body less rigid than a few minutes ago when, with eyes still heavy from sleep, she had answered the knock on her door and let Jim into the room.

Now, as Jim finished, she turned to face him and asked gravely, "Did he have a family?"

Jim shook his head. "No. He was single."

"Parents?"

"He never talked about 'em if he had any. He was a lonesome man, Miss. Didn't have many friends and didn't seem to want any. I doubt if there's a man in the outfit even knows where he came from."

"You'd better ask and let me know if I can do anything."

Gail was trying her best to keep a hold on her nerve and not let her thoughts flee in wild disorder before the panic that threatened her. She asked matter-of-factly, "How do we know we can trust this Frank Erbeck?"

"He pulled Dave out of that fight in Scalplock," Jim told her. "And I saw him come close to gettin' killed last night. If he'd taken us up there on purpose, he'd have beat it before the stampede, wouldn't he? I think he's tryin' to help."

Gail remembered then the things Martha Mills had told her of Frank and her suspicion of the agency rider eased somewhat. "You say he's waiting for you out beyond town?" she asked.

Jim nodded. "Doesn't want the Major to spot him," he said. "He don't seem to think much of the outfit he's workin' for. It was his idea that we should get across to Scalplock without spreadin' this story of the stampede. He thinks Dave will know what to do."

"He's probably right." Gail thought of something then that brightened the look of her hazel eyes with sudden determination. She said abruptly, "I'm going with you."

Jim's glance quickly narrowed. He gave a slow shake of the head. "It's fifty miles, a hard ride," he said. "Besides, what could you do to help?"

"I can at least find Mr. Torrence and return his money. The Major paid me for those horses last night."

"You could give me the money to take to him."

"No," Gail said positively, "I'm going. There's nothing I can do here. And if you find Santell I want to see him."

The impassiveness of grudging acceptance settled across Jim's face. "Suit yourself," he drawled. "I can get a buggy for you. Erbeck says there's a fair road across the pass."

Gail tossed her head. "No, I'll ride a saddle." She added, with a measure of stubborn pride, "You're forgetting that I was raised in Texas. I should imagine I haven't forgotten everything I learned."

"What about . . ." Jim hesitated, confused, then blurted out, "What kind of a outfit will you wear?"

"Pants," Gail said. She did her best to

keep a straight face as Jim blushed. "Yesterday I bought a pair just like yours. Martha Mills, a girl I've met here, was going to take me out to one of the Indian camps today. We were going to ride. Now if you'll give me ten minutes, I'll meet you wherever you say. Can you get me a horse?"

"That'll be easy." Jim hesitated, then asked reluctantly, "You're sure you want to go?"

"Of course I do."

"Then I'll be waitin' down below," Jim said, and left.

From where he waited at the edge of a pine clump half a mile out the north trail, Frank saw them coming and was puzzled by the identity of the second rider. The light wasn't yet strong enough for him to make out any detail except that Jim's companion was slight and sat the saddle too stiffly.

He didn't recognize Gail until they were within fifty yards of him. In the brief interval before he reined the steeldust out into the trail ahead of them, his thinking was confused with this new complication of having the girl along. He didn't for a moment doubt her purpose, having sensed that she was headstrong and willful. But the prospect of this added difficulty to a ride that was to be a hard one at best didn't please him; and when they came up on him his face was set with a strong reserve.

Gail sensed that at once and was the first to speak, saying directly, "I know you're not going to like it, but I'm coming with you."

Frank touched his hat politely and drawled, "Glad to have you."

"No, you're not," Gail said soberly. "But I have as much at stake in this as anyone else. I have a right to be here." Then, even more directly and intuitively, she said, "You know some things you haven't told us. I hope you'll decide to tell Dave Santell what they are."

Frank was caught off guard and drawled lamely, "What would I know that you don't?"

"Why my foreman was blamed for helping Breen steal that herd. Also," . . . And now she was doing some guessing . . . "why the Major's police aren't out now, hunting the men who took those cattle off the reservation last night. Weren't the Major's men watching the herd?"

Frank didn't speak for a moment, trying to gauge something he hadn't suspected in this girl. He was perplexed by a change in her that was hard to define; she seemed more confident now, less helpless and at the same time thoroughly as feminine as when he had had that brief glimpse of her three nights ago on the street in Grade with Martha.

At length, he told her warily, "You're askin' the same questions I am."

"But you know some of the answers to them. For instance, you know why you were in Scalplock the night Santell was there. You know why you got him out of that fight."

Frank was caught short without an answer. His first impulse was one of anger. But when Gail smiled, he couldn't help grinning. "All right," he drawled, "you asked for it, here it is." Then, bluntly, honestly, he told Gail and Jim Land all he knew of the trouble of the past four days. He didn't spare himself in his confession, even admitting that he had been blackmailed into working for Wilce.

"So there you have it," he said at the last. "And if I'm not wanted just say the word and I'll pull out."

Jim said flatly, "You stay."

Gail's glance hadn't once left Frank as he talked. Now she said, low-voiced, "I can see why Martha thinks as she does about you. Of course you stay."

Frank, wondering at his feeling of relief and a strange new liking for this girl he hadn't liked at all until now, said gravely, "Thanks."

They went on up the trail as the first full blaze of sunlight touched the snowfields topping the highest peak of the Ironstones.

XIV

Ed Torrence had run his horse all the way along this high trail above his place, leaving far behind the man Breen had sent down to Wheel to summon him. Now, pausing briefly to breathe his badly winded animal, he looked out across the small hill pocket and saw the horses and cattle scattered there; and the fiery blaze of his anger burned hotter.

It was a clear bright day with a cool breeze tempering the glare of sunlight shining out of an azure sky. The smell of rainwashed earth and pine put a fresh tang in the air. The sheer escarpment of the eastward lofty rim dropping half a thousand feet from the shoulder of the peak close above was slashed with the brilliant reds and blacks of rock seams, an awesome and majestic sight as it towered over the grassy break in the aspen timber footing it.

Yet none of this impressed Ed Torrence. For his temper bore a sharp and wicked edge. Spotting the spiralling blue smoke of a wood fire at the downward edge of the timber, he gave a rough yank on the reins and put his tired horse down there.

Breen saw him coming and laid aside his breakfast plate and stood up from his crouch by the fire. His broad and blocky and still bruised face bore a wide satisfied grin until, watching the approaching Torrence, he caught the stormy look on his face.

Seeing that, he breathed softly to the man nearest him, Pete Holmes. "Now what the hell's the matter?" and waited as Torrence swung aground. He was afraid of the Wheel owner, afraid of Torrence's unstable temper and afraid of his gun; and now he tried not to show it.

Torrence advanced three paces, staring hotly at Breen from across the fire. For a brief space of time no one spoke or moved; except that the fat Holmes slowly and carefully edged farther from Breen.

"I told you to use your head!" Torrence blazed in a sudden outburst. He gestured angrily toward the cattle and the horses, scattered beyond on the grass. "So you do this!"

"What's wrong with it, Ed?" Breen asked as mildly as he could.

"Wrong with it!" Torrence mouthed an

obscene oath. "I've paid for those horses is what's wrong! They're mine! So you steal 'em and maybe kill a couple men doing it! What did you think the McCune outfit would do? Just laugh it off? And Wilce? You expect him to talk them out of getting the law in there? And in a damned sweet hurry?"

"I didn't think —"

"Right! You didn't think." Torrence's voice had the sting of a whiplash. Abruptly, the last weak leash to the man's temper broke. "You knothead! You blundering fool!" Then, with salty oaths and bitter condemnation, Torrence heaped more abuse upon the bigger man.

Only when he paused, too drained of invective to go on, did Breen have his chance to speak. "You'll lay your tongue on me once too often, Ed," he said.

Torrence's face went dark with rage. In a sudden cat-like stride, he came around the fire. His arm struck out and he slapped Breen across the face hard with his open palm. Then, a derisive ugly smile on his face, he stepped back and let his hands hang loose at his sides.

"Come on, make your play!" he drawled. And now he was all at once cool and wary, and there was a cold killing light in his eyes.

Breen's face had paled to a sickly pallor.

Hate was in the glance he focused on the Wheel man. But there was fear there, too, a naked fear that was embarrassing for the others to see. The big man's hand was within finger spread of his holstered gun. Yet the fear visibly paralyzed him, took away all his brute strength and left him a weakling.

Finally, he shook his head. "No, Ed," he said, "you'd kill me."

Torrence laughed. It was the mocking laugh of a man half insane with anger and hate. "You're yellow, Breen," he said. "Yellow as the liver spots on a fevered steer."

"I only thought I was helpin'," Breen said.

His disgust crowding him beyond speech, Torrence turned away and went to his horse. It was a tribute to his hold on Breen that the big man didn't then draw his gun and shoot him in the back. Not one of the four others around the fire would have brought him to an accounting for such an action. Still, that deep and long nurtured fear stayed Breen's hand.

It was a different Torrence who spoke down to them from the saddle, a man coolly and swiftly appraising the job at hand.

"Breen, you're to bunch these horses and drive them down to the holding meadow above Birkheimer's," he said crisply. "You'll need one man to help. The rest of you push the cattle on north and lose 'em. I want the job done fast. Leave the horses and lay over somewhere and don't hit town before tomorrow night, Breen. Got that straight?"

One of the men had the courage to say, "Okay, it's as good as done. Only don't blame Ray for this, boss. We all decided it was a good idea."

Torrence fixed that man with a level hard stare. "Breen's supposed to have a head on his shoulders," he drawled. "The rest of you weren't hired to think." And with that he reined his pony around and started off toward the far end of the pocket.

They watched him and said nothing for a time, each man feeling that last cutting remark as having been directed at him alone.

It was Pete Holmes who finally growled, "He makes a big shadow these days. Why the hell didn't you let him have it, Ray?"

Breen didn't take his eyes from Torrence's retreating figure as he replied, "There's time for everything. He'll never comb me over again."

There was a brittle edge to his voice that let them know he meant it.

Gail had remembered the name of Doc

Faris's patient and now, half an hour after riding into Scalplock and inquiring the way to the Warren house, Frank and the saddlemaker waited in the deep obscurity of the big cedar fronting the yard. Doc was in the house with Gail and Mrs. Warren, while Jim had gone up the street toward the lights of the saloon on learning from Warren that Dave was being held there.

Tom Warren had much to tell Frank, of Ed Torrence bringing Santell in yesterday, of the second fight the night Frank had been across here, of the sheriff's expected arrival.

Presently, Doc came out onto the porch and down the steps and they came over to meet him in the pale wash of lampglow shining from the living room window. Through that window the calendar clock on the far wall showed the time to be ten-twenty.

"She wants to see Santell," Doc announced. He saw then that Jim wasn't with them and asked, "Where's Land?"

Frank nodded upstreet. "Said he'd be back in a few minutes. He has the same idea."

The medico looked at Warren. "Think it could be arranged, Tom? For her to see Dave? Your wife's fixing her up with a dress."

In the halflight, the saddlemaker's rugged

face showed doubt. "You know how they listen to me around here, Doctor," he said. "I doubt if they'll let her."

"She ought to be getting some rest," Frank put in. "That was a tough ride for a woman to take."

"Just what I told her." Doc sighed exasperatedly. "But there's more of the McCune in her than I suspected. She says she's going to see Dave and she means it."

He turned away, looking up the street as the slur of a man's quick step came to them. Shortly, Jim came up out of the shadows, saying excitedly, "It'd be a cinch to bust him out of that whiskey joint. There's a back window and a door. With two men at the back and two in front we could hold 'em till he got away."

"Gail wants to see him and talk with him before we try anything," Doc said.

"It ain't any place for a woman, Doc," Jim said. "Let's go ahead and get him out and do the talkin' afterward."

Doc shook his head. "Then they would have a case against him. It's no go, Land, not unless he wants us to. He's given his word he won't make a break, that he'll wait for the sheriff."

"He won't have a lot to say about it if we take him, will he?" Jim asked truculently.

Frank put in, "Let's wait'll the girl's seen him. There's plenty of time. Where have they got him?"

Jim laughed dryly. "At the back table, sittin' in on a stud game. It's sure sociable for an arrest. I looked on for a few hands. They didn't know who I was and Dave didn't let on. Who's that gent that deals blackjack every time he gets his hands on the deck, Doc?"

"What does he look like?"

"Sort of tall. Good lookin' ranny with dark hair. He sure likes that game of twenty-one."

"Sounds like Torrence, from what you say. He seems to be managing things. They played last night, too, and Dave won about thirty dollars."

"When's the sheriff supposed to get in?" Jim asked.

"Tomorrow morning," Doc said. "They had to send over to Fort Bewell and he was out north of the town helping his boy put up fence. I wish I knew more about him. Tom, what kind of a man is he?"

"Good as they come," was the saddle-maker's ready answer. He added pointedly, "He's never been called up here since he was elected. And the sheriff before him wasn't. He don't think much of us. Last time I saw him he asked why I didn't move out before I caught onto Scalplock habits."

"Then Dave's got a good chance of getting off?" Jim asked.

Tom Warren shook his head. "Not the way it looks now. Birkheimer and Spence and Sid Apple all swear it was Dave that shot Mordue."

"Who are they, this Birkheimer and Spence?" Frank asked, with a dry edge of anger in his voice.

"They run cattle over east in the hills."

Doc said feelingly, "I wish I could be sure about Torrence. He's a queer one. The way he's treated Dave, you'd almost think he was for him. Yet he was the one that brought him in."

Just then the door opened and they all looked that way. Gail came out onto the porch, leaving the door open behind her.

She was wearing one of Mrs. Warren's calico print house dresses, a plain dark green one. She had gathered its ample folds tight at her narrow waist and its simple straight lines heightened her willowy slenderness. Doc, looking at at her, was thinking, *Now I know why I've been thinking she isn't pretty. She's better looking than a pretty woman.*

Aloud, he said, "Gail, I wish you'd give

this up. There's nothing we can do for Dave until the sheriff gets here."

"But I want him to know how wrong I was about him," Gail said.

"He knows that. I told him."

"Your telling him isn't the same as his hearing it from me." Gail's head tilted a little in that stubborn way so typical of her as she came down to them. "I want to see him, doctor. Take me to the jail."

"He isn't in the jail. They're holding him in the saloon. That's not quite the place for a young woman to be at this hour of the night."

"I wouldn't care if they were keeping him in a bawdy house," Gail said stubbornly. "Now let's not argue about it any longer."

Doc sighed, said, "All right, you asked for it." He looked at the others. "I'd better be the one to take her. No use in our all going. Tom, show them where they can stable the horses."

He touched Gail's arm and they went down the walk and past the three tired horses tied to the rail under the big cedar that shaded most of the small yard.

"Tired?" the medico asked as they turned up the rutted street.

"Not now, but I probably will be later." Gail laughed huskily, adding a little guiltily,

"You know, doctor, so much came back to me today. So much I'd forgotten. A week ago I was so proud of things like my dresses and the manners I've learned these last few years. Tonight I'm proudest of the things dad taught me down on the ranch when I was just a girl. You don't know how good it was to discover this morning that I still knew how to ride."

Doc said gravely, "John McCune would be proud to hear you say that."

"I wish —" Gail stopped there.

"That you could tell him this?" Doc asked, sensing her unspoken regret. "No. There's nothing to make up. John McCune wanted you to have the fine things. Where he was wrong was in thinking they meant everything. If he had to raise you all over again, he'd do exactly as he did, send you to a fine school and teach you all the blue blood nonsense he never learned himself. He had no regrets."

Doc laid a gentle pressure on her arm. "Girl, it's to your credit that you've learned what's important and what isn't. Never waste time looking back. It's what's ahead that counts. Take it from an old man who took much longer to get next to himself."

Having spoken this truth out of his own obscure experience, Doc walked on in stolid silence, as proud of this girl as though she were his own daughter. It was deeply satisfying to have witnessed the change in Gail McCune since that first glimpse he'd had of her climbing out of the stage that day in Grade, her skirts held close and her expression one of clear distaste, as though the dust and filth of that isolated town would contaminate her. Gail had changed her sense of values, had matured a great deal since coming here; and Doc was now proud of her.

The lights of the *Elite* came up out of the darkness and now, as they turned in toward the saloon, Gail took his arm, as though relying on him for support. He could feel her hand trembling and he tightened the bend of his elbow to reassure her. After that, her hand was steady.

They stepped up onto the walk and three men loafing before the saloon's swing doors moved quickly and respectfully aside at sight of them. One stumbled in his surprise and fumbled with his hat, jerking it off. Doc reached out and pushed the doors open and they stepped inside.

The harsh glare of the unshaded lamps made Doc squint. The confusion of sounds, the clink of glasses and the click of chips and the loud talk gradually died out. The air was tainted with the odors of whiskey and tobacco. Doc and Gail passed between the corner bar and its facing faro layout, men moving out of their way. In these several seconds the sounds in the room had faded out completely and it was still now, so still that the scrape of a chair at the back poker table where Dave Santell sat made a loud and grating noise.

There were upwards of twenty men in this small room. With few exceptions, they stood or sat surprised in the attitudes they had been in when Gail and the medico entered. The bartender held a bottle tilted over a customer's glass. The faro lookout was leaning sideways on his high stool; he had just removed the cigar from his mouth and targeted a spittoon below him and now he stayed that way, bent over, his attitude ridiculous looking. A player at the front poker layout sat with arms half encircling a scattering of chips at the table's center; he had just won the hand and had been surprised in the act of pulling in his chips.

Gail's face showed no sign of unease or embarrassment as her eyes calmly met the probing glances that, once colliding with hers, dropped quickly away. From the moment she saw Dave at that back poker table, her glance didn't leave him. She and Doc came in on that table and Dave and another, a handsome man — she was to learn later that this was Torrence — stood up. Three watchers at the alley windows behind the table shifted uneasily. The others there were too surprised or confused to more than stare at her.

Doc said, "Gentlemen, this is Miss Mc-Cune. She would like to speak to Santell. Privately."

Ed Torrence said at once, "Certainly," and looked at the others. And now they came up out of their chairs.

It was Birkheimer who frowned, asking querulously, "How come, Ed?"

"What harm can it do?" Torrence asked. "Santell's given his word he won't make a break." He stepped out from the table then, setting an example for the others. He pulled his chair farther back, indicating that Gail should take it.

A look passed between Birkheimer and Blaine Shotwell, owner of the *Merchandise.* Shotwell understood that look and said, "Huck's right, Ed. She can talk to Santell if she wants. But we stay where we are."

Torrence fixed the store man with a level enigmatic stare. "You two have been ridin' Santell raw," he drawled with deceptive mildness. "Lay off. He's being held on suspicion. You act like he'd already been tried. Now let's clear out."

Reluctantly, grudgingly, Shotwell and Birkheimer left the table and went to the bar. "Thanks, Torrence," Doc said as Gail took the chair the Scalplock rancher had offered.

Torrence said, "Don't take too long," and joined the last man in leaving the table.

Now that she was looking up at Dave, who stood across the empty table, Gail was momentarily confused by the unbroken stillness of the room, by the knowledge that most every man there was regarding her with bold interest. She had pictured meeting Dave alone in a jail and the presence of all these witnesses made her forget what she had come to say.

But when Dave smiled easily and drawled, "Glad to see you, ma'am," she felt better. And now she noticed the marks of the fight on his strong flat-planed face and felt a twinge of guilt at having been the chief cause of his getting into this trouble. At once her indecision left her and it was as though she was alone with him; she even forgot Doc, who stood close behind her chair.

"I'm sorry for what I've done to you, Santell," she said. She put down the small prodding of pride that warned her she was making herself humble before this tall grave man, and added impulsively, "I've been wrong about a lot of things. I should have trusted you as my father did. I — I just didn't think."

"Things came too fast for any of us to do much thinkin'," Dave drawled.

"They hurt you the other night," Gail said softly, and there were tenderness and concern in her hazel eyes. "It was all my fault."

"It wasn't so bad," Dave said, and he smiled again. "I got in some good licks myself."

Abruptly, Gail was at a loss as to how to go on. He had made her confession so easy and the absence of any resentment in him only heightened her feeling of guilt.

Doc must have understood her feelings, for now he leaned over the table and said quietly, "We've got some help, Dave. We'll get you out of here tonight."

Dave shook his head. "Won't do, Doc. I've told Torrence I'll wait and see the sheriff. If it was only the others, I'd have been out of here before this. But Torrence has been white about it. He's kept 'em from gangin' up on me."

Doc's face took on a quick flush of irritation. "You're being a fool, Dave! Think of the spot you're in. You're framed tighter than you were in Grade. They'll make it stick."

"I understand the sheriff's a good man. He'll straighten it out."

"How can he?" Doc asked savagely, low-voiced. "They can produce a dead man. At least three of them will swear you killed him. No one but you can swear you didn't. You'd be found guilty in any court of law in the country! Use your head! Let us get you out of here while we can!"

Dave had seen Blaine Shotwell approaching; but Doc, wholly engrossed in driving home his point, hadn't. When Shotwell spoke close at his elbow, the medico was startled.

"Time's up," the storekeeper announced bluntly.

Doc straightened, looking at Dave and breathing a long and wearied sigh. "You won't change your mind?" he asked.

"Can't." Dave's glance went to Gail once more and again the gravity left his lean scarred face. "Don't worry about this," he said.

"Who's worried about him?" Shotwell asked dryly. "You shouldn't be. He's nicked us for plenty tonight."

Gail gave Shotwell a glance of disgust and turned from the table, coming face to face with Ed Torrence. He held his Stetson in his hand and his look was one of apology. "Sorry you didn't have more time," he told the girl. "I stalled 'em as long as I could."

"You were very kind," Gail said. Then: "You're Mr. Torrence?"

He nodded.

"Then I owe you some money, the money you paid me for the horses. My men lost them, you know."

"I'd heard about it," he said. "But I don't want the money back until we've had a chance to take a look around. We might find 'em up in the high country."

"But I'd rather do it my way."

He smiled and said offhandedly, "Anything you say. But I still want those horses bad enough to go look for 'em. Suppose we talk it over tomorrow."

Gail thanked him. She had a parting glance for Dave and, taking Doc's arm, faced the stares of that roomful of men again as she went back past the front poker layout and the bar to the swing doors.

XV

Sound came alive behind them in the saloon as they went down the walk. They were even with the doorway of the *Merchandise* when

Gail burst out, "They can't do this to him! They can't!"

"But they will," Doc said tonelessly. "Did you see them gloating over it, Shotwell and Birkheimer? They and a few others run this country. They're crooked to the bone, every man of them! Gail, there's only one thing left to do. Tom Warren can take me out the Fort Bewell trail tonight to meet Sheriff Moore. Maybe if I have a talk with him before they do, they won't be able to hang Dave."

"Hang him!" Gail breathed.

The medico gave her a searching sideward look, saying quickly, gently, "That was a slip of the tongue, Gail. Of course nothing like that's going to happen."

"But —" Gail's voice broke in the face of her bafflement and sudden stark fear; for she knew that Doc was lying, trying to save her feelings.

She was afraid now, terribly afraid, realizing in all its awesome dimensions the enormity of the wrong she had done Dave Santell. Her mind was numbed by what Doc had said. Even after they were back at the Warren house, and she heard Warren and Jim Land and Doc making arrangements to ride at once out the lower road toward Fort Bewell, that numbness seemed to hold her thoughts in a rigid paralysis.

As she left them, Frank told her, "If you need me, ma'am, I'll be bedded down at the saddle shop," and she wasn't aware enough of him even to reply.

She went into the spare room where Mrs. Warren had made up the bed for her. She sat there without lighting the lamp, her face tight and pale with fear and dread. The house was still, so quiet that she could hear Mrs. Warren's even breathing from the next room.

Some minutes later she heard horses pass along the narrow lane beside the house that ran from Warren's small barn lot to the street; this would be Doc and Jim and Warren starting their ride in search of the sheriff.

It was many minutes after that before she was able to think at all clearly. And then the strain of the long hard day began crowding in on her and she was tired, so tired she ached through her whole body.

She fought this tiredness, thinking, *There must be some way of saving him . . . some way! . . .*

She kept repeating this over and over again. She thought of half a dozen things, none of them practical or even possible. They were confused and hazy notions blending with her weariness and she found it hard to keep her mind from wandering. Could she send Frank Erbeck back to Grade for the rest of her crew? No, the sheriff would be here and gone again, with Dave his prisoner probably, before that help could come.

Why had Dave so stubbornly insisted on keeping his word to Torrence? She was all at once angry with him; then regretting that anger immediately, loathing herself because of having once given way to anger and betrayed Dave. Still, it was wrong, very wrong, that Dave should keep his word with men who would never hesitate in breaking their own.

She wondered about Torrence and halfway thought of going to the saloon again, of talking with him and seeing if he wouldn't help. He'd been so nice to her that she found she trusted him. But Doc certainly knew Torrence and would have called on him if he thought it wise.

She remembered then something Doc had said while they talked with Dave there in the saloon. *They can produce a dead man,* had been the medico's words. *At least three of them will swear Dave killed him.*

She wondered if these three men would take money to lie in Dave's favor, rather than against him. Seriously considering this, she knew that there wasn't even time to find these men and try buying them off, for the sheriff would be here in the morning; besides, she didn't have the money.

Her tiredness was so demanding that it took a great amount of will power to think about standing and taking her clothes off. She decided finally that it would be much easier just to lie down and sleep the way she was.

Then suddenly she sat bolt upright, the weariness gone instantly before a startling thought.

The dead man!

Why hadn't Jim or Frank Erbeck or Doc — or even Tom Warren — thought of this?

Hurriedly, she reached down and took off her shoes. She tiptoed into the narrow hallway and stood a moment before the door of Mrs. Warren's room, listening to the woman's even deep breathing. She went quietly into the living room, blew out the lamp and opened the front door only wide enough for her to slip through. The door closed soundlessly behind her on well oiled hinges. At the foot of the steps she put her shoes on. She started up the darkened street, the night's strengthening chill making her hurry.

She found this excitement a new and strangely pleasing experience. Gone now was the feeling of helplessness and dread that had been in her this long day. She had been restless and dissatisfied for as long as she could remember since coming to the reservation; now that was gone, too, as she found herself with something to look forward to, to take pride in, something she was doing on her own.

Strangely, she wasn't afraid at being alone on the street of this unfamiliar hill town. Off to the east the black broken outline of the timbered hills gave her a sense of primitive isolation. Overhead the stars were a bright sprinkling of diamond dust across the cobalt void of the heavens. Except for this small cluster of buildings, she was alone in a wild and virgin country and something about the unsullied freshness and mystery of this still night touched a chord of deep peacefulness in her. She thought she knew now why her father had scorned an easier life, why Dave Santell and all these others were the kind of men they were. She was almost tangibly feeling the last ties to her old life drop away and knew that, from now on, her days would be richer and fuller with a new understanding.

Thought of her errand turned her

thoughts back to her immediate problem and she wondered if she could find Tom Warren's saddle shop without having to hunt someone on the street to tell her. But the first small slab building she came to bore a white and black painted sign below its single front window. Even in this faint star-light she could make it out: *T. L. Warren, Saddles, Harness.*

She stepped up onto the narrow stoop before the door and knocked gently on the panel. Half a minute's wait brought no sound from inside. She lifted her hand to knock again. But suddenly the door swung open before her outstretched hand and Frank Erbeck stood there.

She was about to speak when he said quickly, "Get in out of sight!" As she edged past him, he leaned out the door and looked both ways along the empty street. Then they were standing in a black abyss of darkness, the door shut.

Frank said irritably, "You shouldn't be out alone."

"I know," she told him. "But I've thought of something. You have to help me."

Then, before he could interrupt, she went on in a rush of words: "They have to prove that Santell killed that man, don't they? They couldn't prove it, could they, if the

260

body was gone? They could lie all they wanted to and they couldn't arrest him if there was no dead man."

She heard Frank's sharp intake of breath and caught his low-muttered oath. "Say that again," he drawled softly. "You mean steal Mordue's body, hide it?" . . . She sensed that his question was directed more to himself than to her. . . . "It could be done! They'd be up a tree. It might work!"

"Do you know where they put the dead man?" she asked.

"In the ice house behind the saloon. Warren mentioned it a while ago. Wait! I'll be back in a minute."

He was gone before she knew it. When she whispered, "Frank!" a moment later, there was no answer. Shortly, she heard the faint grating of a door opening at the back end of the shop and after that there was a complete and empty silence.

She had to steel herself against being afraid, for all at once the sound of her own bated breathing seemed loud and frightening in the stillness. The air in here was heavy with the clean mellow aroma of new leather. Gradually, her eyes became so accustomed to the darkness that she could make out the faint rectangle of the street-facing window. Faintly at first, then strengthening, came the regular muffled beat of a man's boot-tread approaching along the walk out front. This couldn't be Frank, and for many moments a real and deep fear gripped her. Finally, she saw the man's black outline pass the window and his steps faded out and once more she got a grip on herself.

Minutes later, that faint scraping of the shop's rear door came to her again. Then Frank spoke suddenly and startlingly out of the darkness, close at hand, sending a shudder of fright through her.

"Not a chance," he said. "The ice house door is square in the light from the saloon's back window. There's a couple of gents sittin' there watching that game Santell's in. I couldn't do it without their spottin' me."

"But you have to do it!"

"I tell you it can't be done." Frank's low drawl was patient, packed with disappointment. "God, I'd give my right arm if we could. They couldn't hold Santell without evidence of the killing. Hating their guts as he does, I'd bet ten to one the sheriff would let him go."

"There has to be a way, Frank!" Gail said softly, but positively. "Think!"

"I am thinkin', ma'am. I tried to find a way to get in the back of the ice house. But it's built of log."

"How about the roof?"

"No. They'd hear me if I started pullin' loose the shingles."

Gail had nothing to say to that. Slowly but surely the excitement of these past minutes drained out of her. And once more she was fighting that earlier helplessness and depression.

Then she thought of something, something that lifted her pulse to the same quick beat it had taken back there in the Warren bedroom.

"What if I can get those men out of there?" she asked. "All of them. How long would it take you?"

Frank said nothing for a moment. Then: "I'd use Warren's buckboard and team. It'd take ten minutes to get it hitched and ready. Then ten minutes more with the saloon cleared would be enough. Five, even. But how could you do it?"

"Don't worry about that. I'll do it! Can you start now?"

"Sure. Any time you say. Where'll you wait?"

"Right here. Will ten minutes give you enough time?"

"Better make it a little longer, in case I have trouble with the team. You're sure about this? What if you run into trouble in the saloon?"

"But I won't."

"All right, you know what you're doing," Frank said. "Think I'll go out this front way. It'll save me some time."

Gail went to the window as he opened the door, watching him go out of sight in the downstreet darkness. For many moments she was held by misgivings and a wonder at her rash decision. But then she thought of Dave Santell, of the quiet reassuring way he had spoken to her. And then she was no longer uncertain.

"It's blackjack again, gents."

Birkheimer grunted his disgust as Ed Torrence called the game he had dealt each time the cards had come to him tonight. It had been the same last night, Torrence naming that game when it came his turn to deal.

"What's the matter, Huck?" Torrence asked. "You can drop out if you want."

"Go on, deal me in," Birkheimer said disgustedly.

"Poker's half luck any way you figure it. The rest is bluff. I can't bluff but my luck is good. Blackjack's all luck. So I play it." Stating this rudimentary belief, Torrence began the deal. "Place your bets and take your lickin'."

"All right, Santell," Birkheimer said in sarcasm. "Put your bet out."

Dave was getting fed up with Birkheimer. Last night it had been the same, Birkheimer never missing the chance to egg him on when his play was slow, sarcasm barbing his every remark when Dave won, which had been often.

Blaine Shotwell was bad enough with his surliness and suspicion, his several awkward attempts at an unpracticed manipulating of the cards. The storekeeper was a poor poker player, for his face betrayed his hands too often. He was losing heavily and didn't have judgment enough to quit. Torrence, of course, was a steady player and did his best to keep Birkheimer in line. Rocky, the Fort Bewell teamster, sitting in tonight's game, was genial and often funny and pleasant company. He was a little ahead. But tonight Birkheimer was worse than he'd been last night.

Just now, as Dave still hesitated in placing his bet, the rancher drawled, "Wake me up when you've made up your mind, Santell."

He was sitting alongside Dave, leaning forward with elbows on the table, his chair tilted back against the wall beside the alley window.

Dave gave Torrence a look and the Wheel

man smiled faintly in understanding.

Dave looked at his down card again. Then, intentionally, he picked up a blue chip, hesitated as he was about to toss it to the table's center, then put it back on his stack and looked at the card once more.

"Maybe someone ought to teach him the game," Birkheimer said goadingly.

Under the table, Dave's right boot moved in the direction of Birkheimer's chair. The toe of his boot nudged the end of one of the chair legs. He reached out farther with it, felt the rung of the chair, and suddenly lifted his leg with a savage pull.

The chair upended under Birkheimer, leaving him suspended off balance for a fraction of a second. Then, with a surprised grunt, he fell backward and wedged down between the chair-seat and the wall.

Dave, without rising, wheeled off his chair and let his weight go down on the man's chest, knees first. The breath left the rancher's barrel chest in a gasping rush. Dave reached up to the table, took Birkheimer's cards and, a hand at the rancher's throat, had stuffed the cards into the man's mouth before Blaine Shotwell pulled him off his victim.

Coming erect, Dave shoved Shotwell away. He stared down at the purple-faced and swearing Birkheimer, drawling, "That's just a suggestion, my friend. Keep your tongue off me."

Men had gathered about the table and now Torrence said easily, "The fun's over, boys. Give Huck some air."

Birkheimer spit the cards from his mouth and struggled to his feet, standing spraddle-legged and with fists knotted, glaring up at Dave.

Torrence spoke again. "Huck, you had that comin'. Careful, or you'll get more of the same."

His words dulled the hostility of the crowd toward Dave, focused it instead on the humbled Birkheimer.

Dave didn't know what was to happen, didn't care. But what did was as unexpected as anything could have been.

Abruptly, someone beyond the table breathed, "God A'mighty! Here she is again." And the crowd's attention at once left the table and shifted to the front of the room. A sudden stillness settled over the crowd.

Passing between the poker layout and the bar for the second time tonight, but now alone, came Gail McCune.

Torrence said softly, meaningly, "This time, remember she's a lady," and he left the table, advancing to meet the girl. Even Huck Birkheimer had forgotten his anger in surprise.

Gail came in beside Dave's chair, looking up at him and saying, "I've been thinking over the things you told me. I'm going to make them show me exactly what happened."

Puzzled looks crossed the faces of those nearby as she turned to Torrence, smiling to hide her nervousness and asking, "I have a right to know, haven't I?"

"To know what, ma'am?"

"To know what happened when that man was killed."

Torrence frowned, still not understanding.

Gail said, "Who was there in the barber shop that night? Who knows exactly what took place?"

"I was," Huck Birkheimer offered. "Santell threw some wild shots after the lamps was busted. Mordue stopped some of his lead. That's all there was to it."

"But how can you be sure it was Santell?" Gail persisted.

"How?" Birkheimer laughed sneeringly. "Because he was the only one that used his iron."

"Couldn't it have been another man?" Gail asked.

"Listen, lady," Birkheimer said, losing what little control he had over his patience. "I was there and I know. Santell wasn't no further from me than you are. I saw the flash of his iron."

"But he says he didn't do it," the girl said. Her obvious unease tempered their annoyance at her insistence. "It's his word against yours. Could you prove that he shot that man?"

Birkheimer heaved a long disgusted sigh. Torrence frowned at him, said sharply, "She has a right to ask these things, Huck."

"Thank you, Mr. Torrence," Gail murmured. "I know how you feel. This isn't a woman's business and I'm meddling. Still, Santell works for me. So I have some rights. Would it . . ." She looked at Birkheimer. "Could you come across the street to the barber shop and show me exactly where you were standing when the shots were fired? And are there any other men here who were there that night?"

Torrence glanced toward the bar. "Spence," he said. "He was in on it."

The room had listened to this discussion and now Gail turned so that she faced the front. "I'd like witnesses to this, as many as I can get. Will some of you come across with us?"

Shotwell had been eying her closely and now drawled shrewdly, "What're you tryin' to prove, Miss?"

Gail swung around on him, her face flushed. "I'm trying to save an innocent man from hanging!" she said hotly. "If more of you were like Mr. Torrence here, we might get to the bottom of this! And when you're speaking to a lady, take your hat off!"

The store owner, taken unawares by her outburst, hastily removed his narrow-brimmed black hat. Gail looked at Torrence, ignoring Shotwell. "I'd like Mr. Santell to go with us."

Torrence nodded. "Sure thing," he said, and led the way to the doors, adding, "We won't need a key. The place hasn't been fixed up yet."

He and Gail and Dave were leaving the walk, starting to cross the street, when an excited hum of voices came alive in the saloon. Shotwell and Birkheimer came next, then Rocky and several others. Then, shortly, the men who had hung back followed, not wanting to miss anything. Earl, the barkeep, scanned his saloon, empty except for a drunk asleep in a chair along the back wall. He shrugged, took off his apron and went along with the rest.

Torrence climbed in through the glassless

barber shop window and opened the door from the inside. He struck a match, found a lamp and lit it. In the far back corner of the shop a heap of debris had been swept against the wall. The shaving-mug rack had been righted and the unbroken mugs, only a few, put back in their places.

Dave had a chance to speak a hurried word to Gail as they stood waiting for Torrence to light the back room lamp. He was close beside her and put a hand on her arm, speaking softly. "What do I do?"

"Help me keep them here," was Gail's hushed answer. Her eyes were smiling and bright and excited and she had no chance to tell him more, for Shotwell came up behind them at that moment.

Gail went into the back room. Torrence grinned and nodded to the glassless door sagging on its broken hinges. "It's not quite the same as it was that night." His face went serious again. "All right, Huck, where were you when the scrap started?"

Birkheimer moved in past Gail and to the left of the door. "Here," he said. "Santell had pulled his gun on Breen and we were all on our feet with our hands up."

"Where was Breen standing?" Gail asked.

"He was sittin'. There by the wall."

Gail looked up at Dave. "And where

were you?"

Dave said, "Right about here."

"Spence, how about you?" Torrence put in. No one saw the quick frown he directed at Birkheimer.

Spence came in through the door and stepped over to the right hand wall. "This's where I was," he said. The rest of the crowd now packed the door and the main room of the shop.

"You were all standing this way?" Gail said. "Then what happened?"

Dave began, "Someone opened the door behind me. I . . ."

"That was Mordue," Torrence put in.

Dave nodded. "I stumbled and got out of the way. Then Breen pushed the table over and knocked the lamp down. I maybe slugged someone with my gun. But I didn't shoot."

Birkheimer argued this. The talk ran on and on.

Over in the *Elite,* the drunk who slept in the chair close to the back poker layout stirred and lifted his chin off his chest. His eyes came open and he stared about him, vacantly at first, then in growing bewilderment. He closed his eyes and shook his head, then looked around a second time. He swore in his befuddlement. Then he spotted the half-full bottle on the poker table close by and got to his feet and walked unsteadily across and picked up the bottle, forgetting at once the strangeness of the saloon being empty.

He was taking his first drink when he heard a dull thud sound in through the nearby open window from the alley. Next, there came the creak of metal scraping wood. The bottle still in hand, he walked to the window to see what was making the noise.

Out there, in the full light from the window, Frank Erbeck was just throwing a tarp over a stiff shape lying in the bed of the buckboard. As the drunk's shadow blocked out the light, Frank swung quickly around.

The drunk grinned down at him, said thickly, "Drink, shtranger?" He held out the bottle.

The drop of Frank's hand toward the holster at his thigh stopped. "Not right now," he said.

The drunk's face stiffened belligerently. "Wha' th' hell's wrong with my whiskey?"

"Not a thing. Only I ain't thirsty."

"C'mon now," the drunk insisted. "You look dry, partner." His voice had risen.

Frank grinned, said finally, "Guess it can't do me any harm," and stepped across and reached up for the bottle the drunk handed down to him. His face was well out of the light below the window's sill as he took a pull at the bottle.

The drunk, leaning on the ledge above him, asked offhandedly, "Gettin' ice?"

"Yeah." Frank handed the bottle back.

"Melts faster'n hell these hot nights, don't it?"

"Sure does. I'll have to get it home in a hurry."

"Well, any time y' need a drink, jusht ashk for Johnny Sowers. Thash me."

"I'll be seein' you, Johnny," Frank said as he swung up onto the buckboard seat and unwound the reins. "Thanks for the drink."

"Shaloon," the drunk said.

He turned from the window as the buckboard rattled away down the alley. He took another pull at the bottle, a long one. He hiccoughed as he put the bottle back on the table.

Going back to his chair, he said, "Yep, any time y' need a drink, jusht ashk for Johnny Showers — Sowers. Good ol' Johnny."

He sat heavily in the chair and was asleep again before his chin touched his chest.

XVI

Sheriff Moore rode up the trail and into town at eight that bright clear morning, accompanied by Doc Faris, Jim Land and Tom Warren.

They halted at the head of the short lane beside Warren's house when Doc announced tiredly, "Here's where we leave you."

Moore shifted in the saddle to look at the medico. He was a shad-bellied man past his prime, with graying hair and a seamed face wind-and-sun burned to the color of tanned new leather. A hard life had given that face a stony dour cast, but now it relaxed somewhat as he said, "I'll do all I can for you, Faris."

"Which won't be much," Doc said. "This bunch of cut-throats has framed Santell tighter'n a tick."

"I know. This is a shady town," Moore agreed readily enough. "Probably isn't a man within miles you'd dare trust any further than you could see him. In my four years wearin' this star they haven't called me over once before. And it's a cinch it hasn't been that peaceful here. But the law says I have to arrest a man if charges are preferred against him. Provided, of course, the charges are reasonable."

"They'll sound reasonable enough," Doc sighed. "They've got a dead man and three liars to say Santell killed him. What more do they need?"

"We'll see," was all Moore would say.

So Doc put his horse down the lane, Jim and Tom Warren following along behind, and the sheriff went on up the street. Frank Erbeck waited in the barn lot behind the Warren house. He saw Doc's beaten weary look, noticed the medico's bloodshot eyes that were sign of a sleepless night and he said, "Cheer up, Doc. We've got good news for you."

"No news could be good the way I feel," Doc said wearily, and slid from the saddle. "What is it?"

"Go on into the kitchen. Gail's there and Mrs. Warren has coffee on the stove. I'll be right with you."

So Doc and Jim went in while Frank and Warren took care of the horses. And in less than five minutes after the medico had wearily taken a chair in the kitchen, all the strain and tiredness was gone from his face as he listened to the story Gail had to tell him.

Up the street, the sheriff was met by Birkheimer and Torrence, who took him directly to the *Elite*. Shortly after that, a buggy drove down the upper trail flanked by two outriders in the brass-buttoned blue uniforms of the reservation police. The buggy turned in at the saloon and, one of the Sioux tying the team to the rail there, Jacob Wilce climbed stiffly down out of the rig, irritable and worn by his all night drive across from Grade.

The Major grunted a curt order to his two stolid-faced police and went into the saloon. His entrance caused but little interest, except that when Torrence saw him he left the sheriff and came straight up to him, saying in a low voice, "You're outside your fence, aren't you, Jake?"

"Have some business with the sheriff," Wilce said.

"What business?" Torrence demanded. "And talk fast, Jake! I wouldn't want Santell to see us together too long."

"I'm turnin' Erbeck in," the Major stated. "He's jumped the traces and I'm through with him."

Relief was plain on Torrence's handsome dark face. "Erbeck's your own affair," he said. "Just keep your nose out of this other thing. You fumbled it once and I don't want you around."

"Erbeck's here, isn't he?"

Torrence frowned. "Not that I know of. Haven't seen him."

Wilce shrugged. "He's supposed to be. He was seen headed this way yesterday." He went to the bar then and took two stiff drinks.

As Torrence once more joined the group at the rear of the room, Sheriff Moore was saying dryly, "Just hold your horses, gents. There's some others who'll be sittin' in on this. We'll wait till they get here."

"Who?" This from Birkheimer.

"Doctor Faris for one. Maybe the McCune girl for another."

Birkheimer glanced quickly, uncertainly, at Torrence. "How come they get in on it?"

The law man gave him a prolonged and cool regard. "Any reason why they shouldn't?" he asked.

When Birkheimer made no reply, Moore took the chair alongside Dave's at the table. He ignored the others, saying, "So you're Santell. I've heard of you from old John McCune. Met him a couple of years back. A good man. Sorry to hear he passed away."

"He was a good man," Dave said, wondering at the law man's seeming friendliness.

"What'll happen to the outfit now that he's gone?" Moore was making it plain that he wanted no discussion of any details con-

278

nected with the crime until he was ready.

"That depends on what the girl decides," Dave said. "Looks like she'll sell out."

He was noticing Wilce on his way back to the table and, as his expression reflected faint distaste, Moore looked that way, too.

"Who'll this be?" the sheriff asked.

"Wilce, the reservation agent."

Moore grunted in irritation, drawling, "I've heard of him."

Wilce approached the table, saying abruptly, "Sheriff, my name is Wilce. I'm agent of the reservation. I want to see you."

Moore had evidently made up his mind about the Major in these few brief seconds, for his reply was a curt, "You're seein' me. What'll it be?"

Wilce glanced around uncomfortably at the others, Birkheimer, Torrence, Shotwell, Spence. Then, seeing that the law man had no intention of talking privately with him, he took a folded grimy paper from his pocket, opened it out and laid it on the table before the sheriff. "Read that," he said.

Moore read. It was a reward notice topped by a legend in bold type WANTED. At length, the law man looked up. "So what?" he asked.

"That man works for me," the Major stated.

Moore's brows lifted a trifle. "Which might put you in bad," he drawled. "It's against the law to protect or hire a wanted man."

"I didn't know who he was until just a short time ago. I've been waiting for a chance to turn him over to the authorities."

"All right, where is he?"

"Here in town, I think."

"You think?" Moore snapped. "Don't you know?"

"I heard he came across here yesterday," Wilce said, uncomfortable before the law man's direct glance and plainly hostile manner.

"You mean you've let him go loose?" the sheriff demanded. "You have police across there. Why didn't you jail him?"

"I — there didn't seem any point in risking getting my men shot up. This Erbeck's dangerous."

Torrence hid a smile with difficulty. Dave happened to look at him just then and wonder at that smile.

Moore said gruffly, "In other words, you haven't done a damn' thing about this man! You were afraid to arrest him. Now you think he's here but you're not sure. Suppose," . . . And he spoke deliberately now, in a dry and mocking drawl . . . "Suppose you corral this Erbeck and see me then and I'll take him off your hands. You'll want to split the reward, of course?" Before Wilce could reply, he added, "That's a bad habit for an officer to get into. So we'll get this straight right now. No split."

Wilce shrugged his narrow shoulders in a fair pretence of disinterest. "I hadn't thought about the money."

"Good. Then there'll be no argument."

The agent's face flushed at this rebuff and, nervously, he made that sucking noise at his tooth. He said, "Another thing, Sheriff. I have some evidence to give regarding Santell. Important evidence. He's suspected of rustling some —"

Moore waved a hand to silence him. "Later," he drawled. "You'll get your chance." He pointedly turned to the waiting group of Scalplock men. "Better get your undertaker in here so I can get his testimony."

"We don't have an undertaker," Torrence said, and by that time Wilce had taken the hint and moved on up to the bar.

"I'll have to have a statement from someone," Moore said. "Anyone'll do." Now he seemed impatient to have the hearing begin, for he took out his watch and looked at it.

"What kind of a statement?" Torrence asked.

"Don't you ever fill out death certificates up here when anyone dies?" Moore asked acidly. "Or do you just bury 'em and forget 'em, like I've heard tell you do?"

Torrence's face colored. But he kept a rein on his temper and said evenly, "Shotwell here is a notary. He'll sign anything you want him to."

"Anything *I* want him to? I don't give one damn about it. It's the law." Moore eyed Shotwell coldly. "So you're a notary, eh? When was your permit issued?"

Shotwell took longer than necessary in replying, "I don't quite recollect."

Moore slapped the table with a gnarled and calloused hand. "There's somethin' fishy about all this," he drawled. "No one to certify a death, a notary with a permit lapsed maybe twenty years. And —"

"It hasn't been that long," Shotwell cut in indignantly.

"And a stranger bein' held for a killin' that took place in a dark room full of armed men," Moore went on, ignoring the interruption. "Somethin' smells. I aim to find out what it is."

On the street, Frank Erbeck walked between

Doc and Jim on their way up from the Warren house. Doc was saying, "We're going to have to play this right. Moore doesn't have much use for —" He abruptly broke off as Frank slowed and fell behind.

Frank said, "That looks like the Major's buggy."

The medico glanced on ahead and at once recognized the buggy at the *Elite's* tie rail. "Sure does," he said.

"Then this is as far as I go. Just forget you saw me. As far as you know, I'm on the reservation." Frank turned without further explanation and went back down the hard packed walk.

Jim said, "Now what would Wilce be doin' across here?"

"Your guess is as good as mine," the medico answered. "Maybe we'll find out. But no one must know Frank's around. He hasn't been seen, has he?"

"Not that I know of. Hope not, anyway."

They entered the saloon and found Wilce at the bar, Moore at the back table with a group of men, including Dave. Doc noticed the agent and walked up to him. " 'Morning, Major," he said affably. "Didn't know you ever travelled this far."

Wilce was more amiable than usual as he replied, "Neither did I, Doctor. But I heard what was going on over here and thought they might need me. They will, too, before it's over."

Doc's level glance betrayed none of the suspicion he felt toward the man as he said, "That so? Well, you might help us get to the bottom of this. Still think Santell was in with Breen on that rustling?"

"I don't know what to think," the Major said, adding, "If he wasn't, I'll see that the charges against him are withdrawn. By the way, where's Erbeck?" He put his question casually, almost indifferently.

"Erbeck?" Doc echoed blandly. "Back in Grade, isn't he?"

"No. I heard he came across here. Not that it matters." Wilce nodded to the rear. "We'd better get on back there. The sheriff wants to get this started."

They had sauntered back a few paces from the bar when Doc said, "Remember that night you arrested Santell and jailed him?"

Wilce nodded, eyeing the medico side-ways.

"Funny thing," Doc went on. "I haven't been able to figure out why I found you outside the jail that night prying loose the bars to the window and Santell already gone."

The agent halted abruptly, stood stock

still. Doc faced around and looked up at him inquiringly, guilelessly. The agent's narrow face darkened now in helpless baffled rage.

"Of course, you can probably explain that to the sheriff, Major," Doc stated, as blandly as before.

Wilce was cornered and knew it. But now, following that brief betrayal of his surprise, he was his usual shrewd and genial self as he smiled benignly at Doc.

There was a long standing feud between these two that was subtle and wary, for neither undervalued the capabilities of the other. Their ways had often conflicted and, usually, Wilce had had the advantage because of his official standing that made his word the law on the reservation.

On the other hand, the medico had gained a reputation for honesty and integrity that galled Wilce. For the agent, as the government's representative, was often forced to tasks that made him out as callous and severe. But Jacob Wilce had given in to his role as the official and, instead of trying to temper it with justice and humanity, had even in his private dealings become dogmatic and overly severe. Occasionally, he would have his moments of regretting this. But not often. Invariably, it was Doc Faris who tortured his conscience by being his direct opposite. For that reason he had come to hate the medico with a deep and vengeful passion.

Just now Wilce's shrewdness came to his aid. "Is that so?" he drawled. "You saw me that night?"

"I should have mentioned it before this," Doc said. "Of course you had a reason for doing it."

The Major's glance narrowed. "Doesn't matter. The point is, I was trying to help Santell."

"So am I, Major."

From the back of the room, Sheriff Moore called impatiently, "Let's get started, doctor."

Wilce said quickly in an undertone, "Maybe I'd do better to stay out of this and just keep my eyes and ears open. I might run onto something that would help clear the thing up."

"Suit yourself, Major."

Wilce nodded. "Exactly what I'll do. You'll hear from me."

With that, the agent turned and left the saloon and Doc, walking on back to the rear table, smiled meagerly at this small advantage he had gained. The hearing would go much more smoothly without Jacob Wilce's confusing testimony against Dave.

As the medico approached the table, Moore said with cutting sarcasm, "I thought we couldn't get along without Wilce."

Doc took a chair and Jim Land came in to stand behind it. "He didn't know we'd already talked it over," Doc said. "It was about those cattle Breen got away with before the herd hit the reservation. He's decided to drop his charges against Santell."

Moore frowned. "One minute he tells me one thing, the next he's tellin' you another." His glowering glance ran from one Scalplock man to another. "Anyone else goin' to change their story?"

The answers of Torrence, Shotwell, Spence and Birkheimer were in the negative.

Moore asked abruptly, "Where's this Breen? Why isn't he here?"

"He went up into the high country with a bunch two days ago to look for Santell," Torrence said.

"He's a known rustler and you let him ride around loose?" Moore asked acidly. It was more than plain that he was enjoying this baiting.

"We didn't know anything about the McCune cattle then, Sheriff."

"He's just as much of a suspect in this killin' as Santell, isn't he? I understand he used his gun in the room that night, same as Santell. Why isn't he here to give his testimony?"

"His bunch isn't due back until tonight," Shotwell put in. "They don't even know we've got our hands on Santell. Wasn't no way to get word to them."

The sheriff shook his head resignedly. "You've sure got queer ways of doin' things up here," he stated. "All right, let's get started on this."

"Just to keep the record straight from the beginning, Sheriff," Doc put in, "who's examined the dead man?"

"No one," Moore grunted. "No undertaker here, no doctor. Not even a licensed notary to sign a death certificate." He pretended not to notice Shotwell's annoyance.

"I can take care of that for you," Doc said. He frowned abruptly, as though struck by a thought. Then: "You know, there may be a simple way of settling this without taking a couple hours arguing it." He looked at Dave, in the chair alongside him. "What caliber gun were you carrying that night, Dave?"

"A thirty-eight," Dave said.

"And what caliber was Breen's?" Doc's glance moved to the Scalplock men, ranged around the other side of the table facing him and Dave and the sheriff.

"What's that got to do with it?" Huck Birkheimer asked suspiciously.

"You'll find out when the rest of us do," Moore snapped. "Answer his question."

Birkheimer drawled, "I don't go around askin' guys what caliber irons they pack."

It was Torrence who said, "Breen carried a forty-four Smith and Wesson."

"Did anyone else use a gun in that room that night?" Doc asked.

Spence said, "No."

The medico laid his palms flat on the table. "Then there's only one thing to do. I'll probe that bullet out of Mordue and we'll see which gun it fits."

Birkheimer glanced quickly at Torrence and Dave noticed it and didn't know what to make of it. "That's a lot o' trouble to go to when we already know the facts," Birkheimer drawled.

"Suppose it is?" Moore said. "The doctor's offered to do it." He admitted, "Fact is, I hadn't thought of it. But it makes sense to me. All right, Faris, get to work." He stood up, thus settling the matter.

"Where's the body?" Doc asked as he came up out of his chair and Jim, behind him, stepped back out of the way.

Shotwell said, "In the ice house out back."

The table emptied and they all, including Dave, moved to the alley door. Birkheimer hung back long enough to edge up to Torrence and demand angrily, "Why'd you have to tell 'em about Ray's iron? We'll be in a hell of a spot when he cuts Mordue open!"

"Just stick around and watch," Torrence replied with a slow smile. "You're forgetting something, Huck."

"What?"

"That slug blew the back out of Mordue's skull, went clear through. They'll never find it."

Birkheimer gave a gusty sigh of relief and was wiping his perspiring broad face as he joined the others in the alley. He was so vastly relieved at what Torrence had just told him that he volunteered to climb the ladder on the face of the high log building to the small door in under the roof peak.

They watched him go up the ladder, push the door open, and reach for the hook of the block and tackle hanging from the protruding end of the roof's big keylog. He climbed in the door and pulled the hook in after him as Spence, below, played out extra rope.

They waited one minute, then the better part of another. Finally Spence called,

"Need some help, Huck?"

Shortly, Birkheimer leaned out of the high opening. "Where was it we put him?" he called down.

"Over there to the right between them two big top cakes," Spence answered.

"How deep down?"

Spence swore in irritation. "You was with me, Huck. Scrape out the sawdust between those two blocks and you'll find him."

"You come up and find him," Birkheimer growled.

Spence cursed again and went up the ladder. He was gone but a moment before his head emerged from the opening and he bawled, "He's gone!"

"Gone?" Torrence echoed from below. "Who else helped haul him up there?"

"Shotwell," Spence said. "But it ain't no use, Ed. He ain't here!"

Torrence wheeled on the store owner. "Blaine, get up there and find him!" he said sharply. "They may've moved him to get ice. Dig around until you find him."

So Shotwell heaved his generous weight up the ladder and squeezed in through the narrow opening. When he finally appeared at the door again, his round full face shiny with sweat, they could see him leaning on the handle of the big scoop used to move the sawdust.

"It's the God's truth, Ed!" he called in an awed voice. "The body's gone!"

Sheriff Moore said dryly, "What kind of a run around is this?"

Torrence's face had lost some of its ruddy handsomeness. He looked angry and ugly and put a restraint on his temper with visible effort. "But Mordue's got to be up there," he breathed.

A significant look passed between the law man and Doc and Moore called acidly to those above, "Get down here." Then, without waiting for them, he turned on his heel and went back in through the saloon's rear door.

As the doctor and Dave and Jim followed, Dave said in a quiet voice, "You don't seem surprised enough, Doc." His dark eyes reflected a faint but unmistakable amusement.

"Just sit tight, Dave. Jim and I know what the tally is," was the medico's cryptic reply.

Shortly, they were all at the table again. Moore's now wrathful glance appraised each man deliberately, accusingly, before he burst out, "Just to keep the record straight again, Faris here met me ten miles out the trail last night and warned me to expect anything. But, by Jupiter, I didn't expect to run into anything like this! You not only frame a man with a killin' that never took place but you expect me to swallow it! No wonder you didn't like the idea of cuttin' into the corpse for the bullet!"

"Look, Sheriff," Torrence drawled with amazing patience, "Mordue was killed that night because I saw him. So did about twenty others. And —"

"Santell," Moore's rasping voice cut Torrence short, "did you see this dead man they're talkin' about?"

"When could I have seen him?" Dave drawled. "It was dark as the inside of my hat."

"Did you ever see the stiff, Doc?" the sheriff asked.

"No. Which is queer when you come to think of it," Doc said. "You'd think they'd at least have wanted me to have a look at him so I could give testimony."

Torrence said bitingly, "Bodies can be stolen."

"Who by?" Jim Land drawled unexpectedly. He nodded to Dave. "Santell's got three friends in this town, me and Miss McCune and Doc here. Four, if you count Warren. Name a time when we could have stolen the body."

"Any time last night," Torrence drawled.

"Sheriff, what time did we hit your camp last night?" Jim asked.

"Right after eleven."

"And what time did Miss McCune and Doc leave here last night?" Jim asked Torrence.

"About half past ten," was Torrence's somewhat hesitant reply.

"Then there's your answer," Jim said. "Doc and Warren were with me. We were at Moore's camp seven miles out, by eleven-thirty. Which means we made last tracks without takin' time out to steal the body. If you think Gail McCune could have done it alone, you're out of your head."

"What about Erbeck?" Torrence drawled.

"Erbeck? What's he got to do with this?" Doc now cut in without batting an eye.

"Wilce claims he came across here yesterday."

"Suppose he did? Did you ever hear of an agency man being a friend of ours?"

"He hauled Santell out of the fight that night. He —"

Once again Moore interrupted Torrence with an explosive, "Where's all this yammerin' getting us? Me, I don't think there ever was a body! Santell was makin' a nuisance of himself so you framed him. Which might work if you had a bought sheriff and could forge a death certificate. You may have bought off twenty people to swear to seein' that body. But you haven't got me bought and your death certificate isn't worth the paper you want to write it on!"

He turned to Dave. "Santell, you're free as air." He fixed a gimlet-eyed stare on Torrence. "If I was half a man, I'd run the whole bunch of you in for a trick like this."

Torrence said with surprising mildness, "Mordue was killed. But this is all right with me. I was never so sure Santell did it anyway. No hard feelin's, Santell?"

Dave said, "Not any, Torrence."

"You can't get away with this!" Huck Birkheimer blazed. "Santell killed Mordue and, by God, if you don't say so, we do! We'll take care of him ourselves if you don't, Sheriff!"

Dave stepped in on Birkheimer and knocked him down with a full powerful swing to the jaw. He stood a moment over Birkheimer, making sure the man didn't move. No one, not even Shotwell, said anything.

"Come along, Doc," Dave drawled finally. "School's out."

XVII

Gail saw them coming down the street past the saddle shop, Doc and Jim and Frank. Only the three of them. She felt the constriction of disappointment settle through her.

But no! That third man was too tall, too broad through the shoulders, too lean-hipped to be Frank Erbeck.

It was Dave!

Suddenly the burden of her depression dropped away and in its place came a gladness that made her want to shout, to cry out in joy. She ran down off the porch and out onto the rutted street and met them there in the heavy shade of the big cedar, trying to keep back the tears of happiness that came anyway.

"We did it, Gail," Doc said, with as broad a smile as she had ever seen on his face.

The glance of thankfulness she gave the medico was brief. She looked full at Dave and breathed softly, "I'm so glad! I've —"

Her voice balled up on her then and she couldn't go on. Impulsively, she held out her hand. When Dave's firm grasp answered hers and he drawled, "I understand this was all your doin', ma'am," she was calm once more. Dave Santell was free. It was as though everything she had ever hoped for had reached fulfillment.

Gail hadn't noticed the tilt of Doc's head that was directed at Jim. She wasn't aware of being alone with Dave until the scuffle of Jim's and Doc's boots on the Warren walk sounded across to her. She realized then that her hand was still in Dave's and withdrew it gently; and once more she was confused for a reason she couldn't understand.

She said, "Could we . . . Let's walk on down the street. There's so much I want to ask you. And, please. You're to call me Gail, not ma'am, Dave." She laughed self-consciously. "Makes me feel like an old woman." She changed the subject quickly. "Were they surprised to find the body gone?"

"I thought Birkheimer was goin' to choke. Shotwell, too." Dave laughed in a way that was good to hear. "The sheriff was fit to be tied. Claimed there never had been a body and that they'd bought their testimony."

"Then you can leave any time you want?"

He gave her a quizzical glance. "Any time."

His tone told her something, and she asked quickly, "You are going to leave now that you can, aren't you?"

He asked pointedly, "What about Breen

297

and those three hundred steers I lost for you? What about the horses? They represent a lot of money."

"Forget them, Dave! Anyone would have made the mistake you did. All that matters to me now is to get away from all this trouble. To get you away from it."

He deliberated this a long moment as they walked on past the last sorry downstreet shack and out the open trail. She saw that his expression was unusually grave, for the clean lines of his face stood out in sharp relief and there was a hard unyielding look in his deep brown eyes.

"No," he said finally, "that won't do, ma'am."

"I asked you to call me Gail," she corrected him. "Why won't it do?"

There was a low-growing juniper shading the side of the trail and he turned aside to it, out of the blaze of hot sunlight, saying, "Maybe you have to be a man to understand. It's like someone breakin' into your house and takin' what they please. Like you knew who it was and didn't do anything about it."

The bank alongside the trail under the juniper was covered with a fine rich grass. Gail sat down there, saying, "No. It isn't like that. Because you don't know who stole those cattle, Dave."

"Breen did."

She shook her head. "You don't care about Breen and you know it. You're looking for the man Breen works for. You've tried to find out who he is, tried hard. Admit that it can't be done and leave before you get into more trouble."

He lifted a boot to the bank close by where she sat and took a sack of tobacco dust from his pocket and built a smoke, not speaking for a long moment. She watched the smooth sure way of his fingers as they evenly shaped the cigarette.

When he had lit his smoke, he drawled, "A man has a hard time livin' some things down. This is one of those things with me. I found out a long time ago that it's easier to lick a thing right now than it is to ride with it on your mind the rest of your life."

"But you're working for me," Gail protested. "If I ask you to do this, it's me that's giving in, not you."

Dave smiled thinly and his steady glance was on her, a little amused. "You fired me back there in Grade," he reminded her.

Her face flushed as she answered, "Don't hold that against me, Dave. I've already apologized."

"That isn't what I mean," Dave hastened

to explain. "A man has his own say about bein' rehired, hasn't he?"

"You don't want to work for me any longer?"

"Not that. There's nothin' I want more. But I don't sign on with the outfit again until I've licked this thing, licked it all the way to the ground and buried it!"

She said hotly, "Dave Santell, you're as stubborn as my father was! Right now you sound exactly like him!"

"Thanks, Gail," he drawled, smiling. "That's quite a compliment."

He saw the flush deepen on her face and knew that he had angered her. He liked her this way, liked that fiery signal of her temper. She was a beautiful and desirable woman at this moment and he was keenly aware of her attraction. The dappled sunlight filtering through the branches of the juniper flecked her hair with red gold. And the slender rounded outline of her body, unconsciously poised in gracefulness, only added to that quickening of interest that he tried to ignore and couldn't.

She said abruptly, looking up at him, her anger dying, "Dave, please do this for me."

But his glance had left her, running on down the trail. He saw something there that made him frown with puzzlement. Then she heard the horses and looked that way to see the eight blue-uniformed riders swinging into sight around the turning immediately below.

Dave said, "The Army. Wonder what they're doin' up this way."

They sat watching the oncoming troopers, led by a lieutenant who sat the saddle more erectly at sight of Gail there by the road. He saluted them smartly as he passed, his ruddy Irish face taking on a pleasant smile for Gail.

When they were gone from sight beyond the turning at the foot of the street, Gail spoke as though the interruption had never been, saying in a hushed, intense voice, "Please, Dave. Please give this up."

He pushed aside his puzzlement over the presence of those cavalrymen at this out of the way spot, telling her, "You'd be the first person I'd do it for, Gail, if I'd do it for anyone. It's not that I'm bullheaded. But a man's got to live with his conscience."

She smiled then, in a warm impulsive way. Abruptly, she laid a hand on his arm bent across his knee. "I'd do it, too, Dave," she said softly. "I'm — well, just a little proud that you wouldn't let me talk you out of it."

She must have sensed then the quick bond of closeness her words had woven between them, for she looked away. And when she next spoke her voice was matter-of-fact and lacking that quality of warmth she had put into it a moment ago.

"What can I do to help?" she asked. "Do you want Jim Land to go back to Grade after the rest of the men?"

"No, I don't need help."

"Then how are you going to go about it?"

"Do a little ridin', keep my eyes open. Maybe go across the hills and follow out that canyon where the horses were lost. And," he added dryly, "maybe have that talk with Breen I didn't get to finish the other night."

"It'll be dangerous, Dave. Anyone who will steal cattle will kill to keep from being found out."

"Just livin' and workin' is dangerous. Any man who has to have a sure thing never grows up."

She eyed him again in that way that was anything but casual. "You know, you *are* like dad was. Little things about you. I can almost hear him saying what you just did." Then, in her impulsive way, she said, "I think I like you, Dave Santell." And now there was no embarrassment in her, no shyness. She had made a simple statement of fact.

He grinned broadly. "You've sure changed your tune."

"I have," she admitted readily, "about a lot of things." She was silent a moment. Then: "Dave, could I stay in the cattle business?"

His eyes opened a little wider. "Why not?"

"How much am I worth?"

"You know more about that than I do," he said.

"I don't mean how much money do I have in the bank," she told him, adding with a low husky laugh, "Actually, the money Wilce pays me for the cattle will just about settle the claims against the estate. I mean how much do I have down in Texas? How much is the ranch worth? How many cattle are on it? It's been so long since I was down there, and the lawyer for the estate talks only in figures that I can't understand. Dad never mortgaged the ranch, did he?"

"No. It was all his as far as I know."

"Is it big? Is it a good one? Could I make a living on it?"

"John McCune always did," Dave said. "It's bigger'n all outdoors and there's cattle on it that've never been burned with a brand. All we had to do to make up the herd was ride out and round up the first three thousand good head we came across. I don't suppose even your father knew how much he was worth. Money never seemed to bother him much. Each year he'd contract enough in sales to keep the outfit rollin' and answer his own needs. He wasn't a big spender. He was satisfied with just enough to get along on."

"I know," Gail murmured, her expression grave before a thought that had come to her. "You didn't know him when Mother was alive, did you? He was different then. He hasn't seemed to care for anything but me since then." She looked up. "Dave, could you and I keep the ranch going? Would you see to things like getting contracts and doing all the things that need doing?"

He nodded, saying soberly, "After this other's over."

"Yes," she echoed lifelessly, "after this is over." She sighed as she stood up. She looked down the trail, then back toward town. There was a clear regret in her voice as she said, "It must all wait on that, mustn't it? I suppose we should be getting back. Mrs. Warren is probably waiting the meal for us."

She took his arm as they went back up the trail. They were silent before the import her last words had taken. Dave was restless and strangely unsure of himself now, hating what he had had to tell this girl, yet stubbornly refusing to change his mind.

They were turning off the street into the Warren yard when Gail tightened the pressure on his arm and said softly, "Don't worry about me, Dave. I'm waiting here, right here, until you can go back to Grade with me. We'll talk about all this again then, not before."

He said, "Thanks, Gail," feeling that his words sounded inane and feeble. But he couldn't think of anything else to add.

XVIII

For this past hour Frank had been lying here on the roof of Tom Warren's saddle shop, bellied down behind the high false front, looking down at the street through a wide crack in one of the weathered boards. Just now he was restless and uneasy over what he saw down there.

A half hour ago he had seen Doc and Jim and Dave Santell go down the street and had rightly concluded that the sheriff had released Dave. Which meant, probably, that his last night's chore of hauling Mordue's body three miles north and caving in a cutbank on it hadn't been wasted.

He would have climbed down and gone

back to the Warren house but for his curiosity over Jacob Wilce being here in Scalplock. The agent had come out of the saloon shortly after Doc and Jim had entered. For a while he'd loafed in the doorway of the *Merchandise.* Then, just before the hearing was over, the Major had gone on up and entered the lunch room above the saloon. He was in there now.

The arrival of the troopers was the thing that now prompted this uneasiness in Frank. He couldn't figure out why they should be here. They had stopped at the feed barn, the lieutenant had said something to the hostler, then the horses had been led out to the corral behind and were now being fed and watered. The lieutenant had crossed over to the walk in front of the *Elite* and had spent some minutes talking there with several Scalplock men and Sheriff Moore.

Just now a man in that group called to Wilce's two police across the street. Frank heard his hail distinctly. "Where'd the Major go?" was what he asked the two bucks.

One of them came across, giving his answer, which Frank couldn't hear. And a moment later a man left the group under the saloon awning and strode purposefully up the walk to the lunch room, turning in there. This was Ed Torrence, although Frank didn't know the Wheel man by sight.

Suddenly a near panic hit Frank. Wilce would doubtless have missed him around the agency long before this. Had he been seen coming across here yesterday with Jim and Gail and had the agent found out about it? If so, then couldn't Wilce be here looking for him? Wasn't that why the Major had brought along his two police, so as to be able to make an arrest? If he was caught here, wouldn't Wilce immediately turn him over to the Army to be held for a federal marshal?

Frank lay there a minute waiting for the agent to appear with the man who had doubtless been sent to the restaurant to get him. He didn't know why he was waiting, for his impulse was to get down to the Warren barn, to saddle and ride for the reservation as fast as a horse would take him.

Another minute dragged by and still no sign of Wilce. Perhaps the agent was finishing his meal.

Abruptly, Frank knew that he must leave now if he was to get away at all. He came erect and, stooping so that he wouldn't be seen, ran to the rear end of the roof. He had climbed up through the trap door in the loft. But now not even Tom Warren, below in his shop, must know that he was going.

He swung down with a handhold on the eaves and fell awkwardly as he dropped into the alley, some ten feet. He went along the alley almost to its end, turning in at Warren's barn, on the street side.

He was in the barn's back stall, saddling his steeldust, when a shadow suddenly blocked the nearby door's wedged pattern of sunlight. He wheeled quickly, right hand stabbing down to his thigh. There stood Dave Santell.

The wariness drained out of Frank quickly as he saw Dave's face take on its quick smile.

"So they let you off?" Frank said, hooking the stirrup over the horn of the saddle while he pulled tight the cinch.

"Thanks to you," Dave drawled. "You should've been there to see it, Erbeck."

Frank worked on without any reply to that.

Shortly, Dave said, "The Major was askin' after you. Doc persuaded him different when he told him he'd seen him breakin' me out of jail the other night." . . . Dave nodded to the saddled steeldust . . . "Goin' somewhere?"

"Back to the reservation," Frank said. "The Army just blew in. Wilce could make it hot for me if he decides to. I'm on my way."

Dave's brows lifted. "You could hide here the rest of the day. They'd never find you, even if they do look. There'd be plenty to do if you stuck with us."

Frank said dryly, "You'll make out all right by yourself." Some of that unyielding stubbornness and pride of the other night was in him again. He had felt the punishment of Dave's fists and, regardless of what had happened since then, that fact still rankled.

"We'll be headed down to Texas in another week," Dave went on, ignoring the refusal. "There's an all year round job waitin' for you if you say the word."

Frank chuckled softly. "Punchin' cattle?" He shook his head. "No thanks. There's easier ways of makin' money."

Dave shrugged then, and Frank was later to thank him for his quick understanding that more lay behind this refusal than appeared on the surface.

"Any time you change your mind, the offer still holds," Dave said. He grinned broadly, adding, "We could use a man handy at raisin' the dead."

"I'll remember, in case that sort of work gets scarce up here."

"It won't, not around here," Dave said.

Then: "Anything else you'd like to tell me about this before you pull out?"

"Such as?"

"Why the Major took the trouble of framin' me."

"You were in the way, I reckon. I wouldn't know for sure."

"So the Major's tied into this, is he? What about Breen? He wasn't really fired then?"

Frank lifted his shoulders in an unknowing way. "Y' got me, Santell."

"Who's Breen tied up with over here?"

"When you find out, let me know." Frank smiled meagerly and reached for the gelding's reins. "That's straight, Santell. I don't even have an idea."

He stiffened suddenly at hearing steps crossing the narrow yard from the direction of the house. Dave noticed the change in him and motioned him to silence. Then Dave went to the door and through it and out of sight.

Frank heard Jacob Wilce's voice say quickly, "That's him, Lieutenant."

A strange voice said, "Santell, put up your hands. You're under arrest. Sergeant, get his gun!"

Steps came closer to the door and Frank drew his gun and lined it at the opening, still gripping the reins with his left hand.

He heard Dave ask, "What's the trouble, Lieutenant?"

There was a dry laugh out there and the lieutenant answered, "Your friend Larkin, up at Bewell, was killed resisting arrest the other day."

"Should that mean anything to me?" Dave asked. "Who's Larkin?"

"There's no use trying to bluff it through, Santell," came Wilce's dry tones. "Larkin was the man you and Breen have been selling those stolen cattle to. He had the gall to turn right around and sell them to the Army. The quartermaster ran across a suspicious looking hide and sent some men out to Larkin's ranch to ask him about it. He lost his head and tried to shoot his way clear. He was killed."

Frank listened, trying to make some sense of what he was hearing. Beyond the steeldust, the barn's big alley door stood invitingly open. Deep inside Frank was still that fear of Wilce finding him here, arresting him and turning him over to the Army. But now he was held here by a strange loyalty to Dave, wanting to help if he could. He kept his gun lined at the door beyond which these men stood, waiting for the unexpected.

Out there, Dave said calmly, "Lieutenant,

there's been a mistake. I've never heard of this Larkin. If anyone was dealing with him, it was Breen and some other man. Some Scalplock man."

"Go ahead!" came Wilce's smooth taunting voice. "Try and crawl out of it! You were here last winter negotiating that new contract with me. You planned this with Breen then."

"I don't even remember seeing Breen last winter."

"Of course you don't! Because you don't want to. And what about Erbeck? What's happened to him?"

"What about Erbeck?" Dave asked.

"He's working with you the same as Breen is," the Major said. "You and Breen and Erbeck at this end, Larkin at the other. How did you run onto Larkin? Did you go out last winter by way of Fort Bewell and see him then?" . . . The agent's dry laugh echoed in through the doorway to Frank . . . "At any rate, this rustling didn't start until after you left, Santell. There's the best proof of all. You're guilty, guilty as hell! You'll be tried in a federal court and get at least twenty years. You'll —"

"That'll do, Wilce," cut in the lieutenant's voice; and Frank noticed that the officer didn't call the agent by his honorary title of

Major. "I'm arresting Santell and that's enough for the present. When Major Royce gets back to the post next week, he'll decide what's to be done. Now come along."

Frank dropped the steeldust's reins and, regardless of knowing now that Wilce was hunting him, carefully edged to the yard door of the barn. He had some wild and reckless idea of stepping out, holding off Dave's guard at the point of a gun and giving Dave the chance to escape. For he knew certainly, absolutely, that these things he had heard about Dave weren't true.

But when he looked out it was to see six of the seven soldiers, their carbines ready, walking away between him and Dave, the lieutenant and Wilce. Beyond them, standing at the street end of the lane, he could see Torrence, Doc Faris, Jim and Gail; the remaining trooper was with them, evidently having been left there by the lieutenant to keep them from warning Dave of what was coming.

Frank's last rash hope of helping Dave died. He might have helped with only Wilce and the lieutenant to watch. But he knew he didn't have a chance against so many.

He watched until the two groups had met at the end of the lane. Then, remembering that threat of Wilce's, he went back to the steeldust, led the animal into the alley, mounted and headed down the steep slope toward the ravine bottom.

No one saw him, no one heard him go. He was headed back onto the reservation, thinking he was safe because Wilce wouldn't be there; he would reach Grade early in the evening, gather up his few possessions and start west into the distant Rockies. There he would be safe for a time.

There was nothing he could do for Dave Santell.

At the head of Warren's lane, Gail was the first to speak as Dave approached.

"We're going to Fort Bewell with you, Dave. There's a telegraph there. I'm wiring the best lawyer in the East to come out and handle your defense."

Dave didn't like the worry and fear he saw on her face. He was quick to say, "No. You'd all better wait right here. As soon as the major hears what I have to tell him, I'll be released. And don't worry about it, Gail. There's been a mistake and we can prove it."

"How?" Doc Faris asked savagely, his cold angry glance settled on Wilce. "They're lying, Dave, and they know it! The whole thing's so absolutely ridiculous that it's laughable."

"Looks that way to me, too," Ed Torrence drawled. "Lieutenant, you can't arrest this man on anything the Major tells you."

For a moment, Jacob Wilce stared at Torrence as though he hadn't heard right. But then he understood what Torrence was doing. He was quick to act his part, blazing, "I have the authority to demand Santell's arrest and I'm doing it. Furthermore, I'll see him convicted if it's the last thing I live to do."

"There's no use arguing this any further," the lieutenant said. He turned to one of his men. "Sergeant, we're leaving immediately."

The sergeant saluted smartly and, detailing two of his men to remain behind, took the others upstreet to the livery barn for the horses.

Dave had a chance to take Gail aside and tell her, "Nothing will come of this. We know that Wilce is against us and we know why. Because he's in on the rustling. Let's give him more rope and see if he doesn't hang himself."

"But it's you they'll hang, not Wilce!" Gail cried softly, that open fear still in her eyes. "I'm going with you. I'm going to send that wire to Philadelphia!"

Dave shook his head. "No. I'll get off. You

and Doc and Jim wait here. Tell Jim and Doc to keep their eyes open. They're liable to run across something that will lead us to the man that's behind all this, behind Wilce and B●en. Tell them —"

"Santell!" Wilce called sharply. He said to the lieutenant, "You'd better keep an eye on him. He shouldn't be talking to anybody."

The officer sighed wearily, glancing at Dave and Gail and saying, "I'll have to ask you not to talk with your friends, Santell."

That parting word with Gail was the last chance Dave had to speak with anyone. Twenty minutes later he rode out the street on the buckskin, flanked by outriders whose carbines lay ready across their saddles.

XIX

Torrence didn't get a chance to speak to Wilce alone for the next half hour. Then, just as Wilce called to his two police that he was starting back for the reservation and went to his buggy, Torrence sauntered over to him.

The agent was once again sure of himself, possessed of that absolute and supreme confidence that had come through his four years of autocratic dealings with the Indians. He now gave Torrence a meaning smile and said, not too loudly, "Not bad, was it?"

Torrence didn't seem so pleased. "Well, not too bad."

Wilce frowned. "We swung it, didn't we? He's under arrest. We're probably rid of him for good. Larkin getting killed was the best luck we've had. Now if you'll keep Breen shut up we'll be absolutely in the clear."

"I'll manage Ray all right," Torrence drawled. "But I wish you hadn't laid it on so thick about Erbeck. Or did I tell you?"

"Tell me what?" The agent's frown had deepened now, worriedly.

"You remember," Torrence reminded him, "that I was investigating Erbeck."

"Investigating him, how?"

Torrence's look was one of exasperation. "Now don't let on like you didn't know, Jake."

"But I don't! What about Erbeck?"

Torrence looked puzzled. "Didn't I tell you about runnin' onto that Bewell man that knew Erbeck?"

"No."

"I was sure I told you, Jake." Torrence gave a shrug. "Anyway, this gent spoke of Erbeck like he knew him. Which seemed strange to me, considerin' what you'd told me about Erbeck comin' from over east somewhere." Torrence paused, eyed the

317

agent with that same puzzled frown for a moment, then said, "Jake, I told you all this once. You've just forgot."

"Go ahead and tell it again then," Wilce said dryly, impatiently.

"Well, I got to thinkin' it was funny this jasper should know Erbeck. So I sent a man up to the Fort to ask a few questions. He got some answers. And they don't look so good. Without wastin' too much breath, Erbeck's a Big Cat."

"A Big Cat!" Wilce breathed, paling at hearing the term Torrence had used. "How can he be? There's a dodger out on him."

Torrence laughed easily. "Any printin' shop would do that kind of a job for regular prices." Once again his look went serious. "You mean I never warned you, Jake?"

Wilce swore explosively; and now his face had gone a sickly gray. "Damn it! Out with it! How can Erbeck be a Big Cat?"

Torrence took his time replying, relishing this moment. By calling Frank Erbeck a Big Cat — the appellation applied to government agents who came unannounced and unidentified onto reservations to investigate irregularities — he had thrown stark and naked fear into Jacob Wilce. Now he struck his final blow, drawling.

"You knew they'd investigate that rustling

last winter, didn't you, Jake? I told you to be careful. Well, Erbeck's a marshal probably. Had that dodger sent in ahead of him to throw you off your guard. Hell, man, I told you once to go careful with him!"

Wilce appeared for a moment on the point of fainting. He tried to speak, couldn't, and swallowed to clear his throat. Then he said in an awed fear-dulled voice, "You never told me, Ed! You didn't!"

Torrence shrugged. "All right, I didn't. But you know now. You haven't given him anything to go on, have you?"

"He was the man I used to plant the money on Santell! He knows about the pass through the canyon. He knows I pushed those cattle up onto the Muddy so Breen could make the last steal!"

Torrence's jaw dropped open in a perfect pretense at amazement. Then his jaw snapped shut and he said scathingly, witheringly, "You damned bungling fool!" He reached out and took a hold with both hands on the collar of Wilce's black alpaca coat. He shook the agent so hard that Wilce's head snapped back. "You mean you've given Erbeck all he needs to arrest us?"

"Don't, Ed! Don't! I swear he doesn't know you're in it!"

Torrence let go his hold, saying mildly yet with an ominous note that made the agent wince, "That's better. He'd better not find out."

"I haven't told him, Ed." For a moment Wilce seemed intent on proving this to Torrence. But then he thought of himself and asked in a hushed, near sobbing voice, "What'll I do? He knows about me."

Torrence shook his head. "I don't know, Jake. What will you do?"

"Is he here in town? Have you seen him?"

"No."

"He was seen coming across here."

"Then I've just missed him." Torrence fastened an appraising probing glance on the agent. "Not losing your nerve, are you, Jake?"

"But he can arrest me on what he already knows."

"Then you'd better kill a horse or two gettin' away from the reservation." Torrence's glance narrowed. "But first, you'd better see to it that you burn those papers, Jake. They won't hurt me if they're found, but they'd sure look bad for you."

Wilce turned, lifted a foot for the buggy's step and missed it and stumbled. Torrence took his arm and helped him climb up onto the seat. The agent looked deathly sick; his face had no color at all and fine beads of perspiration stood out on his face.

"Sorry we won't be able to finish this last deal, Jake," Torrence drawled apologetically. "But with Larkin dead, I'll have to make other arrangements. It may take a month or so. I may even lose those critters up in the hills until things quiet down."

Wilce picked up the reins, his furtive and fearful glance going both ways along the street.

"Better stop out a ways and trade onto a saddle," Torrence said, nodding to the two bucks who had reined out from the rail and were waiting beyond in the street. "You'll make better time. Figure on leaving to-night?"

Wilce nodded dumbly, too rigid with fear to say anything.

"Better ride east and hit the railroad. They won't look for you over there. If Erbeck shows up, I'll try and keep him here so as to give you some extra time."

The agent said, "Thanks, Ed," and, lifting the whip from the socket on the mudguard, laid it across the backs of the team.

His horses went up and out the head of the street at a stiff run.

Torrence waited there until the buggy had rolled out of sight in the trail bend toward the creek. He laughed softly.

He wore a perfectly sober expression when he turned to the walk once more and sauntered down to join Shotwell and Spence under the saloon awning.

"Sort of in a hurry, wasn't he?" Blaine Shotwell asked. "He'll kill them nags if he drives 'em that way. What was ailin' him?"

"Search me," Torrence said.

Shotwell eyed him narrowly a moment to say abruptly, "Ed, you've never told us what your deal is with Wilce."

There was a cool careful appraisal in the glance Torrence put on the storeowner. "All you've got to do is collect your lease money from that piece of land and sit tight, Blaine," he said.

Shotwell colored, said hastily, "I was only wonderin'. No hard feelin's, Ed."

"No hard feelin's," Torrence said, and went on past them and down the walk.

"Touchy, ain't he?" Shotwell muttered as soon as the Wheel man was well out of hearing.

"Maybe, maybe not," Spence said. "As for me, I get paid good for helpin' him work cattle off your land and on up to Larkin's place. I don't remember what any of them critters looked like, I don't even know as I ever noticed one o' their brands. I just sit tight and hope the easy money keeps rollin' in. If I was you, I'd do the same."

Torrence spent only a few minutes at the Warren place. He had gone there hoping to see Gail, for he had an eye for a good-looking woman and the impression Gail had made on him last night was no shallow one. But instead of talking to Gail, he transacted his business with Doc Faris. He supposed the girl was with Mrs. Warren in the kitchen; for the medico went back there to get the money he had paid for the horses and returned it to him.

"Wish you'd keep this money and let me get some men out and try and find those animals," he told Doc.

But the medico shook his head, saying simply, "If you find them, well and good. You can pay for them again. But right now we've got enough to think about without this. Miss McCune prefers to have it this way."

"That's tough about Santell, doctor."

"It's worse than tough. I'm worried, Torrence."

It wasn't until after Torrence left the house, at a little past two, that he remembered he hadn't eaten his midday meal. He went on up to the restaurant.

He was halfway through his meal when

Kemp, the waiter, asked casually, "Seen Breen?"

"Not for a couple days." Torrence went right on eating, not even looking up from his plate.

Kemp grunted a laugh. "He's sure tanked up."

Torrence looked at him as he added, "So plastered it's runnin' out his ears."

"Where?"

"Where?" Kemp frowned. "Where would a man go to get a snootful? The saloon, of course."

Torrence's appetite left him and he pushed his plate away unfinished, deciding not to order the piece of apple pie he had hungrily eyed when he came in. He built a smoke and lit it, going out onto the walk and looking down toward the saloon, trying to decide what to do.

Ray Breen could be ugly when he drank. And, remembering his words with Breen about the horses the other morning, he decided it wouldn't do to go into the *Elite* and order the big man to lay off the whiskey. In reality, Torrence was recalling Breen's look the other morning and was just a little afraid of the big man.

Just then he saw Jim Land come out of the saloon. The McCune man glanced in

Torrence's direction, then climbed to the saddle of a rangy grey horse and went down the street toward the Warren house. But Land didn't turn in there; he kept on going out the lower trail. Torrence wondered idly how long Land and the doctor and the McCune girl would wait here, hoping for Santell's release. Just to think of his having prompted Jake Wilce here at the restaurant this morning with the story that had caused Santell's arrest made him smile now. He was a little vain over having thought it up so quickly. The lie he'd given the agent about Erbeck was really laughable and he enjoyed thinking back over it.

But he couldn't get Breen out of his mind. And now he started for the saloon. He was just short of it when he changed his mind. He crossed the street and went into the barber shop and let Sid Apple give him a shave. But, some twenty minutes later, he was worrying about Breen again. Suppose the big man talked out of turn? There had been hate in Breen's eyes that morning up there under the rim. Would Breen dare to doublecross him?

Finally his curiosity nagged him into heading for the saloon again. And this time he went on in.

Breen lay across two chairs at the back of

the room, snoring loudly. Earl, the apron, got up off his stool at the bar's far end and came up to him yawning, asking, "What'll it be, Ed?"

"Beer."

Earl lifted the lid of the ice chest, reaching for a bottle of beer and Torrence said, "Big crowd you got here." He was the only customer; at least the only one awake.

"Yeah, place is crowded." Earl yawned again as he emptied the bottle into a big glass schooner.

Torrence nodded back to Breen. "Passed out?"

"Cold." Earl smiled.

"How long's he been at it?"

"Not long. But he went at it like he meant it. Killed a pint right off without comin' up for air. Then he had another while he was talkin' with that Texas jasper."

Torrence frowned. "A Texas man in town?"

"You know, that McCune man."

Suspicion flared alive in Torrence, yet he kept from showing it as he took his first long draught of the cool beer. He set the schooner down and said, "You say they were arguin'?"

"Did I?" Earl asked. "Well, they weren't. Breen was talkin' with this bird real confidential about somethin'.'"

Torrence had a hard time not asking the apron point blank what had been said. But he was being careful now, knowing he was onto something. He drained off the rest of his beer, ordered another.

"What could Breen have to say that's so damned important?" he asked at length. He chuckled. "Maybe he was tellin' this Texas man what he did with those cattle he got from Santell."

Earl gave him a serious look, said, "Y' know, maybe he was at that. Once I heard him say to this gent, 'You really want to know who it is?' And the other guy says, 'You don't even know.' That made Breen sorta mad, it looked like. 'Don't I?' he says, and he leans over and tells this Texas man somethin'. 'The hell you say' he comes back at Breen. I didn't hear nothin' else. But right after that Santell's friend goes out of here like he was headed some place. And it weren't no more'n five minutes before Breen folds, right about where you're standin'. Tips over a spittoon and I got to clear up all the muck and help him back to where he is now."

Torrence hurried with his second beer. Finished with it, he left the saloon. His walk quickened as he headed across to the livery barn. He was running when he went in through the doors.

It hadn't taken him long to decide where Jim Land had gone. He was headed for Fort Bewell, too. He was wondering if he remembered that eight mile cutoff across Starvation Ridge well enough to take it.

XX

Somewhere back there two hours ago the gray horse had picked up a stone in his hard run. Jim still cursed venomously and impotently when he thought of it, thought of how the horse had been lamed so that he wasn't good for a faster pace than a stiff trot.

Still, now as the lights of Fort Bewell winked out across the wide flats close ahead, there seemed no reason for Jim to worry. In this last hour of darkness, he had stopped several times to listen. But, as far as he knew, he had the trail to himself.

Evidently, Torrence hadn't seen anything out of the way in his leaving the *Elite* so abruptly. But at the time, seeing Torrence up the street and watching him, he was sure the Wheel man knew Breen had talked. He had been convinced that Torrence would follow him. For that reason, he hadn't even risked stopping at Warren's to tell Gail and the doctor what he had learned from Breen. Instead, he'd half killed the gray covering those first twenty miles — and lamed the animal because he hadn't used his head, because he'd almost run the gray's heart out instead of easing down to a trot now and then. The gray had picked up the stone while at a hard run. The damage had been done before Jim had felt the break in stride.

It didn't matter. The grey would be in shape again in a week or so. What did matter was that he was here at Bewell in plenty of time to find Lieutenant Porter and tell him what he knew. They'd probably release Dave tonight. Maybe Porter would even head back for Scalplock before morning to make good his false arrest. Only he'd have to bring more men this time, for there were others besides Torrence involved in this.

Breen had told everything, about Shotwell collecting lease money from Torrence for the use of that piece of hill land, about Spence and Birkheimer loaning their crews to help work stolen stuff across to the late Larkin's place. And finally about Wilce. The Army was certainly due to make a cleaning. The lieutenant, if he handled it right, was as sure of a promotion as of the sun rising tomorrow morning.

The tired grey carried him down the last

long gentle slope at a broken trot. The trail widened abruptly and he was riding in on the main gate with the shadows of other buildings beyond and the wide expanse of the parade ground irregularly outlined by an occasional lighted window on its far side. A lantern hung from one gatepost, a sentry standing alongside it, standing stiffly yet at ease. At the other side of the gate was a second sentry, standing in that same easy but alert attitude.

The sentry by the lantern moved over between the gateposts as Jim approached, his carbine cradled in the bend of his elbow.

As Jim drew rein, the trooper drawled, "You're half an hour late, mister. No one allowed inside the post after eight-thirty without a pass. You have one?"

"No. But I've got to see Lieutenant Porter right away. It's important."

The blue and gray clad sentry shook his head. "No can do. It'll have to wait till mornin'."

"Can't you send someone in after the lieutenant? Tell him it's about that arrest he made in Scalplock today. He'll see me if you tell him that."

The trooper frowned. He shrugged finally, turned and said to his companion, "Sam, go find Lieutenant Porter. He's probably at the officers' bar. Tell him what this man says."

"And hurry it, will you?" Jim put in.

The second trooper stepped smartly away into the obscurity, leaving Jim exasperated at this unexpected delay. Jim swung down and lifted the gray's right foreleg for another look at the bruised hoof.

"Looked like he was lame," the sentry said.

Jim nodded. "Got a rock caught in his —"
Crack!

The sharp slap of a rifleshot marked the exact instant Jim's words broke off. Tiredly, letting go the gray's hoof, Jim toppled sideways without straightening. He hit the ground hard on shoulder, rolling onto his back.

The sentry bawled, "Post Four! Get across here!" He lifted the carbine and lined it out into the darkness uncertainly. Then, lowering the weapon, he ran around the fidgeting gray and knelt beside Jim as a call ran the line of the sentry posts. From off to the left came the faint pound of a horse going away.

Another trooper ran up out of the darkness. A bugle's clear notes rang out at the far side of the parade. The one kneeling beside Jim said to the newcomer, "Someone shot him from off there in that brush. Have a look, Ralph." The second trooper ran off toward the brush clump.

The stain on Jim's shirtfront told enough even before the sentry ripped Jim's shirt open and saw the small hole on the left side of the broad chest.

Others were coming up now but the sentry paid them little attention as Jim's eyes opened. He told Jim gently, "Just lay quiet, fella. We'll have you fixed up in a hurry." He asked one of the others to get the doctor as he reached down to fold Jim's shirt back into place.

Several moments later, as they stood staring down at him, Jim tried to say something. But he choked and coughed violently, a racking cough that doubled him up and flecked his lips with blood.

The sentry looked away, said curtly, "Get on out and help Ralph, a couple of you. Whoever shot this man went away on a horse."

Half a dozen troopers left the group, running out toward the brush clump where Ralph was groping around in the dark. One of them had a lantern.

When Jim was breathing shallowly again, he whispered something that the sentry didn't catch. The sentry bent closer.

Jim whispered, "Tell Santell . . . it . . .

it was . . ."

The trooper waited a moment for more, then said, "Go ahead. I got that much. Tell Sam what?"

"Santell!" Jim whispered fiercely. He repeated it again. "Santell."

The trooper nodded. "Santell. The man they brought in this afternoon. I know. Tell him what?"

Jim tried to say something else. But the sentry didn't catch it. Then Jim's whole body went rigid in one last vain effort to draw in another breath. His eyes pled with the trooper to understand.

"Just lay quiet," the sentry said, shaking his head to the others and rocking back on his heels. He heard the approach of several others and added, "This'll be the doctor. You'll be all right."

Jim shook his head weakly. His right hand went out and, palm down, beat the ground, sending up little puffs of dust in the lantern light. He tilted his head and looked at his hand then and some of the tension went out of his face.

He lifted that outspread hand from the ground, made sure the sentry was looking at him. Then, slowly his forefinger traced two marks in the dust.

He had just finished the long wavy line of

the second mark when his hand went limp. His head rocked around loosely.

Jim Land was dead.

Dave was lying in one of the bunks in the guardhouse when the shot came.

The two troopers playing cribbage at the small table beyond — one was in for drunkenness, the other for missing guard mount — went to the window, curious about the shot.

"Maybe one of the boys saw a coyote," one of them said.

They heard shouts from across the parade and the other said dryly, "Yeah. A two-legged coyote."

A bugle sounded and there were a few shouts and the sound of men running.

Dave wasn't particularly interested. He had been here for only two hours. It was comfortable and clean in here and they had fed him well, if late. But he was still smarting under the injustice of his arrest and the prospect of having to wait here for six days until the Major's return seemed more ridiculous each time he thought of it. He was made restless before the unaccountable hunch that something was going to go wrong in Scalplock before his release. What that something would be he had no way of knowing. But he was worried about Gail and Doc, about Jim. Jim was a hard man to prod to anger; but something like this might prompt him to a rash act he would regret later.

Presently, as Dave lay there pondering his own problems, one of the troopers at the window said, "Here comes somebody."

"They ain't headed here," said the other. "They're goin' to the commissary."

"Commissary's closed."

There was a moment of silence. Then: "They're comin' here and they ain't wastin' any time about it."

Dave swung his legs off the bunk and stood up. The big padlock on the heavy door outside banged and, shortly, the inner door swung open on three troopers, Lieutenant Porter and the guardhouse sentry.

The officer looked at Dave and said gravely, "Santell, you'll come with us."

Outside, when the door was closed and padlocked again, they headed out across the wide parade toward the post sutler's and the main gate, the swaying light of a lantern carried by one of the troopers behind them casting elongated shadows of Dave's and the lieutenant's legs.

Dave was waiting for something, he didn't know what.

Presently it came as Porter said gently, "I'll have to tell you, Santell. A man's been killed. He was being held by the sentry while they sent for me. He asked for me. Someone hiding in the brush out beyond the gate shot him. He mentioned your name before he died."

"What did he look like?" Dave asked, finding it hard to speak.

Porter described Jim Land accurately, briefly, adding, "He couldn't talk at the end. He made a mark which may mean something to you. They say he managed to whisper a few words. Something like, 'Tell Santell it was . . .' That's all the sentry could make out."

They had straightened Jim out and covered him with a clean unwrinkled blanket. Moths arced around the lantern sitting nearby on the ground, the flutter of their wings a hushed but pronounced sound in the stillness as the several soldiers nearby stood unmoving, respectfully watching Dave go to his knees beside the mounded blanket.

Dave lifted a corner of the blanket and had his brief look at his friend's still face. Then, dropping the blanket's corner, he stood up.

"Where are the marks?" he asked tonelessly; and his sharp-angled face was graven in the taut-muscled planes of cold anger.

Porter nodded to the left of the blanket mound. "There," he said. "It looks to me like a backward S and then nothing but a crooked line. May not mean a thing but he was trying to talk and couldn't. We thought you ought to see them. Who was he?"

"One of my crew," Dave answered. He knelt again as Porter picked up the lantern and held it closer.

Dave studied the marks, trying to read a meaning into them as related to those last words of Jim's. But, as Porter had said, they had no meaning. One looked like a backward S or a loose-formed numeral 2. The other was nothing but a wavy line or perhaps a weak attempt at the letter I. S — I —. What Scalplock name began with those letters? Could it be Spence? Had Jim been trying to write Spence's name and died before he could finish forming the second letter? No. It couldn't be Spence, Dave realized. Spence didn't have it in him to have planned all the nicely interlocking detail of circumstance of this past week.

"Any ideas Santell?" Porter asked, as Dave stood erect.

Dave shook his head, his bleak glance not leaving those marks.

Porter nodded off into the darkness to the

left where several lanterns swung against the darkness. "He was shot by a man who hid in the brush out there. He was evidently followed from Scalplock. We've found tracks and we have one of our civilian scouts following them with a detail. But we can't accomplish much before morning."

Dave had the impulse to laugh at this mockery. Of course, whoever had shot Jim would take good care to lose his sign long before the light of a new day.

He said, "This ought to prove something to you, Lieutenant."

Porter nodded soberly. "I can assure you we'll do everything we can to get the straight of this."

"Let me go back up to Scalplock and I'll get you the straight of it."

"I'm sorry. But I can't do that," Porter said. "This will have to wait on Major Royce." He coughed discreetly, asking, "What are your instructions on burial?"

Dave tried to think and the lieutenant, seeing him hesitate, said, "We could put him in the fort cemetery."

Dave nodded, turned away. Porter tilted his head to the troopers who had accompanied them across the parade and they fell in behind Dave.

All the way back to the guardhouse,

Dave's thoughts were a muddled and meaningless tangle as he groped for a meaning behind those marks Jim had left in the dust. Red Rhea's death had only angered him. But Jim's was different. He had been closer to the Texan than to most any other man in his crew and these past few days had shown him a dogged loyalty in Jim toward the outfit that made his passing all the harder to realize. Jim had obviously come across here with important news. To the very last he had been on the job, trying his best to help. And death had been his reward.

As the door of the big bunk-lined cell closed behind Dave one of the two guard-house prisoners, the Irishman, asked, "What's up, Texas?"

Dave said, "There was a shooting."

"Shootin'! Anyone hurt?"

"A friend of mine. He was killed."

Irish caught himself on the point of asking another question. He said softly, "That's too bad, Texas," and looked away as Dave went to his bunk and stretched his long frame on it, facing away from the light.

The two troopers sat at the center table again, not speaking often and then only in undertones. There was a friendliness about their gravity that impressed Dave, that steadied his thinking a little.

But over the next half hour, as Irish and his guardhouse mate played blackjack, Dave was unable to make any sense of Jim's death, of the errand that had brought him or of those marks he had scrawled in the dust before he died. Something must have happened there in Scalplock this afternoon after Porter had taken him away. The fact of Jim having been so coldbloodedly shot down brought on a gradual but weighty worry over what might happen to Gail and Doc. And Dave was suddenly afraid.

Gail had been much in his thoughts this evening. Remembering her as he had seen her out the trail there below town, right after the hearing, Dave was stirred by a strange new feeling toward her. Until then, Gail had been a headstrong, spoiled girl who had just as impetuously tried to right an error as she had committed it. But now he saw her as a different person from the one he had first met in Jacob Wilce's office there in Grade. Gone were those surface faults that had so irritated him at first. She was now a person of rare and deep understanding. Furthermore, she had become an exceedingly desirable woman.

He tried to think back in detail over their meeting at midday, reading what he could into the words he remembered. He was struck suddenly and excitedly by the knowledge that Gail had come to mean a great deal to him; and, remembering her look, her words today, he sensed that she cared for him.

Irish forgot for a moment his solemnity as he slapped a card to the table and said in a loud explosive way, "There, by damn! Twenty-one! Pay me!"

Twenty-one!

Dave stiffened on the bunk, seeing again those marks the dying Jim Land had made in the dust, remembering how Jim had last night stood behind Torrence's chair in the *Elite* and listened to the grudging banter that greeted Ed Torrence when the Wheel man proposed that the deal, his deal, be blackjack. Birkheimer had even called Torrence Blackjack a couple of times. And Jim had stood there taking it in.

Jim had written those figures in the dust. Twenty-one! Just as surely as though he had spoken the name aloud, those marks pointed to Ed Torrence.

It was absurdly simple now. Of course it was Ed Torrence, had been all along. The man was shrewd and brainy enough to have thought out the complicated processes by which the cattle had been stolen from the reservation since last winter. It would have taken a brain like Torrence's to conceive of the bold plan Breen had executed in relieving Dave of that small herd so close to the reservation. Dave's frameup there in Grade hadn't been overly clever; but the way it had been tied in with Breen's act had taken some imagination.

And all along Torrence had been friendly, actually taking Dave's side against the rawhiding of the other Scalplock men. Until just a moment ago, Dave had respected Torrence, even liked him.

Now the intricate meshes of this tangled web of circumstances fell away and everything was clear.

Dave came off the bunk, went to the door and pounded on it, calling, "Guard!"

Irish turned in his chair at the table, drawling, "What come over you, Texas?"

He couldn't understand Dave's broad smile, even less his slow spoken words, "Soldier, I've just waked out of a long sleep."

XXI

Only one light marked the town at this late hour, past eleven. But for his knowing that that light was shining from the side window of Tucker's back office, that the accountant often worked late and that Wilce was in Scalplock, Frank wouldn't have dared even to ride into the street. But he knew that, for the time being, he was safe. And it wouldn't take long to get his things and leave. Leave for good.

He passed the squat buildings of the mission, set well back from the street, and he had this added visual reminder of his deepest regret at having to leave this country. Under different circumstances, he knew that he would long ago have asked Martha to marry him. And now the prospect of living the rest of his life without her seemed the entirety of his punishment. That, and that alone, was to be the one thing that would matter. Not just now, but for the rest of his life he would be paying for his wrongdoing by being without Martha.

Turning in off the square with its darkened buildings, he rode through the wide open gate of the compound and straight across to the agency, the steeldust's steps muffled by the heavy dust. It lacked only a few days of the first of the month and Tucker would give him what pay was due him. He'd already thought up an explanation for that; he'd lost at cards and needed his pay to settle his debts.

He swung down out of the saddle, tired

and stiff from the long hard ride. He groundhaltered the gelding and went up onto the rear stoop, pushed the door open and stepped into Tucker's office.

Jacob Wilce, in the swivel chair behind the desk, swung around from the filing cabinet. There was instant surprise, then unmistakable alarm patterning his long and narrow face.

Two drawers of the filing cabinet were open. Papers littered the desk, some crumpled and a pile of them disarranged, a few stacked neatly to one side. The brass lamp on the desk was turned high and without its shade; the light was bright.

This much Frank saw as his hand was settling close in to his right thigh. He saw the high wariness on the agent's sallow face and didn't understand it.

Then Wilce was saying with false casualness, "Didn't know you were around, Erbeck."

The agent's ingratiating tone puzzled Frank. "Didn't know you were either, Major," he said.

"Then you'd heard I was in Scalplock?" Wilce asked. He didn't wait for Frank's reply but went on hastily, "I thought of something that needed attending to. Rode a horse back instead of the buggy."

"You came in a hurry."

The agent nodded and seemed to want to swallow yet not to be able to. "Came straight across without following the trail," he said thickly. That explanation didn't seem to satisfy him, for he added, "I'm trying to help the Army get their hands on these men who've been running off our beef."

"Are you now?" Frank drawled, nicely concealing his surprise at Wilce's strange attitude of confession. "Havin' any luck?"

The Major seemed to take some heart from this mild reply, going on hurriedly, "Santell was arrested in Scalplock today. I've been working with the Army on this for some time. We're about to make some other arrests."

Frank's bewilderment was growing at the agent's uncalled-for manner. There was no trace of arrogance in the Major now. Rather, he was abjectly humble, no longer the imperious tyrant who had held the whiplash of blackmail over Frank these past months. The change in the man was hard to understand. But it was there, unmistakably. Jacob Wilce seemed almost afraid.

When Frank said nothing, the agent blurted out suddenly, "You'll be sure and include this in your report, won't you, Erbeck?"

"Report?" Frank echoed. Then, cautiously: "I'll have to think about it, Major."

"But I haven't had a thing to do with this rustling," Wilce protested. "You may think I have, but I haven't. They were stealing me blind. Breen was the ring leader and I foolishly fired him instead of turning him over to the authorities."

What Wilce was saying was taking on a broadening implication. Frank led him on, drawling, "And here I've thought all along that you were hooked up with Breen."

The Major shook his head violently. It wasn't warm in here, for the windows were open and the night's chill had penetrated the room. Yet the agent's thin face and bald head were shiny with perspiration.

"No, you don't understand, Erbeck. If I'd had enough to go on against Breen, I'd have called in one of you men from the marshal's office long ago. I wanted proof to back an arrest. It took me this long to get it."

"So?"

Frank had a hard time believing his hearing. Wilce had called him a marshal.

"You believe me, don't you?" the agent insisted.

"I'll have to think it over, Major. For instance, I didn't know Santell had had anything to do with this. Remember?" he

346

added dryly, knowing the agent would understand what he was referring to.

Wilce laughed uneasily. "The money I had you plant in his room? That was part of my investigation. I suspected him all along of being in with Breen and wanted to get a confession out of him."

"Is that why you turned him loose?"

"No. He wouldn't talk. So I turned him loose to see what he'd do. He went straight to Breen."

"And half killed him," Frank drawled.

Wilce took a dirty polka-dot bandana from his pocket and mopped his face and head. "That fight was framed," he said. "Today we found out that Santell made arrangements for this rustling with Breen when he was here to draw up a new contract last winter."

Frank merely smiled as the agent finished his explanation. Wilce eyed him guardedly and, as the silence dragged out, he became plainly more nervous.

Finally the agent could stand that direct look of Frank's no longer. He asked uneasily, "Have you brought any charges against me yet?"

More became plain to Frank. Wilce was indeed afraid of him. For some unexplained reason the agent thought this crewman of his was a federal officer. And the fact of Wilce having been in so much of a hurry to get back from Scalplock to Grade had an unmistakable meaning when coupled with this late hour and the litter of papers on the desk. He had been caught in the act of destroying some of those papers, incriminating ones probably.

It wasn't until this moment that Frank spotted the bulging scarred suitcase, the end of which protruded beyond the far edge of the desk. He knew now. He had caught Wilce on the point of leaving, probably leaving the reservation for good.

Taking his cue from the Major's last question, he said blandly, "Maybe I'll prefer charges, maybe not."

"But your word will count. Now that you know the facts, will you tell them I wasn't in any way involved? I'll admit certain things seemed peculiar. But I was only trying to get this thing ironed out."

Frank laughed softly. "You're askin' a lot, Major."

Wilce sagged down in the chair, what little fight there was left in him abruptly gone.

"I knew it," he breathed miserably. "I knew I'd wait too long, that no one would understand."

There was a brief but faint look of defiance in his eyes. "But they can't punish an innocent man. And I'm innocent!"

"Then you needn't worry."

Something struck Frank then so forcibly that he almost laughed aloud. He sauntered over to the desk, letting the idea take quick shape in his mind. He held out a hand and rubbed thumb and third finger together, smiling broadly. "How much?" he drawled.

Wilce looked up, puzzled. "How much what?"

"Money, Major. How much is it worth to have me forget the whole thing until you've crossed the Territory line?"

The slow birth of hope blended with the fear and alarm in the agent's eyes. He pushed up in the chair, sitting straighter. "A thousand," he said.

Frank laughed, softly, derisively. "Come again. You've made a real cleanin'."

"How do I know you won't turn me in anyway?"

Wilce's shrewdness was coming alive again as he indirectly admitted his guilt and saw nothing strange in Frank not accusing him of it in so many words.

"You don't. But if I do, you can cost me my job and send me up for a sweet stretch."

The agent's glance narrowed. "Two thousand and you give me a written receipt."

349

Frank shook his head. "Five and nothing written."

Wilce's eyes blazed defiance. "Five! I haven't got that much."

"You can dig it up somewhere, Major. You took in some nice change on those critters. And there's your split with Ott."

The agent's face reddened. Frank cut short the man's unspoken protest with, "There's enough against you to put you away for life. Five thousand is a cheap buy off."

"What would you report when they find I'm gone?"

"Nothing. I wouldn't know why you left."

Wilce considered this and said finally, "But I don't have five thousand. I could get my hands on maybe thirty-five hundred at the outside."

Frank gave a slow shake of the head. "Five."

Wilce sighed wearily, said, "All right, five," and came up out of the chair. Frank saw the move of his right hand, on his far side, in under his coat. Frank snatched up the nearest heavy object, a pen holder, a pebbled glass jar filled with bird shot. He threw it and it hit Wilce's shoulder, jarring him. Frank's up-arcing fist clipped the Major alongside the jaw an instant later. Wilce slammed back into the filing cabinet, tripped and fell. Frank's boot came down hard on the wrist that held the gun the man had drawn from his shoulder-holster.

"Good thing it didn't come off," Frank said. "You might have been in real trouble."

He stooped, jerked the gun from the agent's hand and tossed it to the other side of the desk, into the wastebasket. "Now let's see what your private bankroll looks like, Major."

The agent was badly shaken when he stood erect once more. Anger and shame whitened his face. But there was fear in it, too; fear that kept him wordless and turned him to the door leading to the front office.

He went to the safe and knelt there and Frank let him swing the safe door open before drawling dryly, "No you don't, Major! That'll be agency money in there. I want a cut on the stake you've salted away."

The quiet positiveness of his voice seemed to wipe out the last spark of fight left in the agent. He came to his feet and, beyond the desk, opened the wide doors of a high wardrobe. At the floor of the big compartment, in which hung his clothes, the Major opened a big drawer. Frank stood close to him, looking over his shoulder, making sure that he made no false move.

Wilce pulled the drawer out and laid it aside on the shabby carpet. He pushed a board in the bottom of the wardrobe and it tilted under his hand to disclose a small secret compartment. Even before he reached for it, Frank saw the thick sheaf of bank-notes.

There was a little more than eleven thousand in the bundle of greenbacks. Wilce squatted on the floor, staring up with a beady eye as Frank counted it.

Finally, Frank looked down. "There ought to be more'n this," he drawled.

Wilce shook his head. "There would be. Only Torrence —"

He stiffened as his words broke off. A look of incredulity, then a smile, came to Frank's face. "So it's been Torrence all along!" he breathed.

The Major seemed about to protest, didn't. A strange twisted grimace intended for a smile patterned his narrow features. He said softly, intently, "Yes, Torrence. And Birkheimer and Spence and Shotwell. I was a fool to ever let Torrence bluff me into it. If it hadn't been for him, no one would ever have known."

Frank said, "Hell, I thought you'd made a real cleanin'." He thumbed several of the bills loose, handed them to the agent.

"Here's two hundred. You'd better spend it buyin' horses. I can give you maybe two days to get away. You'd better go east and hit the railroad. They won't be expectin' that."

The Major took the money, looking down at it with a dull stare. Abruptly, his glance lifted to Frank and there was glaring anger in his eyes. But when he laughed dryly, Frank saw that that emotion wasn't directed at him.

"You'll take care of the others, Erbeck?"

Frank nodded.

Again, Wilce laughed, this time louder. "I'd give my right arm to see Torrence behind the bars! And Shotwell on bread and water! Spence and Birkheimer don't matter. They never had anything before anyway. Remember Breen, too. He was in on it. So was Holmes."

"They'll be taken care of, Major." Frank tilted his head toward the back office door. "Better be on your way."

Some five minutes later, Wilce sat the saddle of a scrawny bay, one of Hult's horses. He looked down at Frank, his face a pale blob against the darkness, the slump of his shoulders pronouncing him an exceedingly humble and chastened man.

But he had a spark of spirit left, enough

to say, "If they catch up with me, I'll see you broken, Erbeck."

"They won't," Frank drawled.

Wilce lifted his reins without a further word. He rode through the gate of the compound and finally his shadow was lost to sight in the further darkness.

Frank waited there, listening to the bay's footfalls fade out into the night's stillness, awed by the weight of the bundle of banknotes he still held in one hand. Here was lifelong security for him, for Jacob Wilce would think enough of his own skin never to mention what had happened to the money. The future might swallow the name of Frank Erbeck, might erase it from men's memory, but the man who had carried that name would never be in want; not with a start like this!

A sudden revulsion was in Frank. Before he had quite defined the impulse, he had turned in through the door of Tucker's now darkened office, crossing it to the front room. His groping hand touched the door of the safe behind Wilce's desk. He reached in, laid the bundle of money on a shelf, and quickly swung the safe door shut and spun the combination. He was breathing heavily as he straightened, thinking of what he had done. But that old self-loathing was gone completely now. He felt somehow clean and refreshed after the decision he had just made.

Regardless of the past, of the killing that lay as a blot on the record of his life, Frank Erbeck knew in this moment that he would never again hang his head. This act of honesty seemed to tip again the balances of his life, weighing out the bad.

Out in the compound once more, his thoughts turned actively toward another thing; and he revised his plans for leaving. He knew that he owed it to Dave to go out by way of Fort Bewell. He would find the officer who had today arrested Dave and tell enough of what he had learned so that Dave would be released. What was to happen to Dave after that was none of his concern.

He went across to the crew shack, finding it empty, knowing that all the crew must now be at the agency camp on the Muddy pretending to be hunting the cattle they had helped Ray Breen steal.

He gathered his few belongings and rolled them into his blanket and crossed the compound again to tie the blanket roll on his saddle.

The steeldust was tired and Frank would have liked a fresh horse. But he would ride the animal anyway; it belonged to him and he didn't want to have a horse-stealing charge placed against him. So he once more mounted the much-travelled gelding and went out the gate and across the sleeping plaza. Suddenly he was trying to imagine the expression that would be on Tucker's face tomorrow when he discovered the bundle of banknotes in the safe; he laughed softly, and again felt that new lightheartedness that had come with having returned the money.

He could have avoided going along the upper street. He could have turned out across the vacant lot next to the blacksmith shop. Farther up, he had a second chance to leave the street by riding back along the wide lot flanking the agency warehouse. Yet something drew him on, keeping him to the street. He realized finally, bleakly, that he wanted one last glimpse of the mission's shadowed buildings, wanted to burn into his consciousness the utter futility of these hopes concerning Martha.

He was almost even with Doc Faris's house when a voice spoke to him out of the darkness of the broad elm tree flanking the medico's yard walk.

"Frank!"

It was Martha.

He drew rein and swung down out of the saddle as she came out to him. The indistinct oval of her face turned up to him as she came close.

"I thought it was you," she said. "I couldn't sleep. I was sitting on the porch when you rode past and I was coming down to see you." He saw her head turn and knew that she had seen the blanket roll. "Where are you going, Frank?"

"Away again."

"For long?"

"Can't tell yet."

He tried to make his tone casual, matter of fact. Yet it didn't deceive Martha, for she said with a rising inflection in her voice,

"Frank, you're leaving for good!"

He knew then that she knew him too well for any pretense to carry. He said flatly, "My time's up here. Now's my chance to leave without any fuss, without anyone caring."

"I care, Frank," Martha murmured. "You know that, don't you?"

He nodded, not trusting himself to speak.

"I've known it was coming," she went on. She laughed uneasily, barely audibly. "I've even planned that you might take me with you. I've bought that horse they've let me ride. I even planned where we would go. It would be Canada. You'd change your name and I would be a Mrs. Smith or a Mrs. Jordan. You'd give me any name. It wouldn't matter so long as we were together."

"But we'd be strays, Martha. In the end you'd grow to hate me."

"Would I, Frank?" she asked softly. And, with a slow shake of the head: "No, never! We'd make a new beginning. It's all I'd ever want. Frank, you're not bad. You did what you did because you had to. The law wouldn't understand that. But we know in our hearts that we're right. That's the only law I care about."

Suddenly he reached out and, tenderly, reverently almost, drew Martha to him and kissed her full on the lips.

"How long will it take you to get ready to ride for Fort Bewell?" he asked presently.

The faint light let him see the questioning yet trustful look that came to her face as she glanced up at him. "It begins here, doesn't it, Frank?" she asked. "Our trust in each other. I'll be ready in ten minutes. Five if you say."

He reached for the steeldust's reins. "Make it five," he drawled softly, his arm about her. And they turned up the street toward the mission.

XXII

The sun's brassy disk had slid from sight over the far flat horizon and in this lingering last full light the mounted troopers of E Troop were lined smartly along the parade, standing retreat and guard mount, the clear strains of two bugles echoing back from the maple grove at the quadrangle's southern limit.

Dave stood at the barred window, behind his two cellmates who leaned on the sill of the opening, watching. Irish said intently, "Up, Daniels. Up front with that guidon!"

"Try stayin' sober and Daniels wouldn't have to learn your job," the other said disparagingly.

The sentry call ran the posts as the troop finally swung right by twos at a smart trot toward the stables. Then, abruptly, the parade was deserted, dust hanging over it in a motionless thin haze. The two troopers turned from the window, Irish suggesting to Dave, "Some cards until they bring our grub? Blackjack, say?"

Dave said, "Later," leaning with one elbow on the window's sill, the trooper's words reminding him again of last night and of seeing Jim lying there so peacefully and of the marks Jim had left behind to point to

Ed Torrence.

Last night's interview with Lieutenant Porter had galled him, made him furious. He had said some strong things to Porter then and this morning, after the service at Jim's grave in the post cemetery. What he had said he had worded so bluntly, with such anger, that his several attempts to see the lieutenant and reason with him since this morning had brought just as many refusals. The cold fact was that he was being held here until Major Royce's return. Porter wouldn't even send a detail back to Scalplock to arrest Torrence.

"He'll be there when we want him," Porter had said last night, adding pointedly, "*if* we want him."

Dave had been broiled bodily and mentally throughout this long day. For the guardhouse was close, oven hot, and little protected from the sun. Dave's inner raging torment against the injustice of being held here was as violent an emotion as he had ever experienced. Yet there was nothing he could do about it and now, at this day's end, he was beginning to accept the inevitable.

He glanced idly down the parade toward the lane that led to the main gate, between the post sutler's store and the quartermaster's storehouse. Most of the evening's activity was centered there, with the store lights already on, groups of troopers idling there and beyond at the post bakery and at the sutler's wagon-yard, where a six-team freight-hitch was unloading. Here, as in Grade, a small hotel occupied the second floor of one of the principal commercial buildings, the post sutler's. The middle window above the combination store and bar was lettered simply, *Hotel,* and access to the rooms was gained by an outside covered stairway.

There were signs of permanence to this post. Two of the barracks were frame-built, their new white paint contrasting favorably with the makeshift slab and log construction of their neighbors. The laundry, the gun sheds and the hospital were newly erected, too, and this scattering of fresh construction seemed incongruous alongside the more primitive and disorderly array of stables, corrals and sheds that were fast being replaced.

At the table behind Dave, the two troopers talked sparsely but sometimes violently over a game of whist. At another time and in other circumstances, Dave would doubtless have found them entertaining. Irish was red-faced and keen witted, the other a New Englander whose slow thought processes laid him open to constant goodnatured baiting. Yet now their talk was only an annoyance to Dave. His brooding thoughts got him nowhere and he would have been better off in calmly accepting this bad turn of luck. Yet he resented, without showing it, the interruptions they made in his constant attempt to think his way out of this predicament.

Just now he turned irritably from the window as the Irishman's loud laughter filled the room. Then, as abruptly as he had left the window, he wheeled back to it again, staring hard across the parade. A moment ago he had seen something that meant little to him. Yet now, and suddenly, it did.

He knew that steeldust horse swinging in toward the wagonyard adjoining the post sutler's, recognized the blocky slouched figure in the saddle. It was Frank Erbeck! The other rider on the smaller bay, slighter than Frank, he didn't know. Only when Frank went across to help Martha down out of the saddle did he know that it was a woman.

The barred door to the guardhouse rattled open and the cook's helper came in and ladled out portions of beef stew into the stoneware bowls of the three prisoners. "Time to eat, stranger," he said to Dave.

But Dave still stared out across the parade and didn't hear him and he looked at the two troopers and shrugged and went out again, the door closing after him.

Presently, the New Englander said, "Get it while it's hot, Texas!"

Dave came across to them then but, instead of sitting at the table, took his bowl of stew back to the window. A moment ago he had seen Frank Erbeck lugging his blanket-roll and the woman's suitcase up the stairway to the hotel over the post sutler's. He didn't want to miss what Frank did next.

"He don't like our company," the Irishman drawled pointedly.

And now Dave turned and the first real smile of the day came to his angular face. "Too much hot air over there," he drawled. "It's cool here." He added, his grin widening, "In about an hour I'll be ready to clean you at twenty-one, Irish."

"A sucker, Bill," the Irishman told the other, straightfaced. But it was obvious that what Dave had said had eased the strained feeling between them.

Dave had nearly finished the stew when Frank reappeared out of the stairway opening across the parade. He met Martha there and they talked for a few moments, Martha then going upstairs and Frank sauntering over to a group of troopers nearby. Presently, one of the troopers and Frank headed out across the near end of the parade toward the officer's quarters.

In the fading light, Dave couldn't be sure, but he thought that the officer Frank was talking to on the veranda of the building was Lieutenant Porter. He grew impatient as the light failed him entirely and he could no longer distinguish anything but lampglow at the windows down there. He left the window finally, drawling, "Ready for your lickin', Irish?"

They started a blackjack game with a nickel limit on the betting. Dave couldn't have told why the sight of Frank had done him so much good; but it had and he played with a sure recklessness that, in twenty minutes, had him a dollar and a half the winner.

He wasn't surprised at the end of that interval when the heavy lock bar on the outside door beyond the small guardroom rattled and, shortly, the inner door opened on Frank Erbeck and a trooper wearing a corporal's stripes.

"Man to see you, Santell," the corporal announced. He tilted his head toward the front guardroom, used by the sentries in winter weather. "You can talk out here."

Dave stepped out past him and into the small room beyond, not speaking to Frank until the cell door was locked, then the outside one closed on the guard and the corporal. Then:

"It's good to see you, Erbeck."

Frank's smile was wry and unamused. "I thought I might help," he said, coming abruptly to the point. "But the lieutenant takes his regulations to heart. They heard today that the major's been delayed another week. You stay right where you are until he gets back."

Dark anger was on Dave's face as Frank went on, gravely, "He told me about Jim. If you say the word I'll head back to Scalplock and settle with Torrence."

"So you know," Dave said.

Frank nodded. "More than you do, likely. Shotwell and Birkheimer and Spence are in on it, too, helpin' Torrence."

"How did you find that out?"

"Wilce." And Frank told of his meeting with the agent last night. He mentioned Martha and the fact that he was leaving the country with her. He ended by saying, with a thin smile. "We were going to be married here. But I figured Porter might remember the name. So we're registered at the hotel as Frank and Martha Horne, brother and sister. I work for you and my sister came up from Texas by train and met me in Grade." . . . He gave a long slow sigh. . . . "I thought I could help, Dave. But Porter's too anxious to keep his shoulder bars in place. Says there's no danger of Torrence high-tailin'. I tell him there is, just as soon as Torrence finds Wilce has beat it."

Dave nodded soberly. "I tried to tell him to go over to Scalplock and arrest Torrence. He wouldn't listen."

"So did I. He said it could wait. He's got a week's trip takin' a paymaster's detail up to the post on Yellow River. The detail leaves at ten tonight. Says he can't spare the men to send to Scalplock. It looks to me like he thought I'd made it all up about Wilce. He's an untrustin' son!"

Dave stood silently a moment, the lack of expression on his face betraying to Frank his bitter disappointment.

Frank said shortly, looking around at the rock walls, "It'd take more'n one man to bust you out of this joint."

Dave nodded soberly. "Couldn't be done. It —"

His head came up and he gave Frank a coolly appraising look. "Or could it?" he drawled. He glanced down to Frank's empty waist, asking, "Where's your iron?"

Frank shrugged. "They made me check it at the store. Post regulations, they said."

"Could you buy another one?" Dave asked quickly.

"I thought of that. But the only thing they'll sell a man is one of those pepper boxes. Four-tens, I think they are, and they don't even handle the shells for 'em."

"Never mind the shells. You could buy one then?"

"Sure. But it'd be empty."

"Do you drink much?"

Frank frowned at the unexpected and seemingly irrelevant question. He smiled briefly. "Who doesn't?"

Dave glanced toward the door, having heard a moment ago the scrape of the sentry's boots on the wooden step beyond the door. When he spoke again it was in a lower hushed tone. "It might be done," he told Frank. "And here's how." He went on, speaking quickly and softly and without interruption.

Frank interrupted with only one objection. "Why so early?" he asked. "You'd double your chances if you made it around midnight when everyone's asleep."

Dave shook his head. "It'll make it pretty late for findin' Torrence around as it is.

Don't worry, I'll make it."

"Not on your own, you won't."

"On my own," Dave stated. "I don't risk your neck along with my own."

"We'll see," Frank said, plainly not agreeing to this last.

Five minutes later Frank pounded on the outside door, calling, "We're through, soldier."

The sentry let Frank out. He came in and was swinging the door shut when Frank called a parting, "See you tomorrow, Dave."

The outside door was bolted. The sentry slanted his carbine under his arm and motioned Dave to the far end of the small room while he unlocked the cell door. He opened it and, stepping back, motioned Dave in.

"Let's gang up on him," Irish said to his partner as Dave sat in at the game again.

That evening, the actions of the man who had signed the hotel register as Frank Horne would have puzzled anyone interested enough to follow and watch him. First, he ate a late meal with the young woman known as his sister. They sat at the lunch counter at the rear of the post sutler's. Afterward, he took her as far as the foot of the outside hotel stairway and on leaving her, kissed her with an exceedingly unbrotherly warmth.

Next, he went back into the store and bought one of the wicked looking pepper-box derringers on display in one of the cases. He asked again for shells for the weapon and was told that there were none.

The noncommissioned officer's and enlisted men's bar was in the big room adjoining the sutler's store. This man calling himself Horne went in there and across to the bar and bought a quart bottle of whiskey. He asked the barkeep for a glass and, getting a heavy big tumbler, proceeded to uncork the bottle and half fill the tumbler and drink it down at a double swallow. He coughed, got red in the face and wiped his mouth with the back of his hand. When the barkeep offered him a water chaser, the interested troopers who looked on heard him answer, "And spoil this? No thanks." He left the saloon as the quiet laughter of the troopers ran along the bar.

Some forty minutes later this Horne pushed in through the saloon's street door and stood spraddle-legged and blinking against the strong light of the lamps. A few of the troopers who had seen him buy the whiskey earlier noticed quite a change in him. For one thing, his curl-brimmed Stetson was gone. His dark straight hair was mussed, strands of it hanging down over his eyes which were now bleary-looking and barely slitted open. He held the bottle in his left hand and it was empty. One sleeve of his shirt was rolled up, the other hanging around his wrist unbuttoned. He looked very drunk.

He ran his tongue over his lips in a dry thirsty way and then started for the bar in the deliberate cautious walk that is typical of the inebriated. He was weaving a little and his unsteady stride took him close past the front poker layout, where three troopers and two civilians played draw.

Just even with the table, he seemed momentarily to lose his balance. He staggered into the trooper in the nearest chair, tried to catch himself but couldn't. He fell elbow-down on the table, spilling the trooper's stacks of chips out across the table to mix with those at the center.

The trooper lunged up, swore angrily, heaved Horne erect and pushed him away. Horne wheeled on the trooper, swung his bottle at the trooper's head, missed, and fell sprawling back across the lap of one of the civilians. This man cuffed him hard in the face and he struck back harder as he came to his feet. Then he wheeled and hit the trooper twice in the face. The fight was on.

That drunken unsteadiness had left Frank the moment he was hit that first time. Now, fortified by his one long drink, he set about creating as much damage as he could in what he knew was to be a very brief space of time; after all, he had come here expecting a beating.

He wheeled away from the first trooper and connected with a hard long roundhouse in the chest of a second, rising from the table. He shouldered the civilian, a small man, backward so that his victim fell onto the table, overturning it and spilling bottles, chips and cards to the floor. He wheeled back out of reach of the trooper he'd just hit and threw his bottle, intentionally missing. It sailed barward and struck a shelfful of glasses there, sweeping them to the back counter in a musical tinkling of broken glass.

Someone hit him from behind, hit him hard and with stunning impact. He turned and slugged and a trooper piled onto his back and he went down.

Someone bawled, "Don't kill 'im! He's only drunk!" and a man's belly-down weight fell across his legs to pin him to the floor. Another dropped knees first on his back, driving the wind from his lungs in a reaching groan. He went limp, pretending to be out.

Two of the post police carried him across to the guardhouse, one holding him by the armpits, the other by his boots.

"He don't fool, does he?" one of the troopers asked, breathing hard under his burden.

They threw him into a lower bunk in the guardhouse. He heard Dave ask, "What happened to Horne?" and one of the police answered, "He just busted up the saloon, is all." Then, shortly, the door closed and through slitted lids Frank saw Dave and the two troopers resume their blackjack game, Dave being questioned on the identity of his drunken friend.

When he was sure they weren't looking and that he was fairly well hidden in the shadow beyond the lamp's reach, Frank unbuckled his belt and unknotted the two bandanas tied inside his shirt. He pulled them from around his waist, the derringer knotted to them. He slipped the small weapon into a pocket of his denims. Then he lifted his boots off the straw-ticking mattress and sat up.

The Irishman was the first to look at him. He fixed the trooper with a gimlet eye, drawled thickly, "Y' hit me, y' big red-faced moose!" He lunged up off the cot then and toward the Irishman who, alarmed now, stood up quickly, saying, "Not me, brother! That was somebody else! Cool down!"

But Frank came at Irish and swung a fist, swung it loosely and intending to miss. He pitched forward against the table, skidding it to the far wall as Dave and the other lunged away.

Dave came up to him, saying sharply, "Frank! They didn't do it! Go back to bed!"

Frank pushed Dave away, for a moment turning his back on the two troopers and handing Dave the derringer. He grunted, "You lemme 'lone, Dave." Then, facing around, he advanced on the New Englander, his fists coming up.

Irish bawled, "Guard! Guard!" as Frank swung on the other. Frank missed and lurched into a bunk upright, barely managing to keep his feet. The lock at the door rattled and the door swung open as Frank was advancing on the short trooper once more.

Dave called quickly, "Horne's tearin' the room apart. Better put him to bed again."

The sentry leaned out the door, laid his carbine on the floor there, then closed the door. He drew his Colt's and drawled, "You gents stay set!" and advanced on Frank with his face set stonily and a hard stare of purpose in his eye.

Dave lined the derringer and said, "Reach, soldier! Drop that iron!"

There was something in his tone that stopped the sentry. He looked back over his shoulder at Dave. He saw the four barrels of the derringer staring at him and his face went slack. Frank stepped in at him then and, with a sudden blow, knocked the weapon from his hand. Frank picked up the sixgun and tossed it to Dave as the sentry lifted his hands.

Dave backed to the door, drawling, "You're not comin', Frank," when Frank started toward him.

Frank said, "The hell I'm not!" and kept coming.

Dave reached behind him and opened the door and wheeled out through it, slamming it before Frank could stop him. He pushed the lockbar into its hanger as Frank beat on the heavy panel, calling, "Dave, damn it! Let me out!" Dave turned then and ran through the open outer door.

Just as he reached the edge of the door-lantern's arc of light, the sentry bawled from the cell window, "Guard! Prisoner on the loose!"

Dave ran out toward the officers' quarters, wanting to make sure that if he was seen they would think he was headed in that direction. But in another twenty yards he swung to the right, toward the stables and the picket line. There, some minutes ago, he had watched the paymaster's detail saddling their mounts for their night's ride.

Off across the parade, a bugle sounded the alarm. Dave knew that every second he could gain was in his favor, so he bawled stridently, "Fire! Fire!" seeing the lamps in the nearby barracks come on one by one. As he ran he opened the loading gate of the sentry's .45 Colt's and thrust the gun through the waistband of his pants, wedging it securely there.

He was breathing hard and his run had slowed when he came to the end of the picket line where the mules and horses were tied. Down at the far end he saw two troopers running out from the near door of the stables. He picked the nearest horse, untied the animal's reins, then fumbled at the knot of the picket rope secured to the heavy ring in the end post.

He worked loose that knot as the troopers halted at the far end of the line, looking off across the parade toward the guardhouse. He dropped the rope, swung up onto the divided seat of the army saddle and let out a whoop that sent the nearest mule shying into the one alongside.

As the mules bolted away from him, breaking from the sagging picket rope, he bent low to the horse's neck and started for the gun sheds obliquely to his right. Somewhere close he heard a sentry cry, "Prisoner escaped! Challenge and fire!" That call went down the line of the sentry posts and died out in the distance.

He was even with a gun shed, then riding the passageway between it and the next, knowing he hadn't been seen yet. The chock of his horse's hooves echoed hollowly between the two buildings, so loudly that he was sure it would be heard.

He came even with the rear of the sheds and reined in there, studying the shadows. Twenty yards to his left he could see the narrow shape of a sentry box. To his right, and farther away, there was another.

Abruptly, shouts sounded nearby, coming closer. He bent close over the gelding's withers once more and gouged hard with the heels of his boots.

The animal left the foot of the passageway in a sudden lunge, nearly throwing him.

A challenge rang across the night, "Halt! Who's there?"

He let his weight sag onto the off stirrup, his head and one shoulder behind the running horse's neck. A carbine's sharp explosion blended with the quick drum of the pony's hooves. The clawing branches of a brush thicket whipped in at his face and shoulders. A second shot spoke from another direction and still the horse's full-out run held steadily, powerfully.

He straightened finally and looked back. The buildings back there were lost in the black blanket of the night. He realized he had been holding his breath and now he let it out in a long relieved exhalation.

Presently, he swung to the right and toward the Scalplock trail, the hard pressure of the gun at his waist reminding him of his errand.

Lieutenant Porter listened to the report of the corporal of the guard. "Prisoner escaped, sir. Santell. He was seen leaving the grounds out beyond the gun sheds."

Porter returned the trooper's salute, swinging around then and telling the bugler, "Go ahead."

The call To Horse rang across the parade and running troopers led their trotting mounts from the direction of the stables, quickly forming a ragged line at the edge of the parade, counting off, urged on by the sergeant's acid tones.

Shortly, the sergeant bawled, "Detail

ready, sir!"

Porter took the reins from his orderly, swinging astride the big black. "Prepare to mount!" he called. Then, "Mount! Left by twos, march!" He looked behind until they were lined out neatly. Then he called, "Gallop!" and used his spurs, heading for the main gate.

All this Frank heard and saw from the guardhouse window. As the last echo of hurrying hoofbeats faded out the trail, he turned back into the room, saying, "What was that game you boys were playin' when I came in, Irish?"

"Blackjack."

"Deal me a hand," Frank drawled, taking the extra chair.

XXIII

Scalplock was restless tonight. It had been ever since Gillis, the mail rider, had arrived shortly after dark with news he thought important enough to bring across without waiting for day after tomorrow's trip with the mail. Jacob Wilce had disappeared from the reservation. It was reported that Tucker had found a lot of money in the agency safe, money that couldn't be accounted for.

Doc Faris and Tom Warren had been on

the street late, listening to the various theories propounded over the Major's strange absence. Some Indians on a hunt over by Crow Butte had heard a rider pass their camp just before dawn this morning and hadn't thought much of it, so Gillis said. Crow Butte was far to the southeast, and if the unknown rider had been Wilce there was every indication that he was headed for the railroad. No one in Grade, not even the agency accountant Tucker, could hazard a guess on why the Major would be headed for the railroad. There was, of course, the probability that he was on government business he hadn't mentioned to anyone. But his manner of leaving had aroused suspicion.

Shortly after the Grade doctor and Tom Warren had gone back down to the saddlemaker's house, the lights there went out. That was just before ten. Now, an hour and a half later, there were still men on the street, their comings and goings given a furtive quality by the lateness of this near-midnight hour.

Ed Torrence, who had been summoned from Wheel, rode down off the east trail about eleven and turned his horse into the livery corral, immediately heading for the *Elite*. Huck Birkheimer met him at the bar, and shortly afterward came to the saloon doorway to call, "Shotwell! Where's Shotwell?" His hail was relayed on up the street until presently the storeowner came down from his house and joined Torrence and Birkheimer at the saloon's back table.

Pete Holmes, the 'breed, had hung around all evening listening to the talk and keeping out of it. Now he sat back-tilted in a caboose chair to one side of the closed livery barn door. He was seemingly drowsing or asleep, for his head rested back against the boards and his wide black hat was pushed down over his face. In reality, he was wide awake. Later, when it was quiet, he would meet Ray Breen down the trail below town and let the big man know what was going on. Breen was keeping out of sight, afraid of what would happen if he met Torrence. He had talked a lot yesterday to that McCune man and couldn't remember what he had said; but he sensed that, whatever it was, he had said too much and that Torrence knew about it.

Just by listening, Pete Holmes could feel the tension that held Scalplock tonight. The undertone of talk coming from the half dozen Wheel and Spence riders loafing under the saloon awning was subdued and cautious. Those men sensed, as the 'breed did, that their future had suddenly become a great deal more insecure than it had been yesterday, or earlier today for that matter. They had guessed at Torrence's dealings with Wilce and now were wondering whether to drift out of the country or await further developments.

Pete Holmes himself was worried. If there was to be any final reckoning for this half year of rustling, he didn't want to be there. He had been involved in everything shady around the reservation for several years and he would rightly be suspected of having been in this. His instinct told him to ride now, to ride anywhere so long as he put the miles between him and Scalplock. But he knew no other country, no other town, and he had a lost helpless feeling that seemed to rob him of any initiative, of making up his mind definitely to anything.

He would wait and see what Ray was going to do. He'd go with Ray, if the big man would have him. He wasn't even sure of that.

Spence's two hired hands presently mounted and rode down the street, cutting close past this near end of the barn to hit the east trail. One of them said, loud enough for Holmes to overhear, "Me, I'm goin' back down to Colorado before they get the

Army in."

It was perhaps thirty seconds after they had climbed out of hearing into the timber that Pete Holmes rose and went back to the corral, taking his rope down off his saddle that hung by a stirrup from one of the posts. He went into the corral and made three casts at his horse and missed. He was made awkward by his fleshiness and it bothered him and he cursed once, soundly, a mean edge to his voice.

Finally, he caught the animal, led him out and saddled. He was in a hurry now and was breathing hard by the time he swung ponderously up into leather. He went back to the street and paused at the front corner of the barn to look both ways. He turned out and down toward the foot of town. It was then that he caught the faint rhythm of a quick-timed hoofpound echoing up from the Fort Bewell trail.

He stopped, sitting motionless, hearing that sound grow slowly in volume. So keyed was he to the feeling of this town tonight, so wary had he become, that he had to know the meaning behind this approaching rider's obvious haste. He glanced on down the street and directly moved down there and into the deep shadow of a tall elm that fronted a house. He waited there, listening to the growing sound.

That drum of hoofbeats strengthened suddenly out of the trail's lower turning. A dog started barking loudly, savagely. Holmes abruptly made out the rider's shape, saw it swing aside and in toward the Warren yard. The horse came to a sudden stop and the rider swung down and crossed the yard toward the house. His shape was shadowy and indistinct. But it was tall and broad enough for the 'breed to recognize him as Dave Santell.

Pete Holmes acted strangely then, prompted by the deep resentment he bore this Dave Santell. He read his own meaning into the urgency of Santell's errand. He reined his horse around and walked him up-street. He turned into the saloon tie rail. Regardless of his loyalty to Breen, he was going to tell Ed Torrence what he had just seen.

There was a lack of any loud talk or laughter in the *Elite* tonight. Men came in off the walks, never more than two or three at a time, went to the bar and had their drinks and talked there briefly in low undertones, if at all. They didn't tarry for long. Most of them were men not often seen in town, men of the high country outfits.

The reason for their soberness and quiet manners was the group at the back table, Ed Torrence, Blaine Shotwell and Huck Birkheimer. Although they had not been told, these men sensed that something important was being decided back there.

About the time Spence's two men rode down the street, headed for home, Ed Torrence was saying, "You're balkin', Blaine. Why?"

"Same reason you are," Shotwell growled, avoiding Torrence's glance. "How the hell do we know what's going to happen?"

"What can happen?" Torrence asked blandly.

"Jake Wilce could have talked before he pulled out."

Torrence gave a slow shake of the head, smiling thinly. "Not Jake. Not knowin' what would happen to him if he did."

Shotwell sighed worriedly. "The offer still stands. A thousand and not a dime more."

"For a quarter section with sixty acres of hay and all that water? Come again, Blaine!"

"What would I do with it, anyway?" Shotwell asked. He picked up his glass, drained the last meager swallow from it, and filled it with beer again. "All I'd do would be to put a man up there to work the hay crops. You get two cuttings a year —"

"Three."

"Three in good years," Shotwell conceded.

"Two tons an acre a year. A hundred and twenty tons. At ten a ton you've cleared your investment the first year."

"If it's so damn' good, why don't you hang onto it?" Huck Birkheimer cut in uncompromisingly.

Torrence didn't like this show of belligerence in those two. He had been able to keep them in line so far, had done it easily. But now they were talking back. They weren't afraid any longer. At least, not of him.

He had the canniness to play this shrewdly now as he said, "You boys know what I've been after. I've got it now. A big enough stake to pull out."

"You're pullin' out at the wrong time," Birkheimer muttered.

"Why is it wrong? Because Wilce turned chicken and ran?" Torrence laughed softly. "We knew he'd do it sooner or later. Why get so spooked? You've got a month, maybe six weeks, before they can bring a new agent in. The government's always slow on a thing like this. In thirty days you can clean out half that herd across there."

"And sell it where?" Shotwell asked dryly.

"Larkin wasn't the only man around Bewell who has a likin' for strange beef at

385

giveaway prices. In a day, I'll find you a dozen others. And they won't be dumb enough to let a quartermaster run onto any stray hides, either. The Army buys its beef dressed. It isn't interested in hides."

Torrence eased down more comfortably into his chair and went on, "You're missing a good bet, you two. Blaine, throw my quarter section in with your lease and you'll have a real layout. You could run a thousand head in those hills and never graze it out. With you and Huck together, you can thin those reservation herds from now until you've grown long grey beards, regardless of who the new agent is. And you'll never get caught at it if you're smart! No one's connected you with this rustlin'."

Birkheimer looked at Shotwell and the reserve he saw on the storeowner's face made him shake his head. "That's our offer, Ed. A thousand from Blaine, five hundred from me. You're lucky to get that. When Santell gets out, he'll bust this thing wide open. We'll be lucky if we aren't run out."

"But Santell won't get out."

The swing doors banged with unusual violence and they turned to look that way, at Pete Holmes striding purposefully toward their table.

He came up, his tea-yellow face tilted back

over his shoulder toward the door. He said in a low tone, "Santell! He's down the street at Warren's."

Shotwell and Birkheimer didn't understand Torrence getting quickly to his feet and saying crisply, "You haven't seen me tonight! You don't know where I am! Get it? Sit down, Pete, and use my glass."

He paused but briefly for their answering nods before stepping to the alley door and going out that way. He ran up the alley to the passageway at the upstreet end of the saloon and along it to its head. He looked out there, identifying two wide-hatted figures standing at the walk's edge.

He called softly, "Gurd!" hearing faintly the slow walking chock of a horse climbing from the street's lower limit.

One of the men turned and came toward him. Torrence said quickly, warned by the approach of that rider from below, "Get across the street and out of sight, Gurd. The same goes for Walt. If anything happens, back my play!"

Gurd swung away, called to his companion, and they crossed the street and disappeared under the awnings there.

Torrence leaned against the corner of the wall, excitement strong in him; there was a little fear, too, although he tried to tell himself it was something else.

Shortly, a rider swung in out of the obscurity and in at the tie rail beyond Pete Holmes' roan. The moment the rider had ducked under the rail and stepped onto the walk, erect, Torrence knew it was Santell. He saw Santell stop and scan the walk, then go directly to the doors and through them.

He eased out of the passageway and, his back close to the wall, moved over to the window. His palms were moist and he wiped them against his flat thighs. There was a constriction in his throat that wouldn't go away when he swallowed. He was trembling a little and the night air seemed to have a deeper bite of chill than he had felt a moment ago. He put his hand on the butt of the Colt's at his thigh.

Reassured by the feel of the weapon, he stooped and looked in through the window where some of the inside paint had flaked away. He saw Santell standing there in the room's center, hands on hips, saying something to Birkheimer and Shotwell.

His fingers tightened about the handle of the gun and he smiled in a way that seemed almost gentle.

Ray Breen had been waiting here two hours, growing more impatient as the wheeling stars overhead told him that it was nearly midnight. Pete Holmes had promised to be here at eleven, which made him already a good bit late. Because the 'breed was usually prompt at a time like this, Ray Breen was worried.

He had ridden as close as he dared to the last house, Lowell MacGruder's, at the lower end of the street. He had tied his horse in a thicket well back from the road and come on afoot to the lower line of the yard fence, which was close enough considering MacGruder's dog. He waited now hunkered down in a waist-high trough washed off the road's edge and emptying downward toward the bottom of the cut.

All this long day he had been tormented by the thought of what Torrence would do. Meantime, he had been physically miserable, with a headache, a sick stomach and an intolerable thirst for a drink of whiskey, knowing it was the only thing that would put him on his feet again short of the next two days. He had consumed a great deal of liquor yesterday and, as always, was paying for it.

He remembered little of what he had told that McCune man, only that he had talked a lot and, from what Earl said, of the wrong things. The barkeep had last evening spoken of Torrence's questions. That had been enough for Breen. Half drunk still, he had made tracks away from Scalplock last night, riding all the way to the cabin above Torrence's where he and Pete Holmes had been living. He'd sent Pete on in to town, arranging this meeting here; and he had taken his blankets and left the shack and slept up in the timber, fearing that Torrence would come.

He knew his time was up here and supposed he should be on his way out. Yet the thought of Torrence's bullying still rankled and he wasn't leaving quite yet. He was curious to know what had happened as the result of his talk with that friend of Santell's. He hoped, and yet feared, that he had betrayed Torrence. He wondered what was coming of it all.

When he heard the rider approaching from the lower trail, he crawled farther back into a deeper part of the wash and waited. He wondered who would be headed into Scalplock in such a hurry. He recognized Dave Santell in the brief two-second glimpse he had of him crossing the mouth of the wash; he also made out the US jaw brand on the horse and wondered at it. He heard the savage yapping of MacGruder's dog close by, then the abrupt dying out of the horse's run.

Suddenly, with rare insight, he knew why Santell was here. A fierce exultation was in him and at once his fears and wariness left him and he stood up out of the shallow wash and stepped into the trail, turning townward.

The dog, still barking, rushed at him as far as the yard fence. But he paid the animal no attention as he once again heard Santell going on up the street, the horse now at a walk. He knew then that Santell had stopped briefly at Warren's.

Coming up on the livery barn, he angled over to the walk there. He saw Santell ride in front of the *Elite's* lights, turning in off the street. He walked on slowly, thinking to go on until he was opposite the saloon. He could watch from there.

He was taking the three steps that led to a higher level of the walk in front of the bakery when he saw a man's indistinct shape move in over the walk ahead and disappear in the deeper shadow in front of the barber shop. He stopped and wheeled quickly into the head of the steep-pitched alleyway beside the bakery, vastly relieved that his approach had been so soundless.

Looking toward the saloon, he noticed Santell's high shape briefly outlined in the swing doors. He waited, breathing shallowly, sensing in the appearance of that man by the barber shop that someone had been forewarned of Santell's coming.

His glance went back to the saloon windows and stayed there. He saw Torrence, stooped, come into the light and crouch there at the far window's edge, peering in.

He drew his .45 and cocked it, trying to judge the distance between him and Torrence, sure now that Santell had walked into a trap.

It was fifty yards across there, he supposed. Too far for accuracy. But it wouldn't hurt to try.

XXIV

Dave wished now that he'd gone on in at Warren's and wakened Doc. At the time it seemed pointless to disturb the medico and the others and he hadn't wanted to make his explanations anyway. He had been drawn on here to the saloon by the same fierce urge that had been with him all those forty miles from Fort Bewell — to find Torrence, to line a gun on the man and to have it over with.

Just now he knew Birkheimer and Spence were lying. Torrence wasn't around, they said. He saw that he would accomplish nothing by pressing his questions and he know he'd been foolish in coming here without first seeing Doc or Tom Warren.

So now he made a last try, drawling, "The Army's about ten minutes behind me. Lookin' for Torrence, too. They've got a half baked idea he's the man they're lookin' for. I wanted to let him know. Now does one of you go find him and tell him to get out of town, or do you want him arrested?"

Pete Holmes' angry glance left him, swinging to Shotwell. The 'breed said quickly, "Where'd Ed go just now?"

Shotwell cursed and leaned over and struck the 'breed a backhanded blow across the mouth. And behind Dave the shattering of the window made a sudden jangling sound that brought him wheeling around, his hand stabbing to the gun at his belt.

He was aware of several things just then. Of Earl, ducking out of sight behind his counter, of a chair's quick scraping behind him, of Torrence's half-lit face showing beyond the jagged hole in the window, of Torrence's gun settling into line. And, finally, he knew that the upswing of his own gun was to be too late.

A shot blasted out on the street. Glass burst inward from the upper sash of the window and Torrence's head pivoted and his gun wavered as he looked out across the street. Dave lunged, jarring hard against the bar, and lined his .45.

A gun's red wink lined in through the lower window opening and he felt the breath of a bullet fan his neck. He thumbed two swift shots through the window, then whirled and sent another at Birkheimer, on his feet and drawing. He saw Birkheimer jarred back against the wall, saw the man's heavy jaw sag open as he dropped out of sight, amazement and pain etched on his broad face. Shotwell and Holmes were moving toward the alley door.

Another shot boomed in from far out across the street and there came the quick pound of boots against the walk planks immediately beyond the window. Dave stared over his sights at the lamp over that back table and he pulled the trigger, seeing the lamp spray apart and the flame go out. With a reaching swing of his arm, he struck the only remaining lamp, nearly overhead, and felt warm coal oil run down his hand as the lamp shattered and it was suddenly pitch dark. He swung away from the bar, letting the weight of his shoulders overbalance him.

He hit the floor already rolling as another gun spoke out front. The bullet ricochetted in a high whine off the bar face and he heard its *thwunk!* as it lodged in the saloon's rear wall. The alley door slammed suddenly and he knew that Holmes and Shotwell were gone.

From behind the bar, Earl bellowed, "Don't shoot this way!"

Dave said, "Lie down and you'll be safe enough," as he got to his feet and ran back along the room. He was remembering that he had no extra shells for this Colt's he had taken from the sentry at Fort Bewell. That hadn't worried him until now; he hadn't supposed that he would need more than the five shells in the gun.

Going back along the room, he collided with the center table and tipped over a chair, the sound coming loud and startling in the stretched-thin stillness. Someone on the street yelled something he didn't understand and then suddenly guns came deafeningly alive out there, pouring their fire in through the windows and whipping this pitch dark room with whistling death.

He reached the back table, pulled it aside, and groped there in the corner until he felt Birkheimer's soft bulk. He touched the man's shirtfront and his fingers came away sticky and damp. Then his fumbling grasp felt of Birkheimer's hand and the gun fisted in it and he had to bend the fingers back to pry the gun loose.

He shucked a handful of shells from the dead man's gunbelt and, the shots out front having slacked off, he went to the open alley window and looked out. He could see nothing in this blackness except a heavy sprinkling of stars overhead. He threw a leg across the window's sill, then dropped to the alley below.

The rainwater tub was full to brimming from the rain of several days ago. He stood on its edge, reached for the overhanging eaves and swung up onto the roof at his second try. Out on the street now men were calling back and forth and he clearly heard Torrence's voice rise above the others, shouting, "Out back! Someone cover the back!"

He hunched over and ran carefully along the roof to the front. Ten feet from the roof's edge he went to hands and knees and crawled until he was staring down over the awning, three feet below, across to the far side of the street. He saw a man over there leave the line of an awning post and walk quickly to the narrow opening between two stores.

"Must've got him, Ed," someone called from over there.

Then, from directly below, came Torrence's reply. "Who was that down below?"

"Breen," came the answer. "He's beat it. But he got Gurd."

Dave swung his legs over the roof's edge and, Birkheimer's gun in his right hand, eased his weight down onto the awning. A board creaked but the sound was instantly blotted out by the swift-timed burst of three shots from beneath the awning.

Torrence called, "Earl, you there?" and the barkeep's answer sounded muffled and unintelligible from inside the building.

Dave was kneeling at the outer edge of the awning now. He had rammed the gun in his belt. He crossed his hands close to the roof's edge and threw his weight out and down, turning so as to straighten his arms. He felt the sudden strain on his shirt dislodge the gun as he was falling. He heard it thud onto the ground close by his boots just before they hit. The drive of his fall took him to his knees. A gun flashed redly at him from less than ten feet away as his groping hand reached for Birkheimer's weapon.

His hand closed on it and he swung it up at the vague shadow under the awning that was Torrence. The Wheel man's .45 blasted out again and a driving blow at his left shoulder rocked Dave back out of his crouch and sprawling flat on his back. Yet, in falling, he swung the gun up and lined it and thumbed back the hammer.

For an instant as he lay there before he squeezed the trigger, he heard the muffled thunder of many running horses sounding up from the lower end of the street. Then he fired, and he saw Torrence's indistinct high shape move at the bullet impact. He fired again, feeling pain in his shoulder now. He didn't know whether he hit or missed; for Torrence was no longer there.

He rolled over and, with his good hand, pushed quickly erect. From behind him an explosion drove out at him and he wheeled and targeted a man running out from the awning there, bringing that man down. He ran in toward the spot where Torrence had stood, looking down to the walk but seeing no one lying there. The thud of running steps echoed faintly up out of the passageway alongside the saloon. He ran to the head of it, into it, thumbing two shots that made his ears ring in the narrow corridor.

Back there a man screamed. But then again came that pound of boots, slower-timed now. Dave kept on running. He fired once more, then reached to his pocket for shells and reloaded, pausing.

It was quiet in here now, except that he

caught again the sound of riders running up the street; it was a muffled faraway sound now but it drove Dave on with a desperate need for finding Torrence.

He hugged the wall at the foot of the passageway, knowing that Torrence would be out there somewhere and that he would be watching this opening.

A bugle call sent its ringing notes over the town. What he had heard, then, was the detail that must have followed close on his heels all the way from Fort Bewell.

In sudden desperation, he lunged from the foot of the alleyway. A gun laid its hollow blast at him from the direction of the icehouse, the bullet-thud in the wall barely two feet from him blending with the explosion. He swung right, toward the icehouse, dodging, weaving, throwing two shots across there. The wink of a gun answered him and he was too slow in targeting and answering it.

Coming in on the icehouse, he dodged to the left at the last moment, following its long wall down the steep slope. He rounded the back corner, slowing to a careful walk, listening. He could hear orders being called on the street and once he knew he heard a saber rattling against the stock of a carbine. Yet those sounds pierced only the outer fringe of his consciousness. He was trying to hear something else as he flattened to the back foundation logs of the icehouse a scant foot from the corner of the wall.

Finally he did hear it, a faint slurring sound that was close. Then he imagined he caught a man's labored breathing. It was all he needed.

He lunged out, far beyond arm reach of the wall corner, and wheeled. He saw Torrence standing there not five feet away. He jerked his gun up, thumbed the hammer and let it fall.

It was as though he had been squeezing the trigger of Torrence's weapon; for the two .45s blasted out at the same instant.

A hard blow at his right thigh spun Dave half around. He swung back again, holding the gun at his hip, lining it carefully in the sudden knowledge that he had but one shell left.

He saw his bullet drive Torrence back to the wall. Torrence buckled at the waist, went to his knees. He straightened and his hand lifted, swinging his gun deliberately into line.

Dave threw the Colt's with all the strength left in him, strength that was fast ebbing before a sudden dizziness and great pain in his shoulder. He saw the heavy weapon smash Torrence in the face. The man screamed hoarsely, a scream that suddenly ended on a high awesome note. Then every bone in Torrence's body seemed to go soft. He simply melted to the ground, face down.

Dave tried to step over to him but his right leg buckled and he went down and rolled over once, down the slope away from Torrence. He lifted his left knee under him and started crawling up toward Torrence. But then the night went blacker and he couldn't see. He stopped fighting that fading of his senses.

They found him that way, Sergeant Griffin of E Troop and two of his men with a lantern. The sergeant sent one man back up to the street for the doctor with a curt word, "Tell him to hurry."

On that eleventh early morning after the shooting, they walked out the trail below town to the juniper where the grass grew green and lush. Dave sat beside Gail, glad to have the weight off his bad leg; for the muscle ached a little where it was healing.

They had been speaking of several things, of Shotwell's confession and of Breen having turned on Torrence that night and then getting away, and finally of Frank and Martha, who must by now have crossed the border into Canada.

But their talk died out and as they sat by the tree there was an awkwardness between them, something unspoken that each felt the need of putting into words. The air was fresh and beginning to lose its chill as this after-dawn sunlight streamed into the valley, thinning the blackness of the pines along this far ridge.

"Smoke, Dave?" Gail asked. These past few days she had learned to roll a smoke passably well, helping him because it was awkward for him with his arm in its sling.

He nodded and she took his tobacco and papers, laughing a little at her laborious efforts. But she managed it and was even able to light the match with a flick of her thumbnail, man fashion.

"We could start back today," Dave said presently. "It's not as hard ridin' as it is walking."

"Two weeks, the doctor said. You have three more days, Dave."

"He hasn't seen me for a week. How would he know what shape I'd be in?"

But Gail didn't seem to be listening. She had clasped her hands about her knees and now leaned back, looking out across the valley. She was a picture to take a man's eye, the sun making spun dark copper of her hair, her slender tall figure gently curved, her expression faintly smiling and at ease.

"I want to forget all this, Dave," she said abruptly. "Let's never come back here again."

Dave nodded. "We could bid on the Fort Laramie contract this winter and let this one go."

"How long will it take us to get back home? Texas, I mean."

"Three days to the railroad. Another week from there on."

"Is the house pretty, Dave?" she asked, turning to him.

"Not very. It was once, they say, when your mother was there. Needs paint now. Most of the curtains are gone. And the flowers have died out. It's a man's place."

"Would they mind me too much?"

"Who? The crew?" Dave laughed. "They'd work themselves gaunt tryin' to please. Did you ever know a bunch of men not to like a pretty woman around? They're a good bunch, Gail."

"I know. Jim Land was good." There was keen regret in Gail's tone. But she went on quickly, not wanting that mood to catch her, "Where do you stay when you're on the ranch, Dave?"

"In the house," he said. "Won't take long

for me to clear my junk out of your way, though. I always did like the bunkhouse best anyway. Not so lonesome."

She gave him a look that was warm and touched with something quick and alive from deep within her.

"Would it be lonesome for you if I was there, Dave?" she asked softly.

At first he wasn't sure. Then he was, and his arm went out and he drew her to him with that look still in her eyes.

We hope you have enjoyed this Large Print book. Other Thorndike, Wheeler, and Chivers Press Large Print books are available at your library or directly from the publishers.

For information about current and upcoming titles, please call or write, without obligation, to:

Publisher
Thorndike Press
295 Kennedy Memorial Drive
Waterville, ME 04901
Tel. (800) 223-1244

or visit our Web site at:

www.gale.com/thorndike
www.gale.com/wheeler

OR

Chivers Large Print
published by BBC Audiobooks Ltd
St James House, The Square
Lower Bristol Road
Bath BA2 3SB
England
Tel. +44(0) 800 136919
email: bbcaudiobooks@bbc.co.uk
www.bbcaudiobooks.co.uk

All our Large Print titles are designed for easy reading, and all our books are made to last.